MW01138024

THE SHADOW RAVENS

CIPHER

AILEEN ERIN

First Published by Ink Monster, LLC in 2014
Ink Monster, LLC
34 Chandler Place
Newton, MA 02464
www.inkmonster.net

ISBN 9780989405089

Copyright © 2014 by Ink Monster LLC

All rights reserved. This book or any portion thereof
may not be reproduced or used in any manner whatsoever
without the express written permission of the publisher
except for the use of brief quotations in a book review.

For my writing family-you know who you are. ;)
You make me a better writer, and more importantly, a
better person.
Big hugs.

Chapter One

CIPHER

It had taken me three excruciating days of nonstop hacking to work my way into Alpha Citadel's mainframe. My fingertips were raw, and the case of energy drinks I'd downed to keep me awake was giving me the shakes. I leaned toward my monitor, my nose nearly touching the screen as I searched for anything that would make my hackfest worth it.

Breaking into any system was always a little dangerous, but going into Alpha Citadel's mainframe... That was taking the risk to an extreme level of insanity. People got killed for less. And yet here I was. Hacking where no one had hacked before.

Except my dumb ass had actually done it.

The first time I'd tried it, I barely escaped with my life. If I got caught this time, I'd be lucky to be shot on sight.

I wasn't a lucky person.

The alarm I'd programmed alerted me that the Citadel's Green Helixes—their DNA-modified tech specialists—were on to me.

Shit. I slammed my hand down on the table and

my collection of anime bobble-heads started jiggling back and forth, as if telling me to calm down.

Good advice. I still had a little bit of time. I tapped the figurines to stop their movement as I assessed the situation.

I was bouncing my IP all around the world to hide my identity but that didn't really matter as a warning scrolled along the top of my screen. My bots in the Citadel's com channels started picking up all kinds of bad news. Drones were being readied. The squads at every Void outpost had been notified and were now on standby.

A trickle of sweat rolled down my hairline and I brushed it off on the collar of my T-shirt. I had to find out what stopped the Red Helixes' abilities. I was a ticking bomb without the intel, but staying in the mainframe much longer wasn't going to help anything.

I closed the alert window. The Green Helixes would find me if I didn't log out within the next nineteen minutes. They were that good. I started a timer on my monitor to count down, beeping every thirty seconds, and set it for fourteen minutes. That should give me enough time to leave the trailer park if I wasn't out of the mainframe by then.

I pushed a piece of my dyed blue hair behind my ear, and tried to focus on what I was doing instead of on the drones that could be headed my way any second. There were hundreds of databases here, too many for fourteen minutes. Running an automatic search would send the Greens straight to me. It was a crapshoot.

I blew out a breath, trying to calm my nerves, and

started scrolling through manually. I must've scanned nearly a thousand file names before I found one that could be relevant. Really fucking relevant.

"Helix Research," I read the name aloud as if that made it more real, but it didn't disappear.

It couldn't be this easy. They wouldn't just have it there, would they?

The file icon had a lock symbol on it. I applied my trusty algorithm, and held my breath. Ten seconds and it opened.

I was in. This was it. It had to be. Only the need to be quick stopped me from bouncing in my chair with excitement.

Inside the folder was a list of nine files. Each named for the different helix classifications. The tenth file was unnamed. Probably a trash folder.

Holy fucking shit. But where's the damned Red Helix folder?

The helix tattoos were a sign that a person's DNA had been monkeyed with. Each color-coded tattoo had a unique subcutaneous design built into it. No one could fake them. No one would dare try. Most helixes and the genes that went with them were coveted—all except the only one that could be given at birth. Babies with unstable DNA got marked with a Red tattoo, tagging them for reprocessing.

Which was a nice way of saying they were killed at birth.

I understood the danger of the Red Helix well. Mine was on my left hip. I never found out who'd gotten me out of the system alive, but I had a nice party trick from my messed-up DNA—the ability to harness electricity. Touching anyone when I was pulling voltage killed them. To keep the rest of the populace safe, I tried to stick to myself.

I rolled my shoulders back, releasing the tension, as I went through folder after folder. There had to be something about Red Helix abilities somewhere in one of these databases. I just had to find it.

The timer buzzed. Twelve more minutes.

A few keystrokes had me in the Black Helix database. If nothing else, grabbing the personnel files would help me figure out who was going to come after me. Knowing key players' faces could mean the difference between getting away in time or being caught. A subfile was marked combat videos. I clicked play on the first one, and a new window opened.

The fighters moved blindingly fast. Ruthless. I knew some self-defense, but if I came up against a Black Helix—experts in warrior arts and military strategy—I'd be screwed. They'd been modified for strength and stamina and trained in about every form of martial arts known to man.

I copied the whole Black Helix database to my drive so I could study it later.

The timer beeped again. Ten minutes left. I had to keep moving.

Since there wasn't a Red database, I opened the next best one. The file was simply named "Seligo" for the immortal ruling class. They had the UV Helix—the ultimate in modded DNA. All aging and disease had been scienced away from them a couple hundred years ago and now they were like a plague of ruling roaches. The fuckers never died. The Seligo were the reason why society was on the verge of collapse, and they were clueless about it. Oblivious to anything that didn't directly involve them. Dipshits.

The clock beeped again—eight minutes.

Why in the hell isn't there a file on the Reds?

I ground my teeth and moved on to maybe the next best thing. I opened the Seligo files. A list of sub-database files filled my screen. Each was named for a member of the Seligo class in alphabetical order. I scrolled down, looking for one name. Jack Parson.

I blinked a few times, wondering if it was a mirage.

Nope. This was the real deal and could make all my hacking worth it, even if it wasn't what I'd wanted.

Jack Parson, my uncle, was the bane of my existence. He was the man who had my parents killed and the reason I was on the run. The asshole had almost caught me a few times, but almost didn't count. Not to me.

Inside the file were a bunch of subfiles. I open the first, and scans of Jack's brain filled my screen. Six of them were labeled "Pre-DNA Modification" along the top. The remaining six were "Post-DNA Modification." Some of the colors changed in the scans, but I had no idea what the medical notes meant. I closed that file and found one that had his latest status update. I copied it, then scrolled down the list of remaining subfiles, quickly searching for anything else that caught my eye.

Another beep sounded. Six minutes left.

Why wasn't there a Red Helix folder? It had to be here. They had to have at least some kind of research. I couldn't be the only Red still alive. That just couldn't be possible.

In my frustration, I gathered electricity before I

could stop. I could never control my Red Helix ability when I got emotional. My breaths came in short gasps as the current ran through my body, making my skin tingle. The lights flickered and I backed away from my computer. I didn't have time to replace another fried system, especially not now. The Greens would make it impossible to hack in again.

The last spark of electricity left my body, leaving me a little drained. Food or sugar would help, but that'd have to wait.

There was only one place left to check. That last unnamed file. I said a little prayer and opened it.

Most of the files in the sub-database had "Shadow Raven" in some form in the name or "SR" and a number or a date. Except for one.

I glanced down at the glowing tattoo on the fleshy bit of my right hand, between my thumb and first finger. A tiny silhouette of a bird in flight. I'd had it for as long as I could remember, but I had no clue what it meant.

It couldn't be a coincidence that there was a database named "Shadow Ravens" mixed in with the helix info, could it?

I didn't have time to figure out which sub-file was most important, so I went to the last one.

"Lady Eva," I murmured. Who the hell was Lady Eva?

Inside the file was a folder named "memos." It seemed like a good place to start. Short and sweet pieces of information. Inside were a ton of files numbered with dates. The most recent was from yesterday.

To: Dr. Nagi

The greeting alone froze me in my chair. Nagi? As in The Doctor Tenma Nagi? His face plastered almost every piece of Seligo propaganda, and reading a letter meant for him sent shivers down my spine. The guy was the source of every great Seligo achievement in genetics, and rumor said he pulled all the strings in the senate. This info was from the absolute top of the command chain. I held my breath as I kept reading.

> *Lady Eva has stolen another Red scheduled for reprocessing. The Red was taken from our facility before support could arrive. This one wasn't logged in any of our systems. We have a leak. I suggest immediately detaining and interrogating all who were at the facility and had any contact with the Red and/or its family. Please see attached files for reference. Will be awaiting your approval.*

There was a link to the file in question. I clicked and multiple feeds popped up from hospital cameras. The images showed a force of people in all black. Tactical masks covered their faces. The only identifier was the tiny glowing raven in flight on the shoulder of each of their shirts. It looked just like my tattoo.

But why? I'd never even heard of this group before.

The forces moved as one, clearing floors and suppressing threats. No one working at the facility was hurt. Just zip-tied and watched. The most impressive thing was how fast they moved. It was so well choreographed. I didn't see any hand signals or coms. It was like they shared a mind.

The video was short. Less than two minutes. They were in and out of the hospital with the Red baby.

The Shadow Ravens were fighting against the Seligo? If I hadn't been watching the video, I wouldn't have believed it.

I went back to the file on Lady Eva. This was someone who could help me. The first memo was from over four years ago.

> *To: Col. Santiago*
> *From: Corp. Marshall*
>
> *The Chicago sighting has been confirmed. See attached file. She has fled the area. All leads are being investigated. Requesting another squad to be dispatched to Evanston as we expand our search.*

The attached file was a picture. The woman was flanked on all sides by big, hulking guys. She looked at the camera, as if to tell them that she was still around. Daring them to come for her. Her halo of red hair would've caught anyone's eye.

My heart sped.

This was it. This could really be it.

I laughed, clapping my hands, before readying my fingertips on the keyboard. The lights flickered. I blew out a breath as I tried to copy the files. The lights were strobing out of control as jolts of electricity ran up my spine. It made me lightheaded, but I couldn't give up.

I was almost there. Just a few minutes... I tapped my fingers on the table as the files transferred.

The timer beeped.

Fuck. Only two minutes left. Where the hell had the time gone? I'd gotten too caught up and now I was out of time. I needed those files.

Fifty percent.

I should've been copying from the get-go. The thirty-second countdown was going off and my heart beat in my ears.

An alert popped up on my screen. The Greens had narrowed down my location to the Arizona Voids.

The lights flickered faster, and popped.

No. No. No.

I pushed away from my computer, but it was too late. Every last light blew in a cascade of flashes. The RV went dark, and yelling echoed from the surrounding RVs.

The stench of burnt electronics filled the cramped room. "Shit!" My computer was charred. "Shit! Shit! Shit!" I wanted to cry. I wanted to punch the wall, but beating up the Griz—my beloved RV—wouldn't fix this. It wasn't her fault. It was all mine.

I had a moment to grieve the lost information before the instinct to run kicked in. I wasn't sure how close the Greens had gotten or if they'd dispatched a squad of Black Helixes from the Arizona outpost, but I wasn't waiting to find out. I swung into motion.

The electrical panel hidden in the floor was fully insulated. I opened it and grabbed a new battery. The palm-sized power unit was icy in my hand. I sealed the compartment tight and went outside to access the Griz's main boards.

It was nearly pitch-black in the trailer park filled with thousands of mobile homes, RVs, and trailers. The silence was eerie. Just the muffled sound of people talking. Cars in the distance. And the sounds of the desert. None of the usual mishmash of TVs, games, and music.

I climbed to the top of the RV and looked out. In the distance, flashing blue and red lights swirled. The Black Helixes were close, but not to the park yet. Besides those lights, the darkness spread as far as I could see. That had to be more than five transformers dead. Months without a slip, and now I'd practically taken out an entire quadrant of the Arizona Void. Exhaustion over the cyclical nature of my life—land somewhere new, lose control of powers, run— weighed down my heart. I didn't want to do this anymore, but that didn't change the fact that it was time for me to bail. I had to start again. If I had time, I would've cried with frustration and anger. I was finally starting to have a life—a friend—and now I had to go.

I didn't have even a minute to breathe. I'd be upset later. Once I was safe and far away from here.

A quick switch of batteries and I had power. The charred remains of the old one were trash. I unhooked the water, power, and sewage lines—yuck. I locked the door and went to the driver's seat. I gave myself a second to say goodbye to this chapter in my life. I'd really liked it here. I'd never had a reason to assume I could stay, but I'd still hoped. It was dumb— really dumb—to get my hopes up. I knew better than that.

Well, that's everything.

I started the Griz and put her in drive. I was about to hit the accelerator when someone pounded on the door.

I was suddenly cold.

Oh God. They'd already found me. I was so dead. I froze with fear, unable to move.

The knock came again. I prayed to God they wouldn't shoot through the door.

"Cipher! Where're you going?"

Thank God.

I strode to the door. "Cut it out," I said as I swung it open, finally stopping the racket.

Mona stood at the bottom of the steps. She was wearing a microscopic green sequined skirt and a white flowing tank that hinted at modesty, or it would've been if it wasn't mostly see-through. Her straight blonde hair hung loose down her back, and her brown eyes narrowed at me.

She was dressed up. Had I forgotten something?

"Where the fuck are you going, bitch?"

Mona had a way with words. When I first got to the Arizona Void, I ordered food every day from the taco place where she worked. Mona was the delivery girl. Somehow she managed to weasel her way into my life, and I was glad she had. She could be a real pain in my ass, but Mona was like a sister to me when I couldn't think of anyone else I'd even call a friend.

"You were leaving, weren't you?" She asked. Her words were clipped and angry. "Without saying goodbye. We had plans. And I brought you dinner."

I stared at the sack as I considered what to do. My first instinct was to close the door and run. Not because I didn't want to see Mona, but because I wanted to keep her from getting hurt. But closing the door would hurt her, too, and the list of people that cared about me was exactly one person long.

I waved her in, and took the bag. Inside was my favorite—a bean and cheese burrito with extra jalapeños and a caffeine-rich bev.

She wasn't going to make this easy. "We had plans?"

"Marx's at seven. Remember?"

No, I didn't, but Marx's was my favorite gaming zone. Mona liked to go because she had a thing for nerdy guys. I liked to go because I liked to game. I would kick the guys' asses, and when they came to hit on me, I'd point them her way. It was a win-win. Even if Mona thought I should be dating.

What she didn't know was that I wanted to date, but I couldn't. With all the running, I hadn't had time to even go on a date let alone worry about kissing a guy. It was a complication that I couldn't afford.

Maybe one day.

I should've messaged her before trying to bail, but I couldn't stick around. It was too dangerous. "I'm sorry. I can't stay. *I have to go*," I said, willing her to understand.

Mona didn't know everything—we'd never talked about what I could do—but she'd seen the lights flickering and I'd blown a lightbulb in her mobile home once. She'd been around me enough to take an educated guess as to what I was, even if Red Helixes and their abilities were more urban legend than fact to most everyone.

"You don't have to leave. There's a spot in my area of the park that opened up today. Move her there. No one will know you stayed and whoever you're running from this time won't ever guess that you stuck around. I'll even go log you into Jimmy's system under a fake ID when he's open next week. Just don't go."

"I… Mona…" God. I didn't want to hurt her, but staying wasn't really an option. "I have to."

"I thought you were my best friend. And you were supposed to help me learn about computers so I didn't have to work this fucking job anymore." She paused to let that sink in.

This sucked. I didn't want to let her down, but the risk…

"I know you have issues, but no one is going to find you here. There are too many RVs. Too many trailers. It's one of the biggest parks in all the Voids. Besides, if anyone does come, you have me. I have your back. We'll take off together."

I wanted to stay, but I couldn't put her in that much danger. "If I stick around and you get caught up in my past, you could end up dead."

Her bottom lip trembled. All the fierce anger was gone. "You can't leave me."

I stared at the ground. Mona had a long history of being left behind. She'd told me bits and pieces, and it wasn't pretty, but it was why we'd connected in the first place. There weren't too many girls our age alone in the Voids. It wasn't easy for us to survive.

I didn't want to add to her sadness. It was going to break both of us when I left.

"Don't go." Her pleading stabbed at my heart.

This—*this*—was why I never made friends. They made you do stupid things. It was careless to stay.

Went against all logic. Beyond dumb. But the thought of leaving again, starting over, felt like too much weight on my soul. It was dragging me down. Especially when Mona wanted me to stick around. No one had ever cared enough to even notice that I was going.

Still, I couldn't believe I was even entertaining the thought.

This was a terrible idea, but I was tired of running. A couple more weeks couldn't hurt much, could it? No one would be able to find my RV in this park. It was huge. Needle in a haystack huge.

And those couple of weeks could help get Mona on her feet. She'd have a more stable income. A marketable skill. I could leave here guilt-free. Say good-bye and even stay in touch.

"Where's the empty spot?" The words slipped out before I could stop them.

God, I hoped I didn't regret this later.

She jumped, wrapping her arms around my neck, nearly strangling me. "Thank you! Thank you! You won't regret it. We're going to have so much fun! We'll be super close neighbors!" She screamed as she bounced.

I hugged her for a second before stepping back. "Okay. Close the door. Let's get her moved."

At least now I knew I should be looking for the Shadow Ravens and Lady Eva. Finding them wasn't going to be easy, but it was more than I had twenty minutes ago. A starting point to begin my next search for information was better than nothing at all. And bad decision or not, staying would make it easier to replace my charred setup.

Whatever else happened, I had to get back online. I had a Lady to find.

Chapter Two

KNIGHT

The gym had emptied hours ago, but I was still working out. Sleep wasn't going to happen anyway. Whatever my deal was, sticking around the Shadow Ravens compound wasn't helping.

I punched the bag, giving it everything I had. Yesterday had been hard. We'd stormed a hospital to save a Red baby. She was safe in our nursery and would be reunited with her parents when the danger passed. But for every Red we saved, there were ten more that we didn't. It was a depressing statistic, and I hated it.

Being a Shadow Raven full-time was what I wanted, but for now I was stuck living a double life. Working for the Black Helixes—running tech on missions—wasn't my idea of fun. Each time I was called for an op, my soul got a little darker, but I had to stay in the system. At least until I found the one Red I wanted to save more than anything.

The problem was I couldn't find her no matter how hard I searched.

"Marquez?" A voice cut through the sound of my

gloved fists slamming against the weighted bag.

"Yeah." I was breathing heavily, which said something about how hard I was pushing. I had a dual helix, Black and Green, tattooed on my forearm. Warrior and tech. My DNA had been modified to peak performance level. I was stronger and faster than any unmodified human could dream of being. Damned if I didn't wish I were normal some days. Working out to the point of exhaustion would only take a third as much time.

A towel smacked me in the head and I caught it before it fell to the ground. Wiping my face, I turned to see Lady Eva. She was a pixie-ish redheaded woman who commanded a serious presence despite her size.

"I have some information I think you'll be interested in." She handed me a tablet.

I finished wiping myself down, and hung the towel over my shoulder. "Yes, ma'am," I said as I took the tablet from her.

"The data for the latest blackout."

I froze halfway through entering my access code. Those words had my full attention.

"Five transformers destroyed," she said.

This was what I'd been waiting for. "You think it's her?" I couldn't help but hope she did as I finished putting in my code.

"I'm not sure. It could be another Red, but whoever it is won't escape attention much longer. The Greens are close to finding her. She's gaining power and losing control."

I scanned the information. Satellite videos showed the area before the blackout. The flash was visible from space.

This was bad. Really fucking bad.

"According to the data, the power levels were fluctuating before the transformers blew," she said.

"Fluctuations?" That sparked a memory.

"Yes. Reports of lights flickering—not the same as a rolling brown-out—rather dips and surges in power. I was hoping you could…"

I wasn't listening anymore. It could be nothing, but maybe not.

Still, the reported fluctuations matched what I remembered from when Emma blew the transformers in our neighborhood all those years ago.

"Marquez?" Lady Eva looked up at me with the question.

"Sorry, ma'am." I needed a moment of quiet. Some time to let the memory flow. "I think I'm starting to remember something, but it's just out of grasp." I paused. She wasn't going to like this at all. "I request permission to use the holo room."

"No. Absolutely not."

"With all due respect, ma'am, I think going over those memories is important. Those moments with Emma when she lost control of her abilities are pivotal to finding her." I'd been asking to do this for years, but had always been denied. I'd even tried to sneak in, but without her approval, the holo room was inaccessible.

"That day was too traumatic. Your father nearly beat you to death."

I clenched my fists. She didn't have to remind me. I remembered that part just fine. "Yes, ma'am. Reliving the past in the holo room isn't going to change it."

"Right. But it *will* influence your emotional and mental well-being. And it's been ten years. Anything you remember will have at least a twenty-five percent bias. At worst, closer to eighty percent."

"It's my brain. My emotions. My risk to take." And I'd risk just about anything to find Emma. She'd stopped my father that day. She was the only reason I was alive.

"It will exert a huge psychological toll. More than living through old fights." She paused and I didn't say anything. "You're not going to let this go."

"No, ma'am." I said the words because she needed to hear them.

"Then I'm on record saying that this is a horrible decision."

"Of course, ma'am." But I didn't give a shit. I was doing it.

She nodded. "Let's go then."

I grabbed my shirt from the corner of the room, slipping it on before following her. Memories flooded my head of that summer ten years ago, and the day that had changed my life. I'd never know why my father started whaling on me that day, and I'd never forget the sight of Emma charging in to rescue me.

Maze-like metal hallways ran throughout the building. Everything at the compound was temporary, or semi-temporary. The site changed every couple of years, and the layout was designed to confuse intruders. Before anyone was allowed to wander around alone, they had to have the whole map memorized.

Eva paused before the door to the holo room and

entered her security code, turning on the room's computer system. "Go on. I'll give you a few minutes before going in. If you have a lead, work it."

"Yes, ma'am." I placed my hand on the holo room's lock.

"Name and rank," the computer prompted.

"Marquez, Hunter. Psi one eight three beta seven one three."

"Welcome, Raven Marquez."

I smirked. Only Lady Eva would give a shit about making the computer polite. Returning the greeting was a habit I couldn't break. "Thanks." The only lasting thing my mom had taught me. Mind your manners.

The room was a massive square with matte-black walls that made the holographic projections as accurate as possible. I pressed twice on the hidden panel beside the door. If you didn't know what you were looking for, you'd never see the panel, but I'd used this room, or one like it, after every major battle I'd been through. As if living through it once wasn't enough, we had to get our brains scanned and watch the replay in high-def 3D to pick out every weakness in our strategy.

I put on the headpiece—pressing sticky electrodes against my skin and scalp.

Being a Black Helix had taught me how to steady my nerves, but even that was a little fucking hard right now. I'd never relived this day before. Only lived it.

I focused on the memory I wanted. "Computer, begin scan."

The 3D holographic projection filled the room. It

was a mishmash of my mom cooking in the kitchen and a dozen other images that reminded me of her. On the side, an image of her coffin flickered as it lowered into the ground.

My mind was scattered. It'd been too long. The farther away from the event, the harder it was to reproduce. It'd been ten years.

I just wanted to see the one thing. Not relive my whole childhood.

I sat on the floor and closed my eyes, focusing on Emma. The color of her light red hair. The sprinkle of freckles across her nose.

I thought about the first time I met her. Even with my eyes closed, I could see the scene start to play out. I almost opened them, but didn't want to get distracted by what I saw. Instead, I let the memory play out as I sat there.

The sun was shining so bright that day. I'd thought she was a dumb kid. I wasn't going to be seen hanging around with some little girl. Or anyone. I was too afraid that they'd ask questions about the daily beatings Dad dished out... No dice.

But eight-year-old Emma had showed up in my backyard at the end of April, with her deck of pink cards and a bright blue frozen gel pack, and my eleven-year-old self couldn't ignore her. I hadn't wanted to take the pack, even if it would stop my eye from swelling, but she hadn't given me a choice.

"This will help," she'd said as she sat beside me in the grass. Our yards were joined into one big space. The neighborhood didn't allow fences.

Accepting help wasn't something I did easily, even when I needed it. I'd stared at that gel pack like it was foul. "I'm fine."

"Don't be dumb." She'd pressed the icy gel pack to my swollen eye, and it felt good. Painful, but good.

"Thanks."

"Wanna play a game with me?"

"Uh." No. I didn't, but I hadn't wanted her to take the pack away either.

"It's just cards. I'm not allowed to use anything with an on-off switch unless my parents are around."

Which was weird. Everyone had a hand console to play with. Even I did. It was old and busted, but it worked. Why would her parents restrict her like that?

With a father like mine, I wasn't about to question her parents' rules. So we'd played cards. She made me laugh, and let me forget about real life for an hour.

After that, she kept coming back. Bringing me food. Telling me about the constellations. She had a way of making me feel like less of a piece of shit. She took away the pain of dad's daily beatings.

Thinking about that memory was bittersweet.

As my thoughts drifted through our relationship, chaotic images flashed across the room. My eyes were still closed to save myself from seeing them, but the bursts of light and color played against my lids. I had to focus.

I concentrated on the day I wanted before finally opening my eyes.

Hiding emotions was part of my training, but as I saw Dad standing over twelve-year-old me, that control was gone like it had never existed. Years of him telling me that I was worthless hit me. I'd believed it then. Sometimes I still believed it.

Fuck that.

"Computer. Pause program."

The image froze in place. The colors were faded, and the projection of my past self was blurry. I focused on the walls. The tiny flower print Mom had put up a few months before she was killed. The projection adjusted. I stood up and walked around to see my father's face. It sharpened—his jawline firmed. His eyes were exactly like mine, a bright sea glass green. Thank God my eyes were all that I had of him. My skin was the slightly tanned tone of my mother, my hair the same black.

I walked back across the room so that I could see the images from the best angle without interfering with playback. "Computer. Resume program."

The scene unfolded in front of me. I knew it was a reconstruction, but that didn't make it any less frustrating. My father kicked me and I rubbed my side. The injury was long gone, but damned if I couldn't feel those ribs screaming in sympathy.

I watched him crack my jaw, and my blood boiled. I wanted him to die again. And again. Age and time hadn't worn down the burning hatred I'd felt toward him. It was always there, simmering under the surface. He hadn't always been such a fucking bastard, but after Mom died, he'd turned into a waste of space. Addicted to all kinds of uppers and downers. Whatever he could get his hands on. He hit me and tore me down any chance he got. It didn't matter how good I tried to be. Nothing helped. No one helped.

Except Emma.

I wanted to fast forward the memory, but skipping something now might take away from what happened next. So I watched, trying to stay disengaged while

Dad ranted about how much of a loser I was. Spittle flew from his mouth and I snorted. It wasn't funny, but coming from him? *He* was the loser. I was just a kid. A helpless, innocent kid. And anyone that picked on someone smaller than themself was a fucking bully.

I took a breath, and let go of some of the anger. If I was being honest, standing there in that room watching it play out, I was a little less bothered by his words. Especially now that I could see the irony in them.

I should've done this years ago.

A small figure ran into the room, her white dress fluttering around her legs as she moved. I couldn't feel anything but joy at seeing the image of her coming to my rescue.

I remembered seeing her that day and being so afraid for her, yet so happy that she'd come. I knew she was strong, I just hadn't known how strong.

"Computer. Pause program."

I stepped closer. Emma wasn't dim and dull like the rest of the playback. Her long, strawberry blonde waves shone in the light. Her hazel eyes were more green than brown, a sure sign she was pissed. I couldn't believe how this little girl had changed my life. She'd entered it with a bang and left the same way.

"Computer. Resume program."

I stepped aside to make way for her, not wanting to ruin the illusion.

"Stop!" She screeched in a high-pitched voice.

I was four years older and had at least thirty pounds on her, but she moved in between my father and me like she could shield me from the next kick. My little avenging angel. She'd been doing that since she moved into the house next door three months before. Not physically stopping my father, but taking care of me.

My father tried to push her away, and my past self's gasp of fear made me shake my head. I wanted to tell him not to worry so much. Emma was small but she could handle herself.

She pressed her finger to my father's chest. A single finger. "Stop!"

The lights flickered twice before exploding, and the power cut.

Exactly what I'd thought. "Pause program. Play back last ten seconds at fifty percent speed."

Slowed down, the lights actually flickered three times. The second time was faster and less bright. Barely perceptible to the human eye.

"Computer. Replay last ten seconds at twenty-five percent speed."

At slower speeds, the flickering lights became more pronounced. I glanced at the tablet, and sure enough—it was exactly as Lady Eva had said. A fluctuation had hit right before the transformers blew.

I thought about leaving before the scene played out, but I couldn't help myself. I wanted to see it, to feel the satisfaction of watching my father hit the floor. "Computer. Resume playback at one hundred percent speed."

Dad gasped, clutching his chest.

Back then, I didn't know what was happening and didn't really care. All I knew was that she'd somehow made him stop hitting me. It was like a miracle.

Now, it was clear she'd jolted his heart with electricity.

Good riddance, asshole.

Light filled the holo room as the door opened. "Computer. Pause program," Lady Eva's voice commanded. "Are you alright?"

I wasn't sure, but I answered anyway. "Yes, ma'am." I turned back to Emma's scrunched-up face. Rage stained her cheeks, making her freckles stand out. It was quite the image.

By saving me that afternoon, Emma had exposed her secret. She was a Red Helix.

Not knowing where she'd gone was killing me. Whether she knew it or not, she needed help. We'd been finding Red Helixes dead in the streets, left where people could find them. It was a warning to Lady Eva. For years, she'd saved every Red Helix girl she could. They always had the choice to join the cause or leave—whatever the parents decided. Most chose to leave, hoping to keep some semblance of a normal life in the Voids.

That was less and less a possibility every day. As gruesome as it was, death was better than ending up on a Seligo lab table.

I exhaled. Wanting to see the rest of the scene warred with wanting to keep it private. Who was I kidding? Anything I put on the computers here, Lady Eva could access. They were hers. "Continue program."

The scene unpaused. I stood back to watch as Emma knelt down beside my childhood self, running her finger down his cheek. "Sorry. Does it hurt real bad?"

My jaw had been broken, so I could only grunt.

Her mother came in and froze. It'd scared me back then. No guests had come into our house since mom died, and now there were two. But her mother knew what the blackout meant—Emma was in danger.

Emma stood, protecting me from her view. "I'm sorry, Mom. I did it again, but it's okay, right? He's a bad guy, too." The plea in her voice made me cringe. How many times did she have to defend herself before that day? How many times after?

Her father and another man stormed into the image, nearly knocking her mother over. "We have to turn her in! She's a *Red Helix*. She's dangerous to everyone around her," said the one I hadn't known.

Now I knew his face well. Jack Parson. I ground my teeth. If I ever found him, I'd end him for what he'd done to Emma and not lose one second of sleep over it.

After a Red lost control and burned down half of New York—state not city—the Seligo went on a crusade against Reds. They'd always been suspect, but that was the final straw. Even twenty years later, anytime someone tried to stop the Red slaughter, the Seligo pulled up pictures of millions of people burning to death.

"So they can kill her?" Emma's father yelled. "How is that an option?"

Her mother picked Emma up and gazed down at me with tears in her eyes. "Please don't tell."

Then they were gone. I'd passed out and woken up in a hospital, but their high-speed chase through the Voids was all over the news. Swarms of Black

Helix patrols followed them until there was a huge pileup with massive casualties, including Emma's parents. Somehow Emma got away. The search for her lasted for months, but eventually the news died down. All our intel said that the Seligo had never found her, but neither had Lady Eva, who'd been searching ever since Emma disappeared. The trail had gone cold a long time ago.

Until the blackout today.

"Rewind program," I said. The scene reversed until right after Emma ran into the room. "Play program." I watched as the lights flickered again. "Computer, calculate the rate at which the energy fluctuates in the program."

"Processing," came the little voice.

"When done, run comparison with data from file…" I paused, searching the tablet for the number. "159S30XC4057."

"Comparison complete."

"What is the percentage of similarity?"

"Eighty-seven percent similarity."

My pulse raced as I turned to Lady Eva. "I'm not sure how reliable my memory is. Whoever blew out the transformers today could be Emma, but it might not be."

"It doesn't matter if it's her. Whoever did it is a Red, and we have to help her."

Lady Eva couldn't predict when a baby girl was going to present with the code anomaly, but she helped when she could. As far as I knew, the Lady was the only one who could stabilize their DNA, but the results were dubious. She'd found that linking the girls to a partner who had the opposite ability helped achieve a balance, maybe even letting them have a normal life. Or it could. If they both agreed to genetic matching.

Emma should've been given that option, but I'd taken it from her by having Lady Eva pair us together. It had been a condition of my joining the Shadow Ravens. It was selfish, but I wanted to be the one to help her find balance. I'd see how she felt about it when I finally found her. I wanted to take care of her like she'd taken care of me all those years ago.

"I want to go to Arizona."

Lady Eva's eyes widened. "That's not wise. It might not be her, and even if it is, the Trials are being held near the blackout location. I've gotten reports that Jack Parson is personally overseeing the proceedings this year. Going could compromise your cover."

I almost rolled my eyes. I didn't mind compromising my cover at all. I hadn't used it for the past six months while I'd been secretly working for the Ravens. My tracking chip was being re-routed to make it look like I was hanging out at my apartment in Los Angeles, but I'd actually been in and out of hospitals saving Reds and tracking higher ups. Lady Eva liked that she could put me back undercover if she needed to, but I was at the end of my rope with taking orders from the Seligo. I couldn't stomach working for them anymore, and Lady Eva knew it. That was why she'd pulled me in the first place.

"You know that's not much of a warning. If someone's going to compromise their cover, it might as well be me." I crossed my arms. "And why the hell is Parson there? It's way beneath his pay grade."

"He suspects a Red is hiding in the area."

I was suddenly cold. Lady Eva was only making my decision clearer. "Get me on duty at the Trials. It's so chaotic there I doubt I'll run into Parson, and even if I do, he won't recognize me. It's been too long. If I don't find her after two days, I'll assume she's moved on and I can start tracking. And if he picks her up, I'll be there."

"Lights," Lady Eva said, and fluorescents bloomed at full power. The matte-black walls were all that surrounded us. Lady Eva searched my face, and then shook her head. "This feels extremely unwise. I'm sending someone regardless, but I'm not convinced it should be you. If this is Emma—"

"If I don't go and she loses control, then it'll be too late for me to help her." Damn it. I didn't want to seem irrational, so I kept it to myself, but I knew this was Emma. My gut was never wrong. "It needs to be me. If you don't agree, I'll defect and go on my own."

"I don't like ultimatums. Especially from one of my top Ravens." I started to apologize, but she waved it off. "This is why I didn't want you reliving this memory. It's affecting your emotions and judgment."

She was being unreasonable. And she was dead wrong. "I disagree. My mind and emotions are clear."

She stared at me hard. "I'll send Oliver and Dex with you. They're on an assignment near that area."

"Fine." I wouldn't turn the backup down, especially from my two best friends. They knew how much Emma meant to me. The need to repay her had driven every step I'd taken since she saved me. And that was exactly why I'd joined the Shadow Ravens.

"You need to be there before morning. You'd

better hurry," Lady Eva said.

"Yes, ma'am." I ripped the electrode assembly from my head, and the holo room doors slid open as I stepped toward them. "Computer. End program. Save file to Knight. Security psi one eight three beta seven one three." My Go Bag was ready at all times. I strode through the Shadow Raven compound, making my way through the complex to my quarters.

My portacom device beeped. The screen's readout told me it was a call from Dex. "What's up?"

"Hey, Knight." Dex and Oliver always called me by my hacker handle. It was what I preferred. "You hear the latest?"

Lady Eva was always fast when handing out orders, but this was really fast, even for her. "Our assignment?"

"Yeah. We're working the Trials."

Dex and Oliver weren't going to like this job any more than I did. The three of us had gone through the Trials. We'd met at The School for Accelerated Learning. As the only guys in the school who weren't from crème-de-la-crème DNA parentage, we'd formed a fast bond. "It was my idea." I ignored Dex's groan. "I know it's bullshit, but it's our best option in terms of finding her and leaves our nights free to search the Void."

"Yeah, man, I get it. I don't want a Red taken, but the Trials? Really? We're going to be like monkeys performing for the masses. You hate that display of bullshit propaganda as much as I do."

The Trials were how the Seligo kept the people happy. The traveling expo went from Void to Void, setting up tents for every helix with exhibitions and games that any non-helix could participate in like an old-school carnival. It made the helixes look cool. And the actual Trials, where kids could win a chance to attend a fancy academy and work toward getting a helix, were bullshit, too. Kids still tried, even though most failed. To pass into the pre-helix path, you had to go through rigorous aptitude testing plus a strength and stamina test. Each part was meant to evaluate the kid's ability in the various helixes.

What they didn't tell anyone was that each kid had to excel in at least two helix categories in order to get a shot at schooling. It was a nearly impossible feat for most kids in the Voids, who were lucky if they had an elementary-level education. If by some chance they made it, but washed out later at school…that was the end of them. The Seligo couldn't afford for the truth about the Trials to get out.

"I hear ya, but I think it's her. I really do. I feel it in my gut."

"No shit?"

"Yeah."

Dex huffed. "I can't believe I'm going back to the fucking Trials… We're in. We've got your back. But you owe me."

I knew he wasn't keeping count, but I had his back whenever he needed it. "Thanks, man. Where are you?"

"New Mexico. About to hit the Arizona border. I'm on my bike. Oliver's behind me. He doesn't like it either. Feels like a good way to get our asses killed."

"Don't be a pussy. Let's just get this done."

"Faster is better."

"That's what she said."

"Asshole."

The double beep sounded, signaling that Dex had hung up. I chuckled as I put my com away.

I coded the lock outside my door and grabbed my pack. I didn't need much.

As I exited the building, the cool Colorado air hit my face. It wouldn't take me too long to get to Arizona. I pressed my thumb to the lock on my bike, and fired it up, praying to every God I could think of that the Red in Arizona was the one I'd been looking for.

I left the Ravens compound finally feeling like I was finishing what I'd started so long ago. Now I had to get to Emma before Jack did.

Chapter Three

CIPHER

I'd pulled apart my computer. Its bits and pieces covered my table and it was official—the comp was toast. So beyond busted.

I banged my head on my desk a few times.

This was beyond sucky. The processor was totally fried. I pulled on a pair of latex gloves and carefully pried it from my motherboard. The sucker was basically brand-new. I'd replaced it before the hack-a-thon, using the last one in my stash. I'd ordered more, but the guy who made them was on the road and wasn't going to send them for another week or so.

There was only one thing to do. I had to go to Marx's and find someone with processors in stock.

Nerves crawled their way into my stomach, and suddenly I wished I'd skipped that stupid burrito. I didn't like making electronics deals in person. Black market parts meant shady people, but there weren't a ton of options.

I grabbed my small backpack and stuffed my wallet and rubber-coated portacom inside. Before I could think twice about my plan, I activated the lock on my door and started toward Mona's.

My gaze darted around as I searched for anyone who might not belong. Anyone with a helix who could be hunting me down.

The manager's building and a pool took up the center of the complex. I'd never gone in that pool. No one with a brain would trust the brown-colored water. The park was packed tight in the shape of a really messed up wagon wheel with rings of RVs and trailer homes around the center building. Getting through the rings was precarious. Little breaks and empty spaces were the only way, and the spacing had no rhyme or reason. My new spot was in the seventy-second ring, around four o'clock if the park were a clock face. The only real problem with this particular park was that they hadn't graveled or cemented the ground. Desert sand got everywhere.

Mona's trailer was five down from mine. It used to be bright yellow, but had faded to a dirty off-white years ago.

Mona answered the door quickly. "Don't tell me you're thinking about bailing."

I cringed. I did tend to bail on her a lot. Probably not my best trait. "No. I'm not going to bail, but I need to head over to Marx's a little earlier than we'd planned."

"Really?" She moved over, and I stepped into her trailer. Her place was a mishmash of colors and textures. For someone else, I'd say the hot pink couch, green carpet, orange pillows, and patterned throw were too much, but not for her. It suited her bright, eccentric personality.

The trailer was smaller than my RV. A tiny room

in the entrance served as living room, dining room, and kitchen. Her bathroom was decent-sized for a trailer, and her bedroom was the same size as mine. Although it looked significantly smaller with all her clothing containers.

"I need to pick up some parts."

She made a face. "You sure about that? Deals there can be a little scam-ish."

"I don't have much of a choice, unfortunately. It's the fastest way and I was kinda in the middle of something when my system blew."

She chewed on her lip. "Okay, but we need to get you dressed in something other than"—she motioned up and down at me—"that."

"Great." I needed to change anyhow. I was still in my clothes from earlier—the ones I'd been wearing for three days straight. Gross.

Mona grinned, showing the single dimple in her left cheek. "You're going to let me dress you? Please, tell me that 'picking up some parts' is Cipher code for meeting a boy."

I rolled my eyes. "No. I'm not meeting a boy." I paused. "Well, I probably am, but not in the way you mean." Anyone who was dealing black market stuff was mega off-limits.

Mona pushed me into her bathroom. "Well, don't count anything out before it happens. Who knows who you might meet?"

The girl had lost her mind. I wasn't meeting anyone good. I had one friend, and that was about all I could handle right now. I was already staying here longer than I should. Avoiding any more ties was priority number one.

One day, that would change. Hopefully. But not yet.

As soon as I was showered, Mona shoved me in a robe and started in on my hair. It was thick and hung halfway down my back. Most of the time it was a wavy mess of tangles, but Mona tamed it to fall in delicate curls. The navy I'd dyed it two weeks ago had faded to a light blue. It had been so long since I'd been my natural strawberry-blonde that I wasn't sure what it would look like anymore.

Maybe tomorrow I should re-dye it electric blue. Or maybe teal.

When Mona started in on the makeup, I grabbed the brushes from her. "I got this."

She stared me down. "You sure about that?"

"Mm-hmm." I fake grinned, showing my teeth.

"You're cute when you smile. But what you did just now with your face was fucking creepy. Don't do that tonight."

"Shut up." I shoved her out of the bathroom. "You figure out the clothes thing. I got this."

She came back five minutes later. "I've got some options…" She took a good look at me and then stepped in closer. I nearly took a step back as she inspected my makeup. "Holy shit. You look awesome."

I couldn't tell if she was being over the top, or if I usually looked like crap. It was most likely the former. "I'm not inept. Just lazy when it comes to girly things."

She grabbed up the clothes and threw them over the empty towel rack. "Close your eyes."

I did.

"Holy shit! You need to do my makeup."

I laughed. Mona got on strings of cursing. Sometimes it was "bitch." Other times it was "fucker." Right now it was "holy shit." It was really cute. "Okay," I said.

"I want to look like that. Will you do exactly that to my eyes?"

I shook my head. "No. I'll use different colors to bring out your brown." I pointed to the closed toilet seat. "Sit."

My eyes were hazel—brown in the center with green around the edge. The ratio of green to brown changed depending on my mood. I'd used dark olive around my eyes to bring out the green, and a semi-sheer chocolate on the lids. With her, I used golds on the lids and a dark chocolate brown shading and liner. For once, Mona took orders well, looked up when I told her to and didn't blink, so I was done quickly.

She spun to face the mirror. "Holy shit. I look hot."

I laughed. "Holy shit. You do!"

"You're making fun of me?"

"Holy shit. Why would I do that?"

She shoved me as she laughed. "Bitch. Let's get you dressed."

"One sec." The last thing I needed to do before heading out into public was cover my raven. I had other tattoos that I'd added to myself. Different stars—some small, some big, some just outlines, others filled in—for every place I'd lived since my parents died. I had thirteen so far, and was hoping that I might be at the end of my adding stars phase. Maybe only one or two more before I was done. A tattoo in Morse code took up space on the inside of my right forearm. It spelled out: *Run to Survive. Survive to Live. Live to Love.* It was my goal. A distant one, but it was there. My light at the end of the tunnel.

I also had my nose pierced with a tiny gold heart, and the left side of my bottom lip pierced with a hoop. I messed with my looks to express myself, but also because without all of it, I still looked like a pre-teen. At barely over five feet, people mistook me as someone they could push around. It was dangerous for them and for me.

But I didn't want anyone to see the bird tattoo. It was tiny—maybe a couple centimeters wide—in the shape of a bird in flight, inked in the fleshy space between my thumb and first finger.

I'd had it since I was little, and I'd always questioned why it was there—did it mean something worse than a Red Helix? I'd never dared ask around, just in case, but I'd figured out pretty quickly that no one else could see it. Even the way the ink shimmered wasn't normal. For a while, I'd almost thought I was crazy and that the tattoo didn't exist, but then I had a run-in with a guy who had an identical one. He'd chased me for miles before I lost him.

Now I tried to remember to cover it before I went anywhere. I didn't like to trust people. Even if we had matching tattoos.

I grabbed the concealer container and paused. With the new intel I'd found on Lady Eva and the Shadow Ravens, I thought for a second about not covering it up. Maybe that guy had been some kind of undercover agent? Had I been wrong to run?

I ran my teeth along my lip ring as I debated. Nothing I'd read in the files said anything about a tattoo, but I'd only scraped the surface of the info before my computer died. Plus, why would Lady Eva want a little girl as a secret agent? I was pretty sure my parents would've mentioned that.

Although the Shadow Ravens' missions involved saving Red babies. Maybe they were the ones who'd gotten me out of the system and they'd marked me for some reason.

On the off chance that I saw someone with a bird tattoo like mine tonight, I'd play it cool. I needed to do more research. Take things slowly. Even if the Shadow Ravens had something to do with the Reds, that didn't mean the tattoos were linked. The logos matched, but assuming things had never ended up well for me.

I swiped a healthy dollop of concealer over it, hiding it from view. "Done."

Mona was giving me a weird look. It must've looked a little odd putting makeup on something Mona couldn't see. "Oookay. Now can we get you dressed?"

"Come on." I pushed her out of the bathroom ahead of me and into her extremely messy room. Clothes were piled high all over the floor. I wasn't sure what was clean and what was dirty, so I just tried to not step on anything. Easier said than done.

We bickered a bit about my clothes, but settled on combat style boots (heels were a no-go for me), black pants so tight I swore they'd tear when I sat—Mona promised they wouldn't—and a shimmery gold tank that both made my milky skin seem less transparent and showed off all the tattoos I wanted seen.

I surveyed myself in the mirror and nodded. "Well played, Mona."

"Hey, I know my stuff." She grabbed a little purse. "Let's hit it."

***

Marx's was so loud you could hear the walls rattling from outside. The thrumming beats of the music mixed with the sounds of gaming. We stepped through the door into the packed club.

It was dark inside, with black lights giving everything an odd glow. A bar took up one side of the room, and a jumbo gaming screen filled the adjoining wall. Up to five people could play on the jumbo. Anyone else had to take a spot at the three rows of L-shaped tables. There were mingling areas everywhere else. Some people at the tables opted to wear headphones, but the jumbo screen played over it all. Music pumped as well, making the club totally chaotic. It had been disorienting the first time I came, but now I was used to it.

Usually I'd head straight to the gaming tables and start playing, but not tonight. I hadn't made many friends here, but after more than two months of kicking ass, people knew me. I had specifics in mind for my replacement part, and I'd bet that someone here had spares on them. It might cost me, but nothing was ever fast, good, and cheap.

"Want a drink?" Mona asked.

Alcohol was mostly off limits for me. I liked to stay alert at all times, but I'd had a pretty crap night so far. Losing control—and burning up my system in the process—had made me feel worthless. "Yeah. Let's get one." Mona's eyes widened, but she didn't comment. She knew me better than to ask.

We made our way through the groups of people hanging out. A few whispers and glances were sent my way, but I ignored them. Mona, on the other hand, didn't ignore anyone. She got caught up talking to some guys, and I moved on ahead to the bar. No one would ever mistake me for being friendly. She'd have more luck with the guys without my awkward self to weigh her down.

The bar top was clear plexi, with lights underneath it to make it look like it was glowing. Half the bartender's head was buzzed short and the rest was cut in a straight bob. Tattoos covered every visible inch of her, giving her an I-take-no-shit vibe that I respected. I leaned over the bar and nodded at her. She held up a finger as she finished serving, then moved my way.

"Hey, Cipher. You're not gaming tonight?" she asked when she got close.

I tried not to show my shock. I was reasonably certain I'd never spoken to her before. She wasn't in the least bit forgettable. "Nah. Looking for something."

"Please tell me you're not after serums."

I made a face. Serums were what the Seligo handed out to the helixes. Sometimes a DNA mod wasn't enough. Serums were needed to keep them young, healthy, and moving fast. On the black market, they went for bank. "Nah. I stay far away from that."

"Smart girl. In that case, anything I can help you

with?"

"Not unless you have a Knight7A9 processor on you." It was worth a shot.

She raised a brow. "That's some fancy tech. You can afford that?"

I was surprised she even knew what that was, but with this crowd, maybe I shouldn't have been. "I do okay." I did better than okay—people paid well for my hacks.

She gave me a long look. "Might want to try Crackhead over there."

Okay, now I was starting to question this girl's brainpower. "I'm sorry. I think I misheard you. You want me to get a top of the line processor from a crack head?"

She laughed. "Not a crack head. The Crackhead." She pointed behind me and I spotted a short skinny dude. His pants looked like they were about to fall off but hadn't, thanks to a belt that was cinched all the way. "He's got lots of black market stuff. He'll rip you off if you don't negotiate, though."

"Thanks…"

"Sandra. And no worries. I've been betting on your games. Always come through for me."

I grinned. "Happy to help."

Mona appeared beside me. She had a knack for timing. "You order yet?"

"Just about to. What do you want?"

"Vodka soda," she said to Sandra.

"And I'll have a French Seventy-Five," I said.

Sandra smiled. "Fancy drink, too. Huh?"

I shrugged. It was a mixture of gin, sparkling wine, and lemon. Depending on what she used to make the drink, it didn't have to be too fancy, but it was better with the good stuff. "Apparently I'm a fancy girl."

Sandra winked at me. "Coming up. Gonna take a sec. I gotta go into the cellar to get the bubbly."

"There's a cellar in here?"

Sandra bent down and opened a hatch in the floor. "Down here. See?"

I hopped up a little and leaned over the bar. "Yeah. Cool. How big is it?"

"Huge. This building used to be mega shady. Whole area was. A few of these buildings are linked together with underground tunnels. They're not long, but long enough that the gang who used to run drugs through here could get away with their goods when the cops showed."

Wow. That was kind of rad. Who knew that there was anything like that here in the Voids?

"Be right back." Sandra disappeared down the steps, and came back a minute later with a bottle.

I had to give it to her, she was a good bartender. She took care making my drink—and used the good liquor—which I appreciated. I didn't drink often, but when I did, I wanted it nice and smooth.

When she was done, Sandra placed it on the bar top with a flourish. I took the chilled glass and sipped. "Excellent." She held out the tab machine. I'd long ago linked my print to a bank account with a fake ID. People had stopped taking cash ages ago. I pressed my middle finger to the screen, paying for both drinks.

I leaned into Mona. "I'm going to go talk to that guy over there."

She checked out where I was pointing and then

shot me an are-you-out-of-your-mind look. "That guy? You don't talk to any guys, don't flirt, but now you want to go hang out with some tweaker? He's a total spaz."

She thought I had the worst taste in guys because I turned down every one she brought my way, but if I was going to take the risk of being with a guy—which I wasn't—it couldn't be for just anyone. He had to be special. I hadn't found that guy yet. "I don't want to go out with him. Bartender said he might have the processor I'm looking for."

Mona laughed, catching the attention of the surrounding guys. "Thank fuck. I thought you'd lost your damned mind."

"Not yet." I hoped. "You okay here?"

She nodded. "I'm getting my flirt on with the cutest nerd across the room. I'm gonna say hi."

I spotted the giant she was making eyes with. He was tall, near seven feet, and ripped with a clean-shaven head. He looked like the kind of guy that could crack skulls. Not the usual gaming club type. But if he was here, he had to be at least a little nerdy. "Go get him, girl," I said as we parted ways.

Crackhead was holding court in the far corner of the club, entertaining four other guys sitting in chairs around him. The closer I got the more I realized why he had that particular nickname. He flailed his limbs around jerkily as he talked in a high-pitched, squeaky voice. It was as if he were so high that he was twitching, but he was having a coherent conversation with those other guys, so he couldn't actually be on something. At least I hoped he couldn't.

"Hey, baby. You comin' to see the Crackhead?" he

asked, standing when I approached him.

Dear God. He was referring to himself in third person. "Yeah. I was wondering if I could have a word."

"Anything for Cipher."

"Have we met?"

"You don't know me, but I know you. Seen your stuff on the web. Seen you here at the club. Whatchuneed, baby? I can get you anything. Even serums." He stepped away from the group to talk to me, and I was grateful for the relative privacy.

"I don't want any of that." I tried not to be creeped out that he knew who I was. Maybe sticking around and destroying on the gaming systems had been a bad idea, but it didn't matter. What was done was done. I hoped Sandra hadn't led me astray. "I'm actually looking for a Knight7A9 processor. Any chance that you have one handy or could get me one fast?"

He whistled. "Wish I had one for you, baby, but don't right now. Too expensive to keep on hand. And Knights are rare these days. Word is the man has been caught up in stuff lately. But I can put some feelers out for you. Come back tomorrow and I'll see what I can scrounge up."

Tomorrow night? I wanted something sooner. "Any way you can get it faster?"

He thought for a second, and then swung his arms. It was like he needed to jerk his body before he could speak. "Tell you what. I got word a little bit ago that a guy's going to be at the Trials. Arrives in the morning. He's a dual helix, but he's cool. Not too into the whole system, if you get what I'm saying. He'll have what you need."

The Trials? I hadn't even known they were going on. This made sticking around so much more complicated. They brought way too many helixes into the Voids. No helix could ever be trusted.

What Crackhead was saying didn't make any sense. If a guy was a dual helix and recruiting at the Trials, then he was definitely hardcore into the system. "I'm not stupid." I started to walk away.

"Wait."

I slowly turned back.

"I'm not messing with you. For reals, baby. Trust me."

Crackhead was out of his mind. I nearly laughed. Of course he was. That was how he got the name. "Dude. I don't trust anyone."

He jerked his body to the side, and I quickly stepped back, sloshing my drink over my right hand. I moved it to my left and wiped my hand off on my pants. Figured. *I get a nice drink and spill half of it on myself.*

"Go check it out," Crackhead said. "Meet the guy or don't, but he'll have what you're looking for. He's legit."

The fact that the Trials were public was the only thing going for them. There'd be witnesses and a crowd to disappear into if things went sour. I should still say no, but I was in a rush.

Two reckless decisions in one night. Why the hell not? "Fine. Where will I find this guy?"

"In the Black arena. He'll be fighting there at noon. Watch him. You'll know when you see him. If you want, stick around 'til he's done, and he'll get you what you need. You don't like him." He shrugged. "You go. It's not like he'll be able to come at you in the middle of a demo."

The first little tingles of electricity ran up my legs. I was nervous, and it was showing. I took a calming breath. "Fine, but you better be right about him."

He held up his hands. "Jeez, baby. For such a little thing, you're tough. Scarin' me."

I snorted. "Come on. You're what—like three inches taller than me and skinnier than hell. You got no room call me a 'little thing.'"

He stumbled back a few steps with his hands over his heart. "You wound me, baby." He held out his hand.

This guy was a total flirt. I shook my head. Was it possible that I kind of liked him? "I can't believe it. I'm actually starting to like you, Crackhead." I took his hand in mine.

He stared at my hand for a second too long. I glanced down.

Oh no. My tattoo. The drink had washed off just enough of the makeup to see a faint glow under it. He had the same tattoo.

"We should talk in private," he said. The squeaky voice was gone and so were the jerky movements.

Yeah. Absolutely not until I had more information. I yanked my hand from his. "Maybe another time."

He nodded. "You know where to find me," he said in a deep voice just loud enough for me to hear over the music. His eyes were calculating, taking me in, and I wondered how I could've ever mistaken him for a crack head.

I swallowed. He wasn't asking questions like the last guy. I just had to play it cool. I searched the room for Mona. She was still with the giant dude. I downed my drink in one go. My nerves were shot, and that was a dangerous thing. The lights flickered softly once. No one seemed to notice, but it was time to make my exit. "Gotta catch up with my friend. I'll see you around."

"Yeah, baby." His tweaker voice was back.

Wow. That was some act he had going.

My hands shook as I put the empty glass on a small table. Everything in me screamed to run. Fast.

But if I ran, he might chase me. *Pretend nothing's wrong.* Then I'd casually book it out of Marx's at the first chance.

I made my way to Mona. "Hey."

"Hey, girl." She was leaning on the 'nerdy' giant, and he was grinning like a fool. The girl was on her A-game.

"How's it going?"

"Good. Oliver here was telling me about working at the Trials. He's a Black Helix."

My eyes nearly bugged out of my head. What was with tonight? And what was a Black Helix doing at a gaming club in the Void? "Cool." I tried to give him a good smile, but Mona elbowed me.

Fucking scary, she mouthed to me. Great. I was trying to be friendly and smile, and she told me I was doing it wrong. Girl was asking for a butt kicking.

"Cipher doesn't get out much," Mona said to Oliver.

"Cipher. That's an unusual name."

"It's her hacker handle."

"Mona!" The name was common enough that it was safe to use—a lot of people used some variation of it because of me—but I didn't go around telling people what I did.

"Really?" he said. He crossed his thick arms, making the muscles bulge out. "That's interesting."

He had the whole intimidation thing down well. "Not really." That was too high pitched. The light above me flickered. This wasn't good. I needed to chill out fast. "Hey, I'm going to get another drink. You want?"

"I'm good," Mona said.

"All right. I'm going to hit the games, but I'm ready whenever you are."

"Cool."

"Nice meeting you, Oliver."

He stuck out his hand, and I saw the glowing bird tattoo.

You gotta be fucking kidding me.

The lights flickered again as I stared.

I stepped back, shoving my hand in my back pocket. "Spilled my last drink. Sticky. See ya' round." I focused on taking evenly paced steps as I went back to the bar and ordered another French Seventy-Five. The alcohol would hopefully help soothe my nerves and avoid any blowouts.

I couldn't leave without Mona. Not until I knew she was with someone safe.

There were way too many bird tattoos going around tonight. Was it all a coincidence? Or was it a sign that I should've left like I'd planned?

Mona laughed, and I heard it even over all the noise.

I sighed. It'd be a damned miracle if I got out of this place without drawing attention to myself.

Chapter Four

KNIGHT

The ride to Arizona from Colorado wasn't bad. I made good time, but checking in took longer than I'd hoped. For a second, I thought Lady Eva hadn't put in the forged paperwork, but everything worked out fine. I got my orders to report at twelve hundred to the arena. Oliver and I had pulled demonstration duties.

I accepted the assignment with a nod, and logged everything into my calendar. I could've ended up with a worse assignment. Talking little kids into trying out and lying about how fantastic our way of life was would be too hard to fake. But beating the shit out of Oliver? That I could do.

The temporary barracks for Black Helixes was set up next to the Trials site. Thirty rows of bunks filled the utilitarian space. It wouldn't give me a lot of privacy, but I wasn't planning on staying here at all— except to sleep. Lady Eva had sent me the info on a safe house that I could use for whatever I needed. First I needed to figure out where Dex and Oliver were, and then I'd head to check out the space. I always preferred to know the hiding spot *before* I needed it. I put in a text to the guys, telling them to get their asses back here, and went about finding a bunk.

Most of the beds were already claimed by the other Black Helixes working the Trials, but I found one with the mattress still rolled up at the bottom of the bed frame. The locker beside it was empty except for the standard white sheets and towels. Making the bed took little time, and I was unpacking my little bit of stuff when Dex and Oliver came in.

"What is up, douchebag?" Dex said. His blond hair fell to his shoulders and he was definitely going to get reamed for it.

"What's up, girlyman?" I loved making fun of Dex's non-regulation hair.

"Don't dis on the locks." He flicked his hair back with a flourish. "You only wish you were man enough to pull off my hair."

"Right." He pulled me in for a quick hug. I hit him on the back before shoving him away with a laugh.

Oliver towered over the both of us. He was a beast, and looked it—at seven feet and change, thick with muscle, and bald—he'd scare even me if I didn't know him. Truth was, he was the biggest softie I'd ever met. The dude cried during sappy movies. "What's up, Ollie?"

"Not much." We did the hug, back hit routine. He tapped a finger to his ear, telling me to engage my blocking tech.

I reached in my pocket and activated it, nodding to him when it was done.

"You found your girl?" he asked.

My girl. The responsibility of the mission weighed on me. I hoped I'd found her. "Maybe."

"Oh, man. That means you're going to settle down. That blows," Dex said as he sat on the closest bunk.

The guy had lost his mind. "No way. I don't have any romantic interest in the girl. Hell, she was just a kid last time I saw her. You know me. I don't date. I do one-nighters. Emma included."

Dex and Oliver shared a look.

"Fuck off," I said. "Just because we're paired doesn't mean we're going to end up together. Working together, sure. But that's it."

"Yeah. You say that now, but we'll see when the two of you are together." Dex crossed his arms as he stared me down. "You're paired because you're compatible in every way. *Every* way."

"Michelle's a Red and she's not romantic with her paired partner."

"Dude. Her partner is her sister. You're not at all related to Emma."

"Whatever." I wasn't sure how I felt about getting involved with Emma romantically. Even if I did the whole girlfriend thing—which I didn't—Emma was still an eight-year-old kid in my head. Anything beyond brotherly platonic care was out of my realm of perception. I placed my five black T-shirts, neatly folded, into the locker. "Where were you guys?"

"Went to a gaming club called Marx's. Totally up your alley. We should check it out tomorrow night."

I lined my toiletries along the edge of my top shelf, labels facing out so that I could see everything, and then rolled up my bags and placed them on the bottom shelf of my locker. Everything was precisely stored. Not that any of this mattered. Five black shirts. Five black pants. Five black socks. Five black boxer-briefs. Plus two civilian outfits—jeans, a gray T-shirt and a white button-down. All generic brands. That's all I brought with me. Easy enough to replace. None of it said dick-all about myself should I need to run. Nothing they could use against me.

I sat in the bunk across from Dex as I weighed the reasons for hanging out in the club. And yeah, the guy was thinking with his dick. "We're not going to be doing much of anything but the mission. No messing around with the local ladies, Romeo."

"I always have time for local fare." Dex shrugged. "And there's a chance she could be at the club."

"Not likely. Emma keeps to herself. Plus, I don't see her as the gaming type." That little girl who wasn't even allowed a gaming console in public? No way.

But Dex's comment about settling down with Emma made me twitch. A little trip over there wouldn't hurt. "Any decent ladies there?"

Oliver whistled. "I met a couple. One was a little thing with blue hair. Cute as a button, but tough. She didn't even crack a smile at me. Her friend was this hot blonde—real friendly. They were still there when I left. We could go back."

I wasn't in the mood to hit a club. Even a gaming one. "I don't know…"

"You don't want to stick around base too much. Didn't you have a run in with Parson a while back? We've already seen him and we weren't exactly hanging around."

I grunted. "It was a long time ago. I don't know if

he'd remember me. Any word on why he's taken over the Trials?"

"He's looking for someone. No one but the top of the chain knows who, though. Wilton's been keeping tabs on this area for a while now. I've reached out. It's why we went to Marx's. The chicks Ollie was hitting up were a total side benny. Wilton was busy doing his thing, so we didn't get to talk to him, but he's gonna let us know—" Dex's com beeped. He pulled it from his pocket. "That's him. Says we should head back to Marx's. He's got info."

"Guess I'm overruled then." I stood up. "Parson and I are most likely after the same girl. The quicker we can get this done, the better."

"You sure?" Oliver asked.

"Maybe I'm being paranoid, but it's the only thing that makes sense." I made sure my locker was secure and followed the guys out the door.

***

Marx's was fully packed when we walked in. It was like any other gaming club I'd been to. The music was too loud and the drinks were flowing a little freely. I didn't mind coming to places like this every once in a while, but tonight it put me on edge.

I spotted Wilton across the room. He was doing his usual cover routine. The guy had built it up for years, playing off his scrawny build and acting like a tweaker. Make someone laugh at you and they didn't think you were dangerous. He was the best at entertaining, so people told him all kinds of stuff. It helped that he kept his Blue Helix well covered. Only the raven on his hand alerted other Shadow Ravens that he was legit.

"Look at you, douche. Haven't seen you in forever," Wilton said in his fake-ass whiny voice. The glasses he didn't actually need made his eyes look too large for his face.

I bit the inside of my cheek to keep from laughing when I looked at him. "What's up, Wilton?"

"I got a booth over here, gentlemen. Let's do some business."

He motioned us to seats in the corner that were completely covered in shadow. The backlights that ran along the edges of the ceiling were burnt out above only this booth.

I pulled my com out of my pocket and tapped the screen twice, turning on the anti-bug software. "What have you got? Any info on why exactly Parson is here?"

"Nah. No word on that yet, but I'm meeting up with a guy tomorrow who has a big mouth. I'll get what I can from him. But that's not why I called you back here."

I leaned forward. "What've you got?"

"Tweedle Dumbs one and two here didn't pick up on the little Raven. They bailed out before I could tell them. The girl has been here for weeks. Her gaming skills are top of the line. Best I've ever seen. Never had the chance to meet her—she's not the friendly type and I've never seen her leave with a guy—but she came up to me asking for a Knight processor."

I raised a brow. Those were mine, handmade from circuits to soldering. And they were expensive. Not too many people in the Voids could afford the price, and I knew just about everyone who could. "What's her handle?"

"Cipher."

That one word took me a second to process. I never thought I'd ever even get close to meeting her. "Cipher is here? And a Raven?"

"Yeah. You know her?"

"She's a legend. So yes, I know her. We talk online sometimes. Are you sure this girl is the real Cipher? A lot of wannabes out there use the name these days."

Wilton shrugged. "That's the name everyone calls her. Showed up in town out of nowhere. Came in one night with her girl, Mona. Been coming in few nights a week since. Sometimes with the friend. Sometimes alone. Kills it on the games. Only total morons bet against her when she's playing. Doesn't drink. Doesn't flirt with the guys. Or with the girls. Just comes to game. Never seen anyone beat her either."

"Fuck. Might be the real Cipher." I shook my head. I'd been talking to her for years now. Sending her gear when she needed it, although she was shifty about where to send stuff. "I thought she was a dude." And I had no idea she was a Raven. How could I not know her if she was a Raven? Was she in deep cover?

"Well, this little one is definitely a girl. You met her, Oliver. What'd you think?"

"Tiny thing? Blue hair? Piercings? Tattoos?"

Wilton nodded. "That's the one."

"Hot." He paused for a second. "Didn't see that she was a Raven though."

"I think she hides her tattoo," Wilton said. "I hadn't seen it before, and you better believe I check everyone who comes in here. Plus the girl broke her usual M.O. She got a drink instead of heading straight to the tables, and then came over to me. Didn't think much of it until she spilled her drink and wiped it on her pants. When I shook her hand, I saw the ink. Still had some makeup on it, but the color was there."

I shook my head. That didn't make sense. "Could be the Red we're looking for or a different one. Could also be some other agent under cover."

Wilton tapped a finger on the table. "It doesn't add up. Why would one of us ever cover our tattoo?"

"We wouldn't," Dex said. "Only another Raven could ever see it. So why hide it?"

"Yeah. But she did. Did you see it, Oliver?"

"No. She wouldn't shake my hand. Stuck hers in her pocket and even took a step back."

Wilton pointed at me. "You see. That's not fucking normal behavior. We check for the Raven on everyone. We make sure to show it. Something's up with this girl." Despite his lack of precise terms, Wilton was an expert in psychology and human behavior. The guy had a photographic memory, too. If he said she was acting shifty, then she was shifty.

"So, she here still?" I asked, glancing around the room for anyone with blue hair.

"Nah. Left just before you got here. Oliver told me the two of you would be battling in the Black arena tomorrow, so I sent her to you. Tiny pixie with miles of wavy, long blue hair. Can't miss her. I'll leave it up to you how you earn her trust."

I leaned back in the booth. "I don't have time for Cipher anyway. I'm looking for a Red Helix. Strawberry-blonde hair. Hazel-green eyes. Small nose, slightly pointed up. Freckles. Roughly five feet eight inches. You seen anyone like that around here?" I showed him my com, displaying the image of Emma captured from my memory scan.

He took the device and studied the image for a second. "You're looking for a little girl?"

"Nah man. That picture is twelve years old. She's twenty."

Wilton studied the picture. "Looks kind of familiar."

I flipped to the age-projection photo, but it didn't look quite human. The eyes had a glassy look from the software generation.

Wilton twisted his head to the side. "I've seen her, but I'm not sure where. How tall is she again?"

"According to her DNA projections, she should've hit five eight with maybe a quarter inch wiggle room."

Wilton rolled his eyes. "With all this precision intel you've given me, it's a wonder I can't think up more possibilities."

"Give me a break. No one's seen her since she was eight and the one image we have is from my brain, so it could be a little off."

Wilton snorted. "Right. Memory from that long ago isn't accurate at all. This is probably more a shadow of what the girl really looks like." He zoomed in, taking in each part of her face separately. "It's on the tip of my tongue. I know I've seen her and recently, but something's off. Something's different. She's changed her appearance to make herself unrecognizable." He zoomed back out and then in again. "Shit. I don't know. Does that look like Cipher to you, Oliver?"

Oliver took my com from Wilton. "No." He

squinted. "Maybe around the mouth and chin? But the eyes and forehead are different. Color is right but the shape is off. Eyebrows, too. Cipher didn't have freckles, but maybe it was too dark in here to tell. And she's short. Barely brushed five feet, if that."

"Yeah. Girl made me feel like a giant, and I'm only five five."

"So Cipher isn't Emma?" I asked, holding my breath while I waited for his answer.

Oliver handed my com back to me. "I don't think so. Sorry."

I blew out a breath. "Would've been too easy." I turned to Dex and Oliver. "I'll do the initial meet with Cipher, and then intro you two, but I need to move on finding Emma. You guys figure out if she's the legit Cipher, and why she's being shifty about her Raven." I met Wilton's gaze. "Do you think she's turned?"

"I didn't get that from her," Wilton said. "She was guarded and distrustful, but mostly spooked. As soon as I recognized her tattoo, she wanted out. Maybe one of us betrayed her?"

"I agree. If anything, this girl was hiding. Must've gotten burned before," Oliver said.

"Either way, we've got her more than covered," Dex said. "You can focus on Emma."

"Yep," Oliver said. "And I know where Cipher's friend works. If she doesn't trust you, I'll get in through there."

"Good." I glanced back at Wilton. "I want you on the streets, at the Trials, at shops, scanning any public area you can get into, searching for the girl in that photo." I checked the time. "I'm going to head to the center of the blackout area. See if I can find anything there."

"You want us to come?" Dex asked.

I considered it, but it'd be easier if I went alone. "No. I got it covered. If I find anything, I'll link you in."

He pulled three little devices out of his pocket. "Want one of these to watch your back?"

I stared at Dex's little bots. He made them himself and always had some stashed in his pockets. They looked like little balls of scrap now, but when expanded, they turned into mini-drones. They usually carried a bit of explosives and could be given minor orders. Like blowing up a small target.

"No, thanks. I'm going to keep it really low key."

"Cool," Dex slid out from the booth so that I could go.

I gave them a nod and headed out. As soon as I was back on my bike, I tried to think about what Emma's next move might be—the only thing that made sense was leaving town. I needed to find out if she was gone already. Sticking around would be pointless if she'd already hit the road.

People packed the Void around the old city of Tempe. High rises were stacked nearly on top of each other, and the traffic was crap. Thanks to my bike, I could weave between cars. The city lights slowly faded as the high rises turned to tiny houses stacked nearly on top of each other and then to endless shanties. Beyond that was the desert. Trailer parks filled up the space as far as I could see. Some couldn't afford anything else and others liked the mobility. Crime ran rampant in the parks, and I hated the idea of Emma in one of them, but that was where the coordinates led.

I slowed when I reached the park gates, but no guards were on duty. The arm of the gate was up. What a joke. This place had dick-all for security.

The park seemed like a maze until I found the pattern in the madness. I slowly made my way through the aisles to the center of the blackout area.

Power had been restored and I had to assume that Parson or his goons had already been by. But they weren't here now.

I put down the kickstand, and turned the bike off. A trailer sat at the dead center of ground zero from my readings. The hints of other tire tracks cut through the sand, but no way to tell if this was Emma's place or not.

I took a wild guess and knocked.

No one answered, so I knocked again.

After the third knock, I decided to let myself in.

Whoever owned the trailer didn't give a shit about security. The lock was old school. I didn't even need a pick. I ran a card along the jamb, and the door swung open.

The smell of extreme B.O. and feces slapped me in the face. It took me a second to stop the gag reflex before I could step inside. Trash littered the floor and paraphernalia jammed the kitchen sink.

I wasn't too shocked when I found the owner passed out in bed. Looked like he'd barely made it there. His feet hung off the edge of the mattress. One of his arms was out of his shirt. And no sign of Emma.

I let out a relieved sigh. As much as I wanted to find her, I'd lose it if she lived like this.

I slipped out and headed for the main office, following the signs to the center of the park. People were always moving in and out of these places. It was par for the course. Most people didn't even register themselves, and if they did, it was under an alias. I didn't expect to find much, but I wasn't about to leave without at least checking it out.

The one-room cement office building was closed. A fence dotted with motion detectors surrounded the structure. Why this crappy park needed an office with so much security was beyond me. But it didn't matter. Nothing was keeping me out of the place.

I pulled out my com and linked it to the security system. I had the key code in less then two seconds. Dumbasses. The security was mostly a facade. The system was active, but the wires from the cameras hung down behind them, clearly not hooked up, and one of the windows was open a crack. The alarm would work as a deterrent for sure, but anyone who really wanted in could get in pretty damned easily.

I stepped into the office and woke up the computer. The screen lit up instantly, already logged in to the park's database. It didn't even prompt for a passcode. The spot I'd checked out was registered to Sam Swan.

I laughed. Sam Swan. That had to be Emma.

The desk chair let out a pathetic squeak as I sat. Samantha the Swan was a character in a children's book series she used to love.

My heart was racing. I'd never gotten this close to her before.

I opened up her file, but she hadn't given any ID or pictures. No information about her RV. From what

I could tell, she paid cash every week so they wouldn't tow her. Sam Swan was a ghost.

I scanned through to see if she'd moved spots tonight, but as I expected, no checkout record was listed.

I put my hands on my head as I thought.

Would she stick around? Or ditch?

The park had more than five thousand spaces with registered occupants, so going door to door wasn't an option.

Where are you Emma?

I'd come back during the day tomorrow and see if the manager had any information. Maybe she'd register for a new spot in the morning. If she didn't, this might be a total dead end.

I locked up the office and headed back to the barracks. I needed to be on top of it in the morning. If Emma had stuck around, she'd be looking for a way out as soon as possible. I needed to figure out where she'd go, and if she had contacts out there…

I was giving this twenty-four hours before I assumed she'd left, and then I'd have to extend the search area. *Nearly fucking hopeless.*

But I clenched my fists. This time, I wasn't leaving for the Raven complex without her.

Chapter Five

CIPHER

I stuck to the shade as I wove between pop-up tents, trying to stop myself from sweating like a whore in church. Scanning through the entrance gate had been hard enough, but the cameras logging in all the faces in attendance put me on edge.

I'd prepared as best I could. My fake ID had my face and fingerprints associated with it, but even with that, I felt unsettled. Scanning in at Marx's was one thing. A Seligo event was a whole new level of dangerous.

It didn't matter that the only helixed people here were the ones working. The rest stayed away from the Voidies. Either way, I was too close to the enemy for any kind of comfort. Plus, swarms of people made me nervous, and this was more than a swarm. I tucked my arms into my sides and focused my gaze straight ahead.

I was going to kill Mona for making me come here. I'd all but decided to not meet up with Crackhead's connection when she banged on my door to drag me out. If it meant me going out in public,

Mona was all for it. And in the daytime, she was even more jazzed. Sunlight did good for you, apparently. My white, flowing sleeveless shirt was lightweight enough that it didn't add to the heat, but it didn't cover me from the sun. Neither did my cut-off jean shorts or sandals. I'd slathered myself in blocker, but I was going to have a million more freckles before the day was over.

As we walked, she regaled me with the benefits of the getting out during the day—something about vitamins and mental health—but I tuned her out. I'd already given in to her so she couldn't complain. If I decided to bail like I wanted to in about thirty seconds, then it'd be all good. At least I hoped she'd understand.

My stomach rumbled as we strode by a stall selling funnel cakes. I didn't know when the last time I'd eaten one of those was, but it'd been a while. The sweet smell was nearly intoxicating.

"Want to grab a bite?" I asked Mona.

"Later. Don't want to be late."

I rolled my eyes. She wasn't going to let me have even a little bit of my kind of fun.

We passed by the Green tents, where helixes showed off their latest tech. Huge screens mirrored what the Green Helix at the front of the demo area was working on. A satellite image zoomed in on one of the Black Helixes who was standing guard along the back fence. He was picking his nose.

"You can see that even from space, we can monitor every person who's been chipped. All I have to do is look you up and bam. There you are. It's linked into every helixes' tattoo," said the shrimpylooking guy in a forest green T-shirt, marking him as a Green Helix.

Oh my God. I stopped walking. That was new and completely horrible. I didn't know the Seligo had this kind of tech. They were monitoring their own people? Were Nagi and the Senate that paranoid?

"Ensuring the safety of those in the Voids is a priority among the Greens," he grinned big, like there wasn't anything nefarious going on with the intel they gathered. "If you're chipped, we can monitor your health and vitals. We can get you help when you're sick. If you get attacked, we can send a Black Helix unit to you within five seconds. We hope to get everyone to leave here with a chip."

If people weren't looking so excited by the idea, I would've laughed, but the crowd cheered him on. Clapping excitedly.

I didn't know what made me sicker. That the Green was trying to sell the audience on monitoring chips, or that the people were actually buying his bullshit. Nobody with a helix gave a rat's ass about helping us in the Voids. This couldn't be as altruistic as he was making it sound.

And these people were going to volunteer to be satellite tracked? Were they all morons?

"Who wants to give it a try?"

The crowed screamed.

"You, there. Who would you like to look up?"

"A Seligo!" A little girl yelled.

"Come on," Mona said, tugging me away from the Green area. "It's this way."

I let myself be pulled away from the Green tents before I jumped onto the platform to give them all a piece of my mind.

Because that would be monumentally stupid.

We headed toward the Black Helix area in the distance. Two huge, black tents stood at the right of the entrance, with a demo stage set up in front of them. People in all black walked among the crowd, visibly showing their Black Helix tats.

"Do you see him?" Mona glanced back at me. Her long blonde waves fell nearly to her butt, and her blue eyes usually caught every male's attention. Today her clothes were adding to the effect—Mona's white sundress was tight, short, and totally backless. The girl didn't own anything that went below mid-thigh. Totally annoying. Not because I was jealous of the attention, but because I didn't want it spilling over to me.

I raised an eyebrow. "I see a lot of hims. Which specific one do you mean?"

"Oliver." She moved faster through the thickening crowd. "He's so tall, we shouldn't be able to miss him."

I wasn't looking for Oliver. The only guy I needed was fighting on the stage. Once I found him, I was out of here.

The closer we got to the Black Helix section, the more antsy I got. I cracked my knuckles as we walked. This was not a place for someone like me, but my need for the processor outweighed anything else.

Even so, I'd be shocked if Crackhead's guy ended up being cool. The only good thing about this crowd was that I'd be able to disappear into it. Even with my blue hair.

It was like everyone in the entire Void had shown

up. Norms celebrated their imperfections, even if they secretly wished they ranked a helix. That meant that most everyone here was pierced and tattooed, with hair colors spanning the full spectrum of the rainbow.

Helixes were all about flaunting their genetic perfection. Most only had one helix tattoo and natural-colored hair. The only helixes I saw were wearing solid colored T-shirts. Some even had badges, signaling that they were the ones to go to with questions. Only helixes who were forced to work ever showed up for these kinds of propaganda shows.

I hadn't seen anyone in a Seligo white T-shirt yet, but that didn't mean they weren't here somewhere. I made sure to keep an eye out just in case. The odds were low that my uncle would be here, but the sooner I was out, the better.

I pulled my hair into a knot at the nape of my neck. I didn't get all the tendrils, but the heavy weight of it was making my back sweat. Plus, less someone could grab if I had to make a break for it. I wouldn't let myself get caught. It couldn't happen. I'd maintained my freedom by keeping to myself and staying on the run, and I was ready to bolt with nothing but the clothes I was wearing if it came down to that.

"I see him." Mona bumped her shoulder against mine. "He's fighting that guy that you're supposed to meet."

I tugged at my lip ring with my teeth as Mona pushed her way to the front the demo crowd. Oliver's bald head was all I could see through the mass. Whoever he was fighting was a little shorter. Not by much though. Mona had to throw a few elbows to get us close to the action. When we'd pushed up to the front, she leaned into the fence that surrounded the circular raised stage, trying to get even closer to the fight.

I didn't blame her. The guys moved fluidly, and even though this was a demo, they weren't pulling their punches. Their feet were bare. Black sweat pants. No shirts. Better to show off their muscles and the helixes tattooed on their forearms.

The two moved so fast, I could barely keep track of what they were doing. The one guy flipped and kicked, while Oliver blocked and spun, throwing another punch. It was a beautiful dance, and it did its job. I glanced down at the little kid next to me. His eyes were wide as he pressed his face to the fence. Even I had to admit, it was an impressive show.

Mona let rip a two-fingered whistle that almost blew my eardrums and I tried to bite back a cringe.

Holy crap. Could she draw any more attention?

She started to climb the fence. "Take him to the fucking mat!" She screamed over the top of it and everyone around us turned to stare.

I was wrong. She could definitely draw more attention.

How long they could keep this fight up? Not that I minded, but both guys were putting their all into each move, and yeah, they were sweating and out of breath, but I would've been unconscious after that much exercise.

The crowd around us shouted and Mona joined in.

There was something about the guy Oliver was fighting. He was handsome, no doubt, but he appealed to me like no one I'd ever met before. It wasn't just the way he looked. I couldn't keep my eyes off him as he moved. My heart sped as the fight continued, and I took an involuntary step forward, my toes hitting the fence. Transfixed. I found myself holding my breath, and I forced myself to look away. It was too much. Too overwhelming.

When I scanned the crowd, every face was riveted, too. So it's not just me.

He was magnetic. That made me feel a little better about staring. I shoved my hands in the pockets of my shorts, and let myself enjoy the display like everyone else.

His gaze met mine. It was as if everything paused for a moment before moving again.

He spun and met my gaze again. I glanced around, trying to figure out if it was really me he kept looking at or if there was some hot chick behind me that he was noticing. Or maybe just Mona?

When I looked back into the ring, he was laughing as he fought. He said something to Oliver, who turned to look at me and Mona. Although none of that was enough to slow their kicks and punches.

How could they be fighting and talking at the same time?

He moved to kick Oliver, but Oliver caught his foot, tossing it away. He flipped through the air three times, and landed in front of me. He slid his fingers through the links. "Hey, Cipher," he said. "I'm Marquez."

His eyes. It was his eyes that got to me. His skin was the most awesome light caramel color, his hair inky black, but his eyes were a light sea glass green that seemed to light from within. They made my breath shaky. My hands clammy.

They felt like home.

"Hi." I managed to choke out. "Aren't you a little busy to be flirting?"

"I'm never too busy for you." He winked.

"Gross." I turned to Mona, whose mouth hung open as she gawked. "Can you believe this guy?" I asked as I jerked my thumb at him.

"Hang around after," Marquez said.

Three things about Marquez hit me like punches in the gut. He had a dual helix on his forearm, a raven in flight on his hand that looked identical to mine, and most shocking of all, I wanted to slather myself all over him.

I already knew the first two, but the third… I was out. I'd never felt that kind of attraction to anyone, and it was way too much for me to even begin to handle.

Marquez kipped up, and I stepped back from the mats.

"Thank you for coming to the demonstration," Oliver said loudly. "If you have any questions about the Black Helixes, you can head over to the tent on the right. You'll find loads of information on what it's like to be a Black and what it takes to earn your helix. Also look for anyone wearing black and sporting a tattoo like this." He waved his hand along his bicep, showing off his Black Helix, except I was close enough to see it also had a bit of green in the pattern. Another dual helix.

The crowd laughed as Oliver bowed.

I took another step away from the fence, but

Marquez was watching me. If I ran, would he follow? If I stayed, would he ask questions or just hit on me?

Hitting on me I could deal with. I'd turned guys down before. Not guys I was attracted to, but the technique was the same. I just had to stay firm.

Mona grabbed my arm. "Where are you going? He said to wait."

I blew out a breath. "Nowhere." Apparently.

"This way." She grabbed my hand and pulled me through the crowd around the back of the demo area.

"Wait there," Oliver called out. "We need a sec."

Mona gave him a thumbs up. I scanned the faces in front of me, but Marquez wasn't anywhere. I hoped he'd get back soon, or else I was bailing.

Maybe I should just go. Like now.

"Hey," said a deep voice behind me.

Chills broke out along my skin. I made myself turn and it hit me again. Stupid hormones. He'd been shirtless a second ago, but with his shirt on…he was still annoyingly good looking. That didn't mean I could act on anything.

I sniffed. What was that? Oak? Man? Wow. Was that really how he smelled? Did his sweat smell good?

I was a sick, sick girl.

"You okay?"

My skin heated.

"Are those freckles?" He went to touch my nose and I jerked back.

"Yeah." But I couldn't let him touch me.

His grin did something melty to my insides. "I like them."

"Ookaaay." I wasn't sure what I was supposed to do with that bit of information. It wasn't like I'd added them for his benefit. They were just there.

He was quiet for a little too long. The way he stared down at me with his hands on his hips, as if he was studying every piece of my face, trying to make sense of something, made me feel like I was coming unglued. "What?"

"Do I look familiar to you at all?"

I crossed my arms, trying to look more severe and most likely failing. "Nope. We just met. Remember? Me, Cipher. You, Marquez. Hello and welcome to five seconds ago."

He laughed and I felt it tingle along my skin. "I hear you're looking for something of mine?"

Of his? No. He couldn't be. Crackhead would've told me if I were meeting the actual Knight. "I'm looking for a special kind of processor."

"Mine are very special."

He was bullshitting me. "A very specific, top-of-the-line processor."

"Aww. You think my stuff's top of the line. That's—"

"Knight!" A voice rang out, and Marquez turned.

No way.

"What's up?" he said to another guy dressed all in black.

No fucking way. He couldn't be the Knight. It wasn't possible. I knew him. We chatted online a lot. I'd know if he had a helix. Wouldn't I?

"Boss man wants a word."

The fun, flirting guy was gone in an instant. His expression turned flat and so cold it gave me chills. I didn't know who the boss man was, but I was glad it wasn't me.

"Be there in five," Marquez said.

"Chatting with a lady fan? No worries. I got your back."

"Thanks." Knight focused back on me.

"Knight?"

"That's me," he said with a nod.

I swallowed. The guy I'd been chatting with for years was a Black Helix. Had I really been friends with the enemy? "Bullshit. Knight's not a helix."

"A dual helix. And yes. Yes, he is." He crossed his arms. "But are you the real Cipher?"

I rolled my eyes. "I am. Prove you're Knight. We talked four months ago. March twenty-sixth. About what?"

He blew out a breath. "Four months ago? March twenty-sixth. Hmm. That was when I was..." He paused. "Right. We talked about a few things. Strategy in FV34. The latest episode of *Along the Shore*. And I think you brought up some lame classic movie."

He was so wrong. We'd gone back and forth for hours about it. "It's not a lame movie. It's hilarious. I can't help it if you have no sense of humor."

He grinned. "I have a fantastic sense of humor. You just have bad taste. Why didn't you tell me you're a girl? Why the charade?"

I used a vocoder whenever I talked online. Protecting my identity was essential. "I like to keep people guessing." I placed my hands on my hips, trying to seem a little bigger and more assertive for my next question. I had to get what I needed and go before he flirted with me anymore. He was way above my skill level. "So, can I have another processor?" Coming here couldn't be a waste. I wouldn't let it be.

"What have you been doing to my babies? I sent you seven a month ago. That should've lasted you years. For real. Years, Cipher."

I couldn't exactly own up to losing control of my powers and frying his gear with electricity. Might as well hike down my pants and flash him my Red Helix. "It doesn't matter how. They got fried, and now I'm out. Do you have one or not?"

"Not. But I can make you another. Just give me a bit."

It took way longer than a bit to make a processor from scratch. This wasn't good news at all. "You don't have one on you?"

He chuckled. "No. I don't have one on me," he said, mocking my voice. "I'm here on assignment. I don't carry much in the way of hardware with me the road."

That wasn't what I wanted to hear. "Okay. A day?"

"Maybe sooner. If you'll go out with me."

I scoffed. "I'm not going out with you. You can't bribe me for a date." I looked at Mona but she was just grinning like a loon. No help at all.

"Says who?"

"Says me!" What was this guy's deal? He was hot, but I wasn't dating him. I didn't date. "A date for computer parts? It's wrong. Unethical."

"I wasn't aware that ethics were involved in securing a date."

Even if he wasn't actually laughing, his eyes were. It was there, bubbling under the surface. He was making me completely uncomfortable and totally enjoying it.

Mona put her arm around my shoulder. "You get

what you need?"

"No." I tried not to sound like a pouting three-year-old and failed.

Knight grinned down at Mona and I suddenly wanted to punch my best friend in the throat.

Jealousy was a bitch. And I had no reason to feel jealous. He wasn't *my* anything. I couldn't afford to have a guy in my life. Knight was dangerous on so many levels... A dual helix. A kick-ass fighter. My best online friend. And so mouthwatering he made me think violent thoughts about my best girl.

"Hey, I'm Mona. Cipher's best friend slash sister slash confidant," she said, sticking her hand out to him.

He took her hand in his, and I wished he were holding my hand instead.

That was so dumb.

"Just the person I need to talk to, then. I'm Knight, and I'm trying to get Cipher to go out with me tonight, but she's not being too agreeable," Knight said as he released her hand. Finally.

Wait a second... All thoughts of jealousy were washed away by insta-panic. Mona was going to jump all over this. She'd been trying to hook me up for weeks now.

Mona squealed and hopped in place. "Perfect. Meet us at Marx's at nine. You can buy her a drink. She can kick your ass at games. You'll fall in love. It'll be a night to remember." She rubbed her hands together.

If I didn't love Mona so much, I'd kill her. What was she trying to pull? I didn't meet up with guys ever. Never ever. And she knew that. Where friends were a liability, getting tangled up with the opposite sex was close to suicide. "No way. I can't go out with him."

"Great. See you ladies tonight," he said, completely ignoring me.

"Good. Bring Oliver." Mona winked.

Panic started to get the better of me. "No. No, I'm not going. There's no date. No date." My voice was high and scratchy.

"There's definitely a date," Mona said.

It was a good thing we were in broad daylight. Otherwise, I'd be blowing lights by now. Electricity was licking the bottoms of my feet, and I let out a breath as I tried to make it disperse. Marquez stuck out his hand and his glowing Raven was plainly visible. I could feel the electricity itching to arc over to him. Like it was craving to zap him.

I wasn't sure if that was my frustration or my attraction or something else, but no matter what, it was bad news. The energy I harnessed had never moved like that before. I wasn't sure what it meant and couldn't afford to find out.

I shoved my hands in my back pockets and took a step away from him. "I guess I'll see you tonight." I spun around. "Let's go, Mona." I wanted out of there so bad, I'd even skip the funnel cake.

I didn't wait to see if she'd follow. She would. So, I kept my pace fast as I could as I moved through the swarms of people.

"What was that all about?" she said when we got to her beat-up silver coupe.

"Nothing."

"That was *not* nothing. That was the definition of

something. I've never seen you give a guy more than two seconds notice, but you flirted with him. And then you ran."

"I did *not*." Okay, so maybe I ran. But I didn't flirt. Wait, did I?

"Yes, you totally ran. I'm sweating, thank you very much." She wheezed. "Jeez. I need to work out." She fanned herself. "You definitely flirted with him. Sort of. Don't worry. We'll work on it."

I didn't want to work on it. Thinking about Knight made my stomach feel like it was filled with butterflies and I didn't like it. Not one bit. He had something that I needed, so I'd show up tonight, but getting tangled with a dual helixed Raven would be asking for disaster.

So, why was he so damned appealing?

Be smart, Cipher. You didn't come this far by thinking with your ass.

"The looks he gave you…they sizzled."

I glanced at her. "How would you know? You were off with Oliver."

"I was standing right there with him. We were both watching you."

Wow. I'd been so wrapped up in Knight that I hadn't noticed them dissecting every word we said.

"Neither of us could believe how the two of you were acting. We shared several meaningful looks about it," she said with an eyebrow waggle.

As much as I wanted to blow off this news, I knew I'd been acting like an idiot. But Knight? That could be his normal. It probably was his normal. With his looks, I was sure he had plenty of experience flirting. "It's because I wasn't what he was expecting." I'd talked to him on and off for years, but we'd never met in real life. For good reason. This was exactly why I went to the trouble of disguising my voice and identity.

Mona shook her head. "You can lie to yourself all you want, but that guy likes you. He *likes you* likes you. You should at least try to give him a shot. See how it goes."

Get a root canal. Clean out the Griz's sewage line. Have my eyes poked out. All these seemed like better, safer options. "I'm getting my processor and heading home. No gaming. No flirting. No nothing."

"If you say so." She tapped her fingers along the steering wheel. "But I think that's a mistake."

"I say so." I wanted to mean that, but I wasn't sure how it'd actually play out.

No matter what I wanted—or my hormones wanted—I couldn't afford any complications. Down the line, maybe we could meet up again. But for now, simple was best. No entanglements.

If I couldn't stick to that plan, I was going to be in a   huge   heap   of   shit.

Chapter Six

KNIGHT

I watched Cipher walk away. The sway of her hips hypnotized me. It killed me a little to watch her go, but I'd see her at the club. Or else I'd go hunt her down.

"You think that was the real Cipher?" Oliver asked as we stepped into a secluded corner of the staff tent.

I shot Oliver a look as I tapped on the anti-bug software. Cipher wasn't on any hot lists, but better safe than sorry—if anyone heard this conversation, it would only raise questions I couldn't afford to answer.

"That definitely was her. Blows my mind that she's the one who's been kicking my ass in just about everything." I paused to consider the question. "Is Cipher the girl I'm looking for? I don't know." I didn't want to use names here. There were too many ears, bug-blockers or not, but I couldn't help thinking about it. I rubbed my eyes as I thought. If that were Emma, I'd be in way over my head. Cipher was a super hot, über-hacker who I'd been a fan of since forever. I'd been trying to hang out with Cipher for years… Emma was the girl who'd saved me. I owed her. I'd rearranged my whole life for her. If these two obsessions were actually one person, she'd own me. "Maybe? I thought I'd know just by looking at her, but I don't. Turns out, twelve years is a long time when you're still growing up." I paused. "But I know one thing."

"What's that?"

"Whoever that is, I want her. Bad."

"That's dangerous." Oliver crossed his arms. "You'll be tied to the one you're looking for. You know you can't start a relationship with some other girl. You'll just end up hurting them both. If you start something with Cipher, it's gotta be your usual one and done."

He was starting to piss me off. "It doesn't have to be a romantic pairing. That's not why I did it." I thought for a second. Damn it. "She had freckles. Her eyes were hazel-green. But I don't remember her lips being so bitable."

Oliver chuckled. "Did you feel a charge off her?"

I knew he didn't mean the romantic kind. "She wouldn't let me touch her." That was something else to add into the might be Emma column. If it were her, she'd shy away from touch. Or maybe she just didn't want some strange dude pawing at her.

I needed proof that Cipher wasn't Emma. I'd run searches on Cipher before, but I'd assumed a lot of things about her that weren't true. Mostly that she was a he.

I needed to get a grip before this obsession really took hold of me.

A guy in black motioned me toward the door.

I sighed. I'd forgotten he'd come to get me while I was talking to Cipher. "I better go find out what the boss needs." I hated that I had to go do this, but keeping my cover meant jumping when Colonel Santiago said jump.

"Catch you back in the barracks?"

I tapped off the bug jammer and tucked away my phone. "Nah. I'm going to head out. I've got a processor to build. Meet me there?"

"Sure thing."

We bumped fists, and I went around the back of the tents to the temp buildings. I knocked twice on Santiago's door.

"Come in." The command came through the door.

I opened it, and a blast of cold air hit me. The movable building held only one office with stark metal walls. The desk bolted to the floor took up most of the space and the only decorations were two folding chairs and the comp screen on the back wall. Everything was highly portable. When the Trials moved, they'd hook a rig to the unit and drive it to the next Void on the tour.

Santiago sat behind his desk. His beady eyes tracked me as I stepped into his office. I was reasonably certain the asshole had given up his soul a long time ago, and I hated what I'd had to do on my last op under his command. It was something I had to live with, but participating had cemented myself into the ranks of the obedient, giving me the access I needed to help the Ravens. But I'd die with a black mark, and hope the afterlife forgave me of my sins.

"Have a seat, Marquez."

"Yes, sir." The chair screeched, metal feet against the metal floor, as I sat. I kept my gaze firmly on his as I waited for him to explain why I was here. Santiago always liked a bit of a power play to start off a meeting.

"It's unusual to see you taking a break from ops to work the Trials," he said, finally.

"I go where I'm needed, sir." I maintained my cool. No need to give anything away. He could be fishing for something or he could be buttering me up for a request. I was betting on the latter.

"You might have noticed that Parson is running the show this go-round."

"I did, sir." My mouth was a little dry, but he'd notice if I swallowed. I kept my breathing even.

His small grin worried me. Nothing good could come of this. "Well, we've had a bit of a problem and since you're here with two of your team members, it crossed my mind that you could help."

"Anything I can do, I'd be honored, sir." Lie. I didn't have time to add bullshit Seligo missions to my itinerary.

"You might have seen the reports that some Red Helix girls have been neutralized recently."

I nodded, not trusting myself to say anything until he fully explained what he wanted.

"It's a problem that they survived. Given, I'm not about to start a witch hunt to find who's been taking out the trash—probably some of those vigilante Ravens people—but it doesn't look good for us that these Reds are turning up dead in public. Orders came down to use the Trials as a cover while we hunt down the few girls last sighted in the Arizona Void."

He pushed a tablet across his desk. "I know this was meant to be a temporary assignment, but I'm requesting that you stay on. You've done good work for me before, and I feel that you can take care of this little problem without it becoming public knowledge."

Over a hundred ways to kill him ran through my head. I could slam his head on the desk and twist his neck before the guy even attempted to react. Channeling my training, I kept my face blank, but I wanted to jump the desk with every fiber of my being. My hands didn't shake with anger as I took the tablet.

The screen showed a list of nine names. Two in this area of the Void. One was Emma. I forced myself to loosen my grip on the tablet before I snapped it in half.

I met Santiago's gaze. "There've been four dead so far. Now you're telling me nine more girls are out there for sure? How did so many get away?"

He shrugged. "It's not a perfect system. Most people don't have the stomach to euthanize a baby when it comes down to it. Even with the known danger. But it's necessary."

Emma did kill my father, so it wasn't hard to imagine why the Red Helixes were so misunderstood. Yeah, she was dangerous, but so was I. Even before I was paired with her. "I understand. Do we have any intel on the abilities these Reds have developed?" I needed to know how much he knew if I was going to stop him.

"Some. You'll find the essential details in each girl's file. Some are more exhaustive than others. Our main target here is Emma Jean Boyd. She's one of the oldest of the bunch, and extremely dangerous. It's been confirmed that she can manipulate electrical current." Santiago leaned over the desk. "This is a dicey mission. Because it involves neutralizing Reds, it'll involve hazard pay as well as a bonus for each Red captured or killed."

As much as the idea of this mission made my stomach clench, nobody else could have it. At least not until Emma was caught. After that, I'd try to pass the orders on to another Raven on the inside. "Count me in, sir."

Santiago grinned, flashing his perfectly white teeth. "I'm glad I was right about you." He stood and reached across the table.

I took his hand, making my grip a little too firm. "Thank you, sir."

"This overrides any of your previous assignments. You've full license to use your time as you see fit and requisition whatever resources you require. Just keep me in the loop with regular reports."

"Excellent. I'll get started immediately and keep you updated."

"Good. See that you do."

"Yes, sir." I tucked the tablet under my arm, and excused myself.

I kept my body relaxed as I moved through the grounds to my bike. Telling myself that this couldn't have worked out better didn't dull my anger. My time was my own now and I was in charge of finding Emma for both the Ravens and the Seligo. Only now the Seligo would be watching me more closely than usual.

I revved my bike and took off toward my safe

house apartment. Time was of the essence. Too many people had Emma in their sights: whoever was murdering the Reds, the Seligo, and the Ravens. I'd bet my ass she had no idea how many people were after her.

***

The apartment that Lady Eva had set up for us as our local safe house was in a towering sky rise. The building took up a full square block, with over two-hundred floors. The unit-size options were tiny, seriously tiny, and microscopic. She'd most likely gone the tiny route, but the lock on the door was legit. Full hand scan, retinal scan, plus an alphanumeric code.

When I opened the door, I found a futon next to a desk. It was currently in sofa mode, but a pile of white sheets and blankets were precisely folded with a pillow on top. An L-shaped couch was hidden in an alcove in the back corner of the room. Dex and Oliver were already logged into a game, their feet propped on the low coffee table as they faced the massive vid screen.

"What's up?" I said.

They grunted as gunfire filled the apartment. I ignored them and checked out the rest of the space. Past the kitchenette, the bedroom had been converted to a workroom for me. All the supplies and tools I could want were piled in clear plastic boxes labeled by part.

It was as if Lady Eva were psychic. She anticipated the needs of her people better than anyone I'd ever met. Damned if I knew how she did it.

The bathroom was stocked with essentials. Spare clothes in the closet. Four different stacks. One for me, one for Dex, and one for Oliver's huge ass. The last stack was miscellaneous girl clothes. Lady Eva always did plan for success.

"I'm going to get to work on the processor for Cipher. Give me an hour."

I didn't wait for their response. Working would clear my head of Santiago and his orders.

As I stepped into the small workroom, I couldn't help but think of Emma. She was the one who got me hooked on computers. She'd brought me my first one. Just a little piece of shit thing that was mostly garbage—I was pretty sure she'd gotten it from a scrap sale. She'd marched over to my backyard and told me that if I learned a skill, it would be worth something when I grew up. Apparently, the girl thought I needed direction. She'd broken her parents' no electronics rule by giving me the unit and showing me how it worked, but her stubbornness had paid off. I never would've showed aptitude as a Green if not for her.

I rolled up my sleeves, revealing my helix tat, as I started to work. The green half showed anyone who cared that I had a brain for science. Both engineering and programming, in my case. Anything tech, I could use, rework, retool. I'd been good before all the modifications, but with all my enhancements, the stuff was second nature.

Maybe Emma really was Cipher?

No, I reminded myself. *She couldn't be. Cipher was way too short to be Emma.*

I finished with one processor, and was still pissed at Santiago. So, I built four more.

By the time I was done working, some of the tension I'd built up was gone. I stepped into the main room. My stomach was on empty. "Any chance there's food in the fridge?"

"We ordered pizza," Dex said without looking away from the game. "And there's beer."

That would work. I opened the fridge and pulled a bottle out, taking a long pull before setting it down and opening the pizza box. I ate the first slice at room temp before nuking another three slices. It wasn't good—typical cheap-ass Void food with soy cheese and additives to the bread that make me feel more full than I actually was—but I ate it anyways.

Dex came to stand in the kitchen with me. "What'd Santiago want?"

I killed the first beer, and grabbed a second, popping the cap off on the countertop. "I'm supposed to hunt down and kill Reds." I pulled the tablet from my pocket and handed it over.

"At least this means we can take over finding them. Fake their deaths and get them to safety."

I leaned against the counter, rolling the chilled bottle between my hands. "How many can we get before they realize what we're doing?"

Oliver joined us, taking the tablet from Dex. "Don't be such a pessimist."

"It's not pessimism. It's realism." I so wasn't getting into a philosophical debate with these two. Oliver was too happy and hopeful, and Dex...well, Dex saw the world in a different way than anyone else I'd ever known. He had a sick sense of humor in situations not normally funny, and never took anything very seriously. In our situation, that wasn't normal. "Anyway. He was definitely withholding info. I'm guessing he's running multiple teams on this, each with different targets. But it's interesting that I got her file in particular."

"Agreed." Dex sighed. "How do you want to play it?"

"Same thing we were planning before. Now that we're off arena duty we're supposed to focus on hunting Reds, and even stay on after the Trials leave the area, but we've got to make up bullshit progress reports." I paused. The guys weren't going to like what I said next. "And if someone's cover is getting blown, it'll be mine. Once I find Emma, I won't be able to keep up a double life anyway."

"The higher-ups are going to be watching us because of our relationship with you," Dex said. "Might be safe to assume all of our covers are going to get blown." He crossed his arms. "Well, I was starting to get tired of this covert stuff anyhow. It was really cutting into my gaming schedule."

I rolled my eyes. Getting found out was going to be an adjustment to all of us. If it happened. "I'm going to change into civie clothes, and I suggest you both do the same. Then we'll hit up this Marx's. See if we can figure out if Emma is Cipher. The details don't line up, but there's something…" Or maybe I was being hopeful. "If not, Cipher might be one of the other Reds on our list—Steph Keane is a possibility. Or could be Devan Coda. None are a direct match, but Cipher's Raven alone is worth investigating. So, we check her out, and if she's not Emma, then you guys take care of her and I'll move on. Cool?"

"Sounds like a plan."

Oliver grunted his agreement.

"Good." I would've taken their opinions into consideration, but it was nice to have them back me up. "Let's get this show on the road. No time for fuck-ups, douchebags."

"Us? Fuck-up?" Dex held his hand over his heart. "I'm insulted, asshole."

Oliver punched my shoulder. "We know what's at stake here. But don't let this get too personal."

He was right, but I didn't see any way around it. This mission to find Emma was personal. Extremely fucking personal.

Chapter Seven

CIPHER

Waiting for a new processor wasn't working for me. I'd never been a patient person and I was itching to get into the files I'd salvaged from the Seligo. My portacom wasn't exactly secure, but it was better than nothing. Still, I couldn't use it from the Griz. I couldn't risk any traces coming back to me.

I messaged Mona telling her I was going back to the city and I'd meet her at Marx's at seven.

You better be there, bitch, she replied.

Don't freak. I'll be there, I answered.

I threw on a pair of black leggings, white tank, and super-thin gray hoodie. I rolled up the sleeves to show my Morse code tattoo, and pulled on a pair of combat boots. I liked to be comfortable, in case I needed to run, but I still needed to look halfway decent. I put on a minimal amount of makeup and pulled my blue hair in a high ponytail. Mona would still say I should've dressed nicer, but I didn't care. It wasn't like I was trying to impress Knight. Okay, maybe I wanted to, but that would've gone against my plan to stay away from him. So I was purposefully dressing low key. I grabbed my little backpack with my portacomp and a few essentials and headed out.

The park was teeming with activity. By this time, the night owls were up again, but it wasn't late enough that the earlier risers were back in bed. The desert sand kicked up around my feet as I moved between trailers and RVs. Transpos went by the gate every five minutes. Any bus would take me straight into the Void proper. There were plenty of rooftops to work from, especially in this area. The rooftops were filled with homeless people, and I could blend easily and get a clear link to any number of secure satellites. I just had to pick a building to work from.

The transpo bus was nearly empty when I got on. The patterned material covering the metal seats was faded and dirt turned the lighter colors to a dingy gray-brown. It smelled like garbage and sweat. When I'd first started taking these buses, I'd tried not to touch anything, but now I was mostly desensitized to the filth. It was part of the joy of living in the Voids. Even though I had the Griz, I'd never drive her into the city. She was too hard to maneuver in the crowded streets.

After an hour and what felt like a million stops, I hopped out at a random spot. I wasn't exactly sure where I was, but that was the point. Logging into my account when someone might be looking was dumb, and doing so in a totally random spot marginally negated that stupidity.

I walked five blocks until I found a rundown building. It was shorter than most. Only five stories. The windows were boarded, but a few boards had been pulled off. Squatters didn't care if a building was condemned or not, only that it had a roof and walls. Sometimes even those were nonessential.

Loiterers ambled around outside the building, but didn't pay me any attention. No one was stupid enough to get in each other's business out here. It was more of a place to either disappear or lose yourself. To forget. I stepped over three sleeping forms—at least I hoped they were sleeping—to get to the chained double doors. Pulling open the heavy metal took a little doing, especially with all the rust, but I managed without pulling a muscle. The smell inside was horrible. Piss, shit, vomit, and alcohol mixed with rot and mildew. The lights were busted out—not that they would've worked if they hadn't been busted. Glass and trash covered the floor. The sole of my shoe crackled when I picked my foot up.

Nasty, but desperation led people to all kinds of crazy things. I knew that better than most.

Shoving my shirt over my nose helped me not gag, and I started to carefully climb the stairs, testing each step before placing my full weight on the wooden planks. I didn't want to die at the bottom of a stairwell.

A few people were camped out on the roof. They passed around a glass pipe and I knew that on the off chance they noticed me, they'd never remember. All they cared about was getting high.

I spotted an empty space off to the side away from the druggies that was as good a place to work as any. I pulled my two-inch by one-inch portacomp out of my backpack. Pressing two buttons, I opened it, expanding the device into a ball. The two projection points lit up, one casting the lines of a keyboard along the rooftop and the other forming my screens—one big, two smaller.

I cracked my knuckles before entering my access code and looked up the position of my usual link. The satellite had a special secure login that I'd designed myself. I had a handful of satellites that I rotated between.

Once I was in, it didn't take long to pull the information from my cloud. As I scanned through the files, it was obvious that not everything I'd been trying to copy had made it. And most of the Shadow Ravens stuff was missing.

Hacking in again—for a third time—seemed like a damned stupid idea, but I didn't have many options. I needed to know more about the Shadow Ravens. Could I really trust a Helix guy with raven tattoos? Were they really willing to help an unstable Red, or was this some front to trap people?

I navigated to the Black Helix files and looked up Sergeant H. Marquez a.k.a. Knight. If I was meeting up with him tonight, I needed to know how deep in this guy was, and how much I could trust him.

Even I could admit that his background was pretty impressive. He'd managed to get through the Trials at thirteen. Fast and strong were a given, but that wasn't the impressive part. Knight was smart. His tests were off the charts, and the combination of skills that had earned him a dual helix made him a really big deal. He served as a ground ops tech, along with two of his classmates—Dex, who had a Blue and Black, and Oliver, who had a Green and Black.

But Knight didn't have a single disciplinary mark on his files. He'd never done anything bad. Nothing to warrant investigation. Pretty impressive for a double agent—especially with how paranoid the Seligo were. They assumed everyone was an enemy. The guy must lie incredibly well—I couldn't let myself forget that.

I clicked on some video clips of his missions. They were a little more violent than I could stand, so I skipped over to the candid images of him in various assignments. The intensity on his face was scary when he worked. It didn't match with the teasing guy I'd met, and the two-faced thing really freaked me out.

As I moved through the file, a pic of him half-dressed filled my little screen and I groaned. He was too much. I left it up…to desensitize myself to his hotness.

Also, because those abs were too good not to look at.

The Shadow Ravens file was frustratingly incomplete. Everything was suspected locations and suspected agents, but nothing was backed up with facts. Apparently the Ravens were kicking the Seligo's asses on the spying front, but that didn't help me any.

I moved on to Jack's folder. The most recent file detailed his mission to hunt down Reds. It was from two days ago. I scanned a recent memo to Dr. Nagi and my blood ran cold.

Power fluctuations reported in the Nevada Void approx twenty-one minutes ago. Sent unit to investigate. Type of fluctuation leads to Devan Coda, not Emma Jean Boyd.

Orders are to capture or kill.

Nine Reds are still unaccounted for. Four have been neutralized.
Update to follow.

-Parson

I hadn't been in the Nevada Voids in a while. I wondered who this Devan chick was. Could I get a warning to her? Or had she already been caught?

Reading through the file and knowing that Jack was actively trying to find Reds pissed me off. I'd always hoped I was the only one he was after... Was his vendetta because of me or because he hated all Reds? Or both?

Either way this had to be stopped.

I fiddled with my lip ring as I thought, running my teeth gently against it. Helping myself was hard enough. How could I begin to help other Reds? Was there a serum we could use? Something that took away or toned down the side effects of being a Red so we could blend in? I'd have to look into that if I could get into the Citadel's mainframe again.

I needed those processors. I had to find a way to control my powers before they got me caught.

There was no avoiding another visit to Marx's. I'd have to trust Knight, at least for this little thing. Then, we could part ways and I'd never have to see him again.

A prick of pain hit me at the thought of never seeing him again. It was so dumb. I didn't know him. Not even a little. We'd had a few conversations online. Nothing major. Sure, I respected him and his work, so it was only natural that I felt some sort of connection once I saw how hot he was, but I couldn't let that attraction get the better of me. Controlling my emotions was essential. I couldn't afford to feel anything for this guy. Not in any real way.

I shut down my portacomp and stashed it in my backpack. I wanted to get to Marx's before Knight did. Positioning myself with the upper hand would help me keep control of the situation.

Any control I could get and keep around him would be a feat.

***

Marx's was mostly empty except for the gamers at the tables and on the jumbo screen. The crowd that gathered to watch was thick at lunch and in the evenings. It was only half past six. In a couple hours, it'd be packed. I usually avoided going up on the jumbo, but with it being so empty, it was okay. The bigger screen made for better gaming.

My avatar—a girl in a hooded robe with a staff—loaded and I started to play against whoever was around. The control panel was a little high for playing at length, but I rolled out my shoulders, trying to relax into it. My fingers flew across the board, sending commands to my avatar as it moved through the 3D world. I lost myself in the fantasy forest, filled with fairies, gnomes, and wizards, casting spell after spell and melting the baddies in giant balls of flame.

Halfway through the game, the three people I was playing against bailed out.

"Fucking Cipher," the last one muttered as he climbed down the stage.

I almost felt sorry for him. "What? Can't keep up?"

"Not with you," he said. "It's no fun getting slaughtered."

I sighed. Maybe I shouldn't have been taking my aggression out on the players, but killing a ton of slogs and a few wicked combo spells had done wonders for my mood. "Come back up. We'll switch modes and play together."

"You mean it?" The guy's voice cracked. He was way too young to be in this bar, but who was I to say anything? He was probably only a few years younger than me.

"Yep." I hit a few buttons and reloaded the game. A few more clicks and we were playing against online players instead of each other.

"I want back in next round," another guy said as he jumped back on stage.

Soon, all seven spots were taken. We strategized on our headsets and I took charge of the group as we hit different dungeons. Time melted away as one scene flowed into another. We fought in a rainforest, abandoned ruins, and a temple city. Before we switched to the alien planet landscape, I heard the voice—the one that made me shiver—behind me.

"I want in. Lowest scorer is out. And we switch to team battle."

"Who the hell is this guy? You can't come in here and take over. We're playing with *Cipher*."

I looked at the boards. "DickBallz is out. And seriously, get a new handle. That sounds like a nine-year-old made it up. It's embarrassing."

"That's because I made it up when I was nine. If I

change it now, I lose my standing," the guy two stations over from me said. His face was bright red and he was sporting more than his fair share of pimples. Poor guy.

"Change the name. I'll get you re-upped," I said.

"Seriously?" His eyes were wide.

"Yes. Just message me on my site. Now make room for Knight or the deal's off."

"Wait. Knight? As in *the* Knight?"

Knight gave me a not-too-friendly look. "Way to announce it."

I shrugged and hit the start button. "If you're gonna play, step up. Otherwise DickBallz is back in."

"The hell if I'm going to let some guy with a lame handle take my spot." He put on the headset and held his hands over the controls.

"We're splitting into two teams." I rattled off some names, trying to keep the skill level even and leaving Knight on the opposing team.

The screen faded and then a desolate alien planet landscape appeared. Jagged black rock formations rose from the ground like knives. I took cover behind one, and the countdown started.

It was a fast, fierce battle. By the time all was said and done, each member of my team had been killed no less than twenty times. I hadn't been killed yet. The guys on the opposing team had all died no less than twenty-five times, and Knight had been killed once. By me.

Knight put his headset down. "Drink?"

I turned around to check the crowds. The area in front of the bar was packed three deep, as people shouted orders to Sandra. The areas between the tables were totally filled as people danced, watched the games in progress, or tried to get lucky. A quick check of my com told me it was nearly nine. Mona was down there somewhere, probably annoyed that I was gaming instead of flirting.

Guess I'd better stop stalling. I'd already beat him at this game. Why not try a different kind of game? "Sure."

I followed him down to the bar.

Sandra patted the bar in front of where she was standing, yelling at the people in front of us to make way. "Another fancy drink for you?"

It was really nice that she remembered. I grinned. "That'd be great."

"I'll take a beer." Knight glanced at me. "Fancy drink?"

"Sure thing," Sandra said and she got to work. This time she didn't have to go underground to get what she needed. She had it ready for me.

"French Seventy-Five," I said.

He leaned against the bar. "That does sound fancy."

I shrugged, trying to play off that his twinkling eyes weren't getting to me, because they totally were. "It's good. You can try a sip if you want."

His grin was startling. It transformed his face and I couldn't look away even if I tried. "I'll try anything of yours that you'll let me," he said.

I tried to look cool, but if the bar were any brighter, he'd see my blush. "That's some line."

"It's not a line." He pulled something out of his pocket. "For you."

The little square container fit in the palm of his

hand. "What's in it?"

"Processors. Five of them."

No way. "I thought you said you didn't have any."

"I didn't. I made them this afternoon."

I'd been impressed before, but now I was blown away. He'd made this many by hand in a matter of hours? How was that even possible?

"What do I owe you?" I reached for the box, but he held it out of reach.

"A date."

I took a step back. I liked to deal in cash-only transactions. But a date? Not going to happen. "No date. I'll pay for them. Normal rate?"

"Nope." His grin meant trouble. "The date clause is non-negotiable."

What was his deal? A date with me couldn't be worth the grand I was willing to pay him. Why would he turn down the money? I didn't trust it. No one wanted a date that bad. Especially not with me. I wasn't sociable enough to be desirable. "Say I agree to a date, how do you know I won't change my mind later?"

"I trust you."

He trusted me? That was going to make me feel like an asshole when I blew him off.

Screw it. I probably wouldn't be in the area long enough to keep the promise. Leading him on wasn't cool, but I needed those processors. "I'll try. Depends on when you want to go. That's the best I can do."

He lowered the box, and I snatched it from him before shoving it in my bra.

"Here you go, Cipher," Sandra said as she slid my drink along the bar.

"Thanks." I took a sip, letting the sweet tang run down my throat. "Perfect."

She grinned and handed Knight a bottle. He paid for both of us before I could stop him.

A thought occurred to me. "Um. So this counts as the date, right?"

"No. A date is when I pick you up at your place, and take you someplace nice and quiet and we share a meal. This is not nice or quiet, and we're not eating. But good try."

I spotted a bowl of nuts on the bar, and grabbed a handful. "I'm eating," I said as I munched.

He gave me a grin that nearly melted my knees.

"There you are," Mona said, cutting off the retort that I was just about to come up with. If my brain would start working again.

Mona wore one of her trademark micro dresses and perilously high heels. If she could pull that kind of outfit off, which she could, why not rock it? Oliver towered behind her with another guy who had shoulder-length blond hair. I'd bet good money he was Dex.

Staying much longer was a bad idea, especially now that I'd gotten what I needed. It was time to go. I downed my drink in one gulp and set the empty glass on the bar. The metal railing zapped me lightly with static electricity as I brushed against it.

Oh no. Losing control here would be beyond bad. "Well, thanks for the date, but it's getting late. Time for me to head home."

"Go? What? No! You can't bail yet." Mona blocked my path to the exit.

She was going to be pissed no matter what. I

couldn't do this whole normal thing. I was a live wire, ready to zap anyone who got too close, and Knight made me feel things I shouldn't be feeling. The hold I had on my ability was already weak. I didn't need anyone around who made me weaker.

"Wanna head out with me or are you staying?" I asked Mona.

"No. You're—" Mona started, but I cut her off.

"Going. Later." I spun.

"Wait." Knight stepped in front of me, blocking my way.

A blast of electricity shot out of me before I knew what I was doing. The lights overhead flickered, and the monitors around the club blinked off and on.

A chorus of curses rang out through the room as the games reset.

I froze.

Shit. That didn't just happen.

I swallowed as the hand around my arm pulled me in. Why wasn't he on the floor? He should be dead.

Why couldn't I feel the buzz of electricity pushing against me anymore?

"Hey," Knight said as he ran his finger down my face. He tilted his head to the side, staring at me. Studying me. But he didn't seem bothered by the voltage that was flowing into him.

There was no way he didn't feel the shock. Why wasn't he letting go of my arm? I struggled to break free, but his grip wasn't budging.

"Emma?" He whispered the words almost reverently.

I gasped. No one knew that name.

Panic swept through me and I stomped on his foot, finally breaking his hold. The little bit of control I'd grabbed slipped away again. The light over my head exploded, raining glass down on us.

His hand gripped my arm again. His light green eyes were wide as he searched my face.

"What did you call me?" I fought to pull away. How did he know my real name?

"It *is* you." He pulled me against his chest and took a deep breath.

What was going on? I squirmed. "Let go." I punched him in the stomach, but he didn't even flinch.

"It's her," he said.

The music shut off as a group of men in all black entered the bar through the side door.

Oh God. How did they get here so fast? Did Knight send them?

The three guys moved as one to block Mona and me from the Black Helixes' view.

I glanced at Mona. "How fast can you run in those shoes?"

"I can run in anything. Why? What's going on? What just happened?"

"You're not running," Knight said.

"Yes, I am. Mona, we need to go. Now."

Knight held my shoulders. "Don't move. Don't run. If you do, they'll see. You have to stay hidden here until they're not looking."

I tried to break free of Knight's grasp, but he didn't let me go. "Your buddies are about to make my life hell. Let go now or I'll make you let go."

He leaned down, talking softly. "There are too

many of them. You can't outrun them, and they're watching for anyone who leaves."

"Staying's not an option. It's run or get caught for sure. At least if I run, I have a chance."

I reached for the electricity, but it was gone—I could still feel it there, but it drained away as fast as I could pull it. As soon as I jerked away from Knight, it was back, stronger than ever, and three more lights exploded overhead.

Knight pulled me into him, blocking me from the falling glass. With his hand clamped firmly on my arm, the current drained away. I reached for it, but it was like he was sucking it all away through his skin.

How could he absorb all that and live? Knight was blocking my ability. "What—"

He shook his head. "Let me help you," he mouthed the words.

I wanted to know how first, but I didn't have time to debate with him.

My best choices were always based on intuition.

It took me all of two seconds to decide that I'd have a better chance getting out of here with him than without. He had a dual helix, but he also had a Raven. He wasn't like any other helix I'd come across.

The Black Helix soldiers were busy cornering the people in the gaming area. They checked IDs, throwing anyone who hesitated to the floor. It was chaos, but that wouldn't last for long.

I spilled my plan. "I'm going to blow the transformers, knock out all communication and surveillance, and get out of here in the dark. But you have to let go of me."

"It's not a bad plan," Oliver said.

At least Oliver was on my wavelength. "I know. Now get your guy to let me go."

"Fine," Knight said. He let go and the electricity was mine again. It licked along my skin as it built. I didn't have long. The electricity would make me a beacon in the room as my skin started to glow.

"Better close your eyes," I said, but Knights' gaze stayed open and focused on me.

I counted to three as power gathered, and then let it rip—hoping I'd built up enough energy.

The lights exploded, raining glass down on everyone. Monitors sparked and went black. Voices shouted.

"We have to hide you," Knight said in my ear.

"We can exit through the cellar. There's a hatch in the floor behind the bar."

"Good. We'll move toward the end of the bar. One at a time, go under the gap." I slid a hand along the plexi surface, pushing behind the people in the way as I felt my way in the dark. When we got to the end, I went around the corner and under, tugging Mona behind me. Knight, Dex, and Oliver stood frozen, blocking the break in the bar from the rest of the room.

What the hell were they doing?

"They're coming this way. Hide. Don't make a sound," Knight whispered.

My pulse raced. "Then we need to run. Now."

"Black Helixes can see really well in the dark. Just stay where you are. Trust me. Don't move."

I felt Mona shaking next to me, and pulled her into my side as I tried to keep a grip on my ability. She grasped my hand in hers, gripping tight. This was why I didn't have friends. I got people killed.

"Marquez," a deep voice said.

I knew that voice. My Uncle Jack. I struggled to keep control of my emotions. I'd never forgive myself if I zapped Mona.

"Yes, sir."

"I shouldn't be surprised to see you here. I heard Colonel Santiago put you on task to find the Red. We got a few fluctuations here tonight, and I took a chance." A throat cleared. "Where's the Red? Have you confirmed that this one is Emma Jean Boyd?"

I put my other hand over my mouth to cover the gasp that wanted to slip through. Knight was the one hunting the Reds? And I'd trusted him?

I hoped I wasn't wrong about him. This could be the biggest fuck-up of my life. The last fuck-up of my life.

Chapter Eight

KNIGHT

The lights were still off, but a few of the Blacks had cracked their chemlights. It was more than enough for me to see every wrinkle in Parson's face. He was a Seligo of the worst kind. Every time I was on a mission under him, shit went fully FUBAR. Civilian casualties were always high, and everyone knew about his wicked vendetta against the Red Helixes. Probably because he'd let Emma slip past him, and rumor said Dr. Nagi was only giving him enough serums to stay alive—nothing more. The guy was aging, and not well.

"Sir, I'd narrowed the search area down to this club and the surrounding area when the lights blew. No physical target yet, but I'm certain she's within a half-mile radius from this spot." My voice didn't waiver. I'd learned to lie a long time ago, and did it well. "Would've called you if you hadn't shown."

He looked around the room, assessing the layout. Five teams of five were working the space, but I was sure the club was surrounded, and more were likely waiting to jump in if the crowd got out of hand.

"Good work. Your record shows you're always spot on about this kind of thing. When I noticed your tracker signal right in the middle of the fluctuations, I knew you had her cornered here." He clapped my shoulder and I wanted to break his face with my fist. "Good work, Sergeant. Fast, too. We've got all the exits blocked. She's in here. I can feel it. She blew three transformers, but this is the confirmed epicenter. We just need to figure out which one she is."

"Yes, sir. If she's still here, we'll find her." My words were harsh and cold. Distant. I crossed my arms. "My best guess is she's hiding with the gamers in that area." I pointed toward the cluster of kids the helix team was interrogating.

"Excellent," Parson said, turning toward the group now huddled in the corner. They were surrounded by one of the teams. Colonel Santiago was with them, organizing their movements. "If she turns up, you'll get a hefty bonus."

"Thank you, sir." *Now fuck off.*

I counted to ten as he walked away before breathing again.

I should've gotten her away as soon as there was even the slightest possibility that she was Emma. Why had I played that stupid game with her? I should've grabbed her and run. Asked questions later. So unbelievably dumb.

How in the hell were we going to get out of here?

I kept it together by concentrating on smooth breaths, even if my heart was racing.

"We have to go," Emma whispered. It was hard not to react to the sound of her voice. A little low with a hint of rasp, like she was a smoker, but I knew she wasn't. She smelled like coconut, not cigarettes.

"Don't worry. I've got you." I continued to watch the team as they moved through the club.

Oliver caught my eye. He pointed to himself and Dex and then nodded.

They were saying they were with me, but that wasn't an option. "No way," I mouthed. They couldn't blow their cover for this.

Oliver moved a little closer. "You need someone to watch her back. You can't get her out of here without getting caught unless you have our help. We're out anyway. Everyone knows the three of us are like brothers. If you leave now, we're screwed by association."

Three Raven covers blown in one night. This wasn't going to go over well. There weren't that many of us within the helix ranks. The Lady put in years of work to secure every covert operative and build cover stories.

She was going to be so pissed.

The tracker deactivation device was the size of a pinky nail, and each of us had one on hand just for this kind of nightmare. I set the micro-needle against my helix and pressed the button, killing the code that linked me to the Seligo satellites.

Dex and Oliver did the same. Had we been outside the blackout zone, the Citadel's computers would've known within a matter of seconds and someone would've instantly scrambled to find out why three helixes just went missing.

With the blackout, we could fall under the radar for a little bit. Long enough to get us out, at least.

Once the system was back online and we showed up as missing from the system, our covers would be officially blown. I should probably regret it more than I did, but I wouldn't hate leaving the lies behind—especially not with Emma at my side.

Now it was time to run like hell. The farther, the faster, the better.

The other Black Helixes were separating everyone in the club into manageable groups. They'd separated the girls from a few guys. The guys started yelling and shoving—one took a swing and in five seconds, that whole side of the room was brawling. The attack team scrambled to control the crowd that was now fighting back.

Time to go.

I dropped to the floor and crawled under the break in the bar. Sandra opened the hatch in the floor. For whatever reason she was helping, I'd take it. She opened her mouth to talk, and I put my finger against her lips. I moved to whisper in her ear. "Thank you."

She was shaking, but there wasn't anything I could do. I had to get Emma out. Now. Taking Sandra with us wasn't an option.

I went down the dark stairs first, grabbing Emma's hand as I moved past her. I put her hand in my back belt loop so she could hold on while I kept both hands free. It also kept her within arm's reach. After years of searching, I'd finally found her. I wasn't about to let her get away again.

Emma pulled Mona along behind her. Dex and Oliver followed, closing the hatch behind us. There was barely enough light to see by. Rows of metal shelving along the walls were stacked high with cases of alcohol. Kegs were piled in groups of three and four, but even in the well-organized room, we wasted nearly three minutes looking for the way out.

"It's an empty room," I said. "We're trapped."

"No," Emma said. "There's an abandoned tunnel system here. Drug runners built them. Sandra was telling me about them last night. We're just not looking hard enough."

I checked my watch. The blackout probably wasn't that bad, and with Parson in the area, the attack teams would move fast.

"Tap the walls. One of them has to be fake," I said.

The guys and Mona each took a wall, but I kept Emma with me.

Metal screeched against concrete. A second later there was another crash.

"We're trying to do this as *quietly* as possible."

"Shut up. I found it. Down here," Dex said. "There's a corridor. It's narrow and made for little people, but this has to be it."

Dex had moved a bunch of kegs off to the side, and punched a hole in the drywall. "Good work." I hunched down and took the lead.

The tunnels were dim. Only small, motion-activated lanterns broke the darkness, but navigating was a basic skill that every Black Helix had to master. Drop us in the middle of nowhere with a blindfold on, and we'd have to find our way home. This required memorizing maps of the major Voids, and I didn't remember seeing any tunnels in this area. That meant the Seligo didn't know about them.

I focused on counting turns and the angles of the tunnels. Getting lost could get us all killed. I tried to keep us headed northwest toward the market district, but the tunnels wound and broke off—some were completely blocked. The crude ceilings and walls made just being down here unsafe. Bits of dirt rained down as cars rolled overhead. How had these paths even held up?

As we moved through, frustration gnawed at me. We couldn't turn back now, but this could easily go south. There didn't look to be a way out and time was limited.

Sweat dripped down my back as we reached a fork.

Voices sounded in the distance.

I motioned for Dex and Oliver to take cover. Not that there was much. Shielding Emma and Mona behind me, I pulled my weapon from my ankle holster.

Three Black Helixes ran through the tunnel in our direction.

"Stop," a voice echoed toward us.

I didn't think about who they were or that maybe I'd fought beside them. I couldn't. Not and still pull the trigger.

Dex, Oliver, and I shot at the same time, downing two of them. The third pulled his gun, but I put a bullet between his eyes before he could fire.

"There'll be more on the way." I didn't dare meet Emma's eyes—killing in front of her didn't make me feel good, but better them than us. Instead, I turned back to the fork in the tunnel. No time to debate. From the way we were going and what I remembered of the area, if we went left we'd end up in some apartment buildings. Right veered toward a shopping district. Shopping was better. More chaos. More people to hide among.

I couldn't believe I was out here without my gear. "Dex. Any chance you got one of those bots?"

"You know I never leave home without them. Why?"

"Send it behind us. If there are more coming, I want to know."

"Sure thing." He pulled a tiny device out of his pocket. It unfolded and expanded, looking like a mini helicopter. He clicked a button and sent it down the tunnel.

Its features were limited to going in one direction and exploding on contact. In other words, nearly useless. But we were desperate.

After another hundred yards a ladder was mounted to the wall, leading up to what I hoped was a manhole cover. "Wait here," I said. Emma nodded and I started climbing.

I lifted the cover just enough to scan the area. The power was still out, and it gave people the perfect excuse to act up. It was chaos out there. People running, shoving each other, and fighting. Looting. Random spurts of gunfire.

Damn it. I should've gone the apartment route. I'd wanted chaos, but this…

Emma stood eight feet below me, huddled with her friend. She got to me. I knew she would to some extent, but not like this. The way she looked. The curve of her hip. And that awful blue hair. I was so screwed, and I couldn't blame it on the pairing. The girl kicked my ass at games. Hacking. Everything about her was a turn-on.

It would've been idiotic to think that Lady Eva could match me with someone who wasn't a fit for me. This girl was going to have me wrapped around her little finger if I wasn't careful. I was probably lying to myself by thinking she didn't already.

But keeping her safe was my priority. That hadn't changed. It was just a little bit trickier.

An explosion echoed down the tunnels. Given the speed the bot traveled, we had maybe five minutes before backup was on our ass.

"We got incoming," Dex shouted.

I dropped down the ladder quickly. "Riots and looting in the streets. We watch the girls, get them to safety. We move fast."

"Where're we headed? Safe house?" Dex asked.

"Not sure yet. We need to get out of here as quickly as possible. The grid is out, but with Parson here—that's not going to last for long."

"We just need wheels," Emma said. "I can hotwire any car. Once we're on the road, it's easy to disappear."

"Not as easy as you'd think with today's—" Wait. She could what? I couldn't hold back the laugh. Emma was out of control. I don't know what I'd expected, but it wasn't this. Not even close. "You can hotwire a car?"

She shrugged. "Sure. Can't everyone?" She pushed me toward the ladder. "But does it matter? Shouldn't we be getting the hell out of here?"

"You might be in over your head," Dex said with a laugh.

"Shut it," I said. "We're going up. I'll lead. You two cover. No one gets Emma."

120

"Who's Emma?" Mona asked.

I touched a strand of her blue hair. "*She* is Emma." Did her friend not know who she was? A buzz of electricity shot past me, exploding the closest lantern. I ducked as shards flew past me. "Something bothering you, Em?"

Another lantern broke and I put a hand on her.

She shrugged it off. "Don't. It feels like you're sucking everything out of me when you touch me. It's unnerving. And no using my real name. No one's called me Emma since I was eight. It doesn't even feel like my name anymore. And no one calls me *Em*."

"I used to call you Em."

She laughed and it wasn't a good sound. "There's only one person who called me Em and he was *not* you. I've never met you before."

"You sure about that?" She looked at my helix tattoo and then back at my face, but I didn't give her time to process. "Let's move."

I climbed up the ladder and pushed the manhole cover all the way to the side. I took a quick look before pulling myself up, and then reached down a hand. "Let's go, Em. *Fast*," I said when she didn't move right away. Her little hand was totally swallowed up by mine when I pulled her out. I tucked her hand back in my belt loop. "Don't let go." I'd run too many missions to count, and I'd never felt so afraid before—the stakes were too high with Emma in the middle of the danger.

"Any chance you've got more of those bots, Dex?"

"No."

Not good, but understandable. "Oliver?"

"Nothing. I wasn't going in for a fight tonight."

Neither was I. The only reason I was armed was because I never went anywhere without at least one weapon.

Mona was next. I kept searching for trouble as I pulled her out of the manhole. "There's a parking lot at three o'clock."

Some asshole rushed past us—not a threat until he tried to grab Emma. "Hey!" She screamed as she wrestled his grasp. I spun, punching my fist through his nose. Blood splattered as he fell to the ground.

People were bumping into us as Dex and Oliver climbed up. Someone tried to pick my pocket, but I grabbed the guy's wrist. "Nice try. Pick someone else's."

As soon as Dex and Oliver were out of the tunnel, I kicked the cover back in place. The guys had been working with me for so long that we didn't need to speak. We moved as one, covering each other as we worked through the mass of people. Looters ran by—carrying as many electronics as they could hold. Kids in filthy rags ran from minimarts with food spilling from their pockets and cradled in their shirts. A fight broke out in front of us—two guys trying to assault a girl—and I moved around it. On my way past I kicked the closest guy's knee and heard the crunch as it broke. Oliver took care of the other guy. It went against the grain for me not to stop, but giving the girl the chance to run was the best we could do.

The parking garage was a five-story structure with stairwells running up the corners of the building. A couple people were partying on the stairs. Trash was kicked against the walls and it reeked of piss and body odor.

"Let's go," I said as we entered the ground floor. A few gangs of kids were already busy breaking into cars.

An explosion went off on one of the floors above.

The touch of Emma's fingers against the small of my back weighed on me. The pressure to get her to safety… My hands were sweating as I gripped my gun. "I'll stop at the best vehicle that can fit us all."

We got a few aisles in, and Emma tugged on my pants. "This one."

I checked the car over. It was a late model sedan painted an unassuming gray. No bells and whistles. "No. We need something faster. Or more sturdy."

"No. This one. No one will look at it twice."

Before I could stop her, Emma slipped away from me. She pushed a few buttons and the door popped open.

She was already in the car. How did she get in the car? "How'd you break the lock so quickly?"

She rolled her eyes. "Everyone knows this model has a hack."

I couldn't help but smile at the snark in her voice.

"The keypad was defective. Most were recalled, but I took a chance on this one. It's a shitpit. Thus, probably stolen." She swept a bunch of trash off the floorboard, sending it scattering down to the garage floor. "Next time you see a beat-up S580, press star-four-zero-eight-zero-six-star-star. Usually works. They're an eyesore, but the horsepower is pretty solid." She twisted so her head was under the steering column and ripped off the panel.

I put my gun away. "I can get the car started. I don't want you to get electrocuted." As soon as the words came out of my mouth, I realized how dumb they were. I was making a hell of an impression on her.

She laughed. "Are you sure you know me? Because, seriously, if you actually knew anything about me, then you know how incredibly stupid that was."

"Habit. Didn't want you getting hurt."

Her gaze met mine for a second, and I felt it all the way to my bones. "That's sweet, but not necessary." She stripped the wire with her teeth. "I'm pretty good at taking care of myself." She flicked the wires together, the engine turned, and she twisted them to hold the connection.

I pulled her out of the driver's seat and pushed her toward the back of the car.

"What? What are you doing?" She tried to wiggle away, but I kept my grip on her arm.

"We're going in the trunk."

"No!" She punched me in the stomach, but it wasn't hard enough to do any damage. "No! I'm not going in a trunk. And definitely not with you."

Was she going to argue with me about everything? God, I hoped not. "Yes, you are. The Seligo will probably get surveillance of every girl who entered that club and you can bet they'll find the blue-haired one who got away. They'll have checkpoints set up to search every car for us. Once we get outside the blackout zone, the cameras will be looking, too. I know it's not ideal, but we're riding in the trunk."

"By that logic, we should all be riding in the trunk. They're going to know about all of us."

"That's why we'll be splitting up soon. The helixes

will follow the three of them on a wild goose chase in this car, thinking we're hidden in the backseat or trunk, and we'll go our own way once we get to a safe house in a dead zone. Eventually they'll ditch this car and make sure they're on tape so it's clear only three of them were together. We'll be off safe, and by the time Parson's people realize it, they'll be too busy backtracking trying to find us to go after the others."

"What if they get caught? Mona's my best friend."

"That's on Dex and Oliver. They'll keep her safe. But I'm here to make sure you don't get caught."

The war she was waging with herself played across her face. She might think she hid her emotions, but she didn't. She was scared and didn't trust me. Not yet.

The trunk popped open, and I climbed in and held out my hand. "Please. Trust me this little bit. I promise I won't let you down."

"I can't believe I'm doing this," she muttered.

Her hand touched mine, and a little wave of electricity ran up my arm. Good thing I'd spent all that time maxing out how much voltage I could take. When I'd first gotten the modifications that paired me to her, I couldn't take much, but it was like a muscle. The more I worked at it, the stronger I got. Now, I figured that I could take about as much as she could give without it stopping my heart or frying my insides.

She stepped awkwardly into the trunk, settling on her side with her back to me. I held her against me, and then reached to shut the hatch. We were instantly in the dark. Her hair fell in my face and I couldn't help taking a whiff—it smelled like coconut.

"Did you just smell me?"

Busted. "Yes. Yes, I did."

"Why?"

"You smell like coconut. It's nice."

She wiggled and her butt rubbed against my crotch.

Keep it together. One hundred thirty-seven divided by three. Four carry the one...five with two remaining.

I gripped Emma's hip to steady her as the car started moving. I didn't want to make her uncomfortable, but I was a guy and even long division wasn't going to stop my body from reacting if she didn't stop wiggling.

The muffled sounds of people shouting grew louder. Someone slammed hands on the trunk as the car jerked forward.

Emma's elbow hit my stomach and I grunted.

"Sorry."

"Don't worry about it." I relaxed, and pulled her into me. I brushed her hair away from her neck and ran my finger along her skin. She was so soft.

"What are you doing?"

Goose bumps ran down her arms, and I wanted to cheer with satisfaction. My touch was affecting her. "Nothing."

"That's not nothing." Her voice was a little more raspy than usual.

I couldn't really argue with that.

"How do I know you?"

"Do you remember me at all?" I was hoping she would just know, but that was probably unrealistic.

"No."

"You haven't asked me my first name."

Emma rolled to face me and I grinned.

She was holding her breath for too long. "You okay?"

"You can't be him."

"Yes, I can."

"How?"

I breathed deeply. "That's a long story. What you did, it got me out. Free. I can never repay it, but I'm going to do my best to make it up to you."

"You don't need to repay me. I did the same thing that anyone else would do...or maybe not exactly the same thing. I didn't mean to...you know...zap him." She said those last few words really softly. "Sometimes I get upset, and I hurt people, but I don't let myself get close to anyone. Not anymore. I'm too dangerous."

"Not to me."

"Yes. To *everyone*."

"Not to me." I sighed. "And I do have to make it up to you. What you did cost you a lot."

"No. I was a ticking bomb. My mom hung onto her relationship with Jack, which was probably the reason everything happened. If I hadn't gotten caught that day, it would've been a different day. It was inevitable. But what happened—"

Shouting came from outside. Dex or Oliver—I wasn't sure who was driving—laid on the horn. Something slammed against the trunk and Emma jerked into my arms.

"Sorry," she said.

"You're okay. I've got you."

"Are you really Hunter?" Her voice was even softer as she asked, like maybe she was afraid of the answer.

"Yes. A year after you took off, I went through the Trials. Earned a spot at the Academy and got my helixes a few years later."

"Why'd you do it?"

I blew out a breath. How much should I tell her? I wanted her to trust me, but there were things about being a helix that I wasn't too proud of. And for a while there, I nearly drank the water. Almost believed the crap they were selling. It wasn't until I was on a mission and did something I didn't think I could live with that I remembered why I joined the helixes.

"You."

"That was a long pause for a one-word answer."

I shrugged. "It's the truth. I heard your uncle ranting about Red Helixes. Before then, they were monsters that would come get you in the night." She laughed, and I took that as a good sign. "But after that, I wanted—*needed*—to pay you back. You lost a lot to save my life, and I knew you were in danger. I figured that by joining the helixes, I could find a way to help."

"And did you?"

"What do you think?"

"I don't know. I mean, I'm here in a trunk with you, but I'm not sure if I can trust you."

She would. I'd make sure of it. "The thing about trust is that it takes time. Remember when we first met?"

"Yeah," her voice was so quiet, I almost didn't hear her.

"It took me a while to trust you. To care about you. But you kept coming back. I'm willing to wait you out. I'll show you that I can be trusted by my actions, not my words. Eventually, you'll know that I'm here for you."

We were quiet for a bit. It would be good to give her some space to think about what I'd said, but there wasn't a ton of that in the trunk of a moving vehicle.

The sounds of rioting quieted as the car rolled on and we passed the thick of the chaos. Emma's forehead rested against my sternum, and I itched to pull her closer yet didn't dare. It was probably my pride, but I'd spent all this time chasing her...now I wanted her to come that last little bit on her own. Patience was something I'd struggled with, but I'd gotten good at it.

I couldn't rush and I didn't need to. With Emma, I was in it for the long haul.

The car stopped, and I pressed my fingers to her lips.

"Identification," a stern voice said.

Checkpoints already? They'd moved faster than expected. "I'm on leave. We're taking a little trip," Oliver answered.

The light flickered in the trunk, and I gripped Emma's hand. Her gaze shot to mine.

"No," I mouthed.

Her eyes were wide as her hand squeezed mine. I could feel her heart pumping, and I couldn't keep the distance anymore. I pulled her flush against me, rubbing my hand up and down her back. "It's going to be okay," I whispered. "Oliver is good at this. Trained for this. Just stay calm."

Her breath hitched.

"You're a Black? What are you doing out here?

Everyone was either called into the Voids to search or sent out to blockades." The man outside paused. "Your chip isn't coming up."

"That's not right. Wait, the green light's off on your unit. You sure you charged that?"

"Yeah. It was working a second ago." He banged something. "Damn it. It's broken. How the hell did that happen?"

Dex. The guy was handy.

"Wow. That sucks," Dex said so earnestly that I nearly laughed.

"We have our coms off, so I don't know what's going on in the Voids," Oliver said. "I requested this leave months ago and I'm not going to let anything get in the way of me, my six-pack, and this girl here. She's freaking hot and has the tiniest pink bikini."

The guy laughed. "I hear you. Well, you better get out while you can. I'm not supposed to let anyone go, but a couple of fellow helixes and their chick should be fine."

The car started moving again.

I focused back on Emma. Her breath came in pants, and electricity licked along my skin—it jolted me like I'd had a few too many cups of coffee.

I pounded on the back of the trunk. "Get us to the safe house. Now."

"What's going on?" Mona said.

"She's having a panic attack." I took Emma's face in my hands. "Breathe with me."

"I should've left. I should've left. Why did I stay when I should've left? Stupid. Stupid. Stupid."

She kept chanting the word and I wrapped my arms around her. "Where're we going, guys?"

"Another safe house," Dex said. "It's on the outskirts of town, twenty miles out. We can regroup there."

I ran my fingers through her hair. "Not long now. We're fine. You're safe with me." She was shaking, and it was killing me. I held on tight.

She was trusting me this much. All I had to do now was not screw it up. I hoped I could be good enough to save her.

Chapter Nine

CIPHER

I knew I was freaking out. It was embarrassing, but I couldn't make myself stop. This was the closest I'd ever gotten to being caught. And it'd happened twice. In less than thirty minutes. How dumb could I be?

I knew what my future would be if I got captured—nonexistent. I'd be dead. Or on a lab table, which was probably worse. I had to focus in on a plan. I was here with people I really didn't know or trust—except for Mona—but I couldn't help her. I could barely help myself. If she ended up getting hurt, it'd be my fault.

I hadn't been this screwed since the day my parents died. I'd been in a car then, too. The sound of the crash—that was horrible. The smells of burning rubber and spilled gas. My parents' blood. Shaking them. Trying to get them to wake up. That split-second decision I'd made—stay with them and get caught or leave them and run—was the worst moment of my life.

I ran. I was pretty sure they were dead. I'd seen

death before. I'd killed before. But not like that. Not with all that blood.

I'd scuttled between cars. Hiding behind them until I got to the edge of the freeway. Running from ditch to ditch. Until I got to a rest stop and met Sally. The nice old lady truck driver took pity on me. Looking back, maybe I shouldn't have trusted her. She should've turned me in, but she didn't. She hid me. Helped me. Saved me.

And here I was, back to that very same spot. In a car. Racing to freedom with an unknown destination. In another car with someone I loved.

What?

No. I couldn't. Those feelings for him were in the past.

How had this happened?

Somehow I'd forgotten how much was at stake. It was all happening again and there was nothing I could do to stop it. It was like these twelve years had never happened.

So, I was freaking out. Fully, thoroughly freaking the fuck out.

The only thing that was keeping me sane was Knight's hand. His steady breathing. His heartbeat. He murmured things to me, but I couldn't focus on his words enough to make sense of them. The only thing I could think of was getting away. Running as fast as I could until I was far away from anyone with a helix.

I needed out of the trunk.

When the car stopped, I slammed my hand against the roof of the trunk. "Out. Out. Out. I need to get out. Now. Please."

"Guys!" he said.

"We heard her. Trying to find the—"

The latch popped and I stumbled out, hitting the ground hard. I climbed to my feet and started pacing in a circle, trying to figure out where to run. The only building within sight was a small, one-story house. The rest was dust and dirt and shrubs and cacti.

Where in the hell was I?

Knight grasped my shoulders and spun me to face him. "Hey! It's fine. You're fine."

The electricity I'd been gathering rushed into him again. How did he do that? Why didn't I hurt him? The ground under my feet was scorched, still smoking. Not even my shoes had been enough to dampen what I'd been channeling.

"You're going to be fine." His words were firm and clear, and they only made me more frantic.

I pushed him away. "You don't know that. You don't know how long, how hard I've been running. How dangerous it is. Last time they got this close I was in a car, too. Only everyone I loved died. I lost everything. And now I'm an idiot. I let someone get close. I put Mona in danger. And you three morons want in, too? That's not only nuts, it's monumentally stupid. Everyone needs to let me go. Let me run on my own. I've been fine so far. I'll keep on being fine."

"And when do you stop running?" Knight asked.

I couldn't look him in the eyes. There wasn't a good answer. At least not one that either of us wanted to hear. "I don't know. Maybe never."

"That's how you want to live?"

I shoved him and he staggered back a step. "You think I want this?" I pulled down the waist of my pants just enough to show the top of the Red Helix tattooed on my hip. "You think I somehow asked for this?"

I heard Mona gasp, but didn't dare look her way. I didn't think I could stand the rejection.

"No," he said quietly. "I don't think you asked for it. But that doesn't mean you have to run. I'm here to help you. *We—*" Knight motioned to the other two guys. "Are here to help you. You don't have to run anymore."

"You'll end up dead, just like my parents. And Sally. Jack and Natalie. Everyone who's ever tried to help me. Every time I slow down, they catch up. I'm tired. Freaking exhausted by all of this. I want to stop this ride and get the hell off, but I don't know what else I'm supposed to do. Staying away from people and keeping moving in the Griz is the only thing that's worked. For five years, I've been okay. But I stop—for weeks, not years, not months and months—but weeks now, and they're all over my ass."

Knight pulled me into him. I struggled at first, but gave in.

"You're losing it, bitch," Mona said.

I laughed against Knight's chest. And then kept on laughing. "Did I ever have it to lose?"

Knight pulled away so that I could see his sea glass eyes. Why hadn't I recognized that color right away? Against his tanned skin, they glowed.

"Give us a second, guys. We'll meet you inside." When the door closed behind them, he said finally, "It's going to be okay."

I shook my head. "Don't make that kind of promise. I'm not dumb enough to believe it, and you

136

shouldn't be either." We were in the middle of the desert. The sounds of the city were long gone. There was no place to hide. No Griz. I was screwed.

"A Shadow Ravens safe house," he said.

I guessed this was it. I was with the Ravens now, for better or worse. Knight, Oliver, Dex—all of them really were Ravens. But whatever my tattoo meant, I wasn't one of them.

"We'll stay here for the night. Re-group. I've got to call in and see what it's like out there."

The idea of sticking around for any length of time still didn't sit well. Not at all. "Shouldn't we keep moving?"

Knight shook his head. "Better to know where to run to before taking off. The Seligo have a long reach, but the Ravens have been slowly gaining ground. We find a route that won't get us caught and we take it."

I liked the 'won't get us caught' part, but it sounded too good to be true. There had to be a catch. "To where?"

"Lady Eva's compound."

There was that lovely catch. "Nope. I'm not going to some place to be experimented on. Not in a million years."

"No one is going to experiment on you."

I narrowed my gaze at him. There was no way he could possibly know that for certain. "Are you sure about that?"

He blew out a breath. "I guess not one hundred percent sure, but close enough. She's the one who saved you and stabilized your DNA when you were a baby. Why would she hurt you now?"

I nearly laughed. "Maybe because I'm not freaking

stable. I have a wee side effect." Hell, I'd burned the sand under my feet. It glittered as the moonlight touched the little bits that had turned to glass.

He grinned, and I knew I was in trouble. "Oh, I noticed."

Which brought up a whole other line of questions. "How do you keep grounding the electricity?" Because that was so not normal. I'd hit him hard. Mega voltage. It was enough to stop his heart for sure, but here he was, standing there looking handsome and calm while I was feeling entirely not okay.

"That's a long story, and part of how I know you can trust Lady Eva." He reached for me. "Let's get settled first."

He wasn't going to get out of it that easily. "You'll tell me later?"

"Promise. And that's one I know I can keep."

I stared at his hand for a second as he held it out to me. This was a fork in the road. Another one of those key choices that would either make or break my life. Who was I kidding? I was already in deep with this guy. "Okay. Fine. Let's go inside."

His smile got bigger. "Good."

"Just don't blame me when this comes back to bite you in the ass."

"As long as you're the one doing the biting…" He winked.

A surprised laugh escaped me. "Oh my God. When did you turn into a flirt?"

He put his arm around my shoulders and walked me to the front door of the house. "You've missed a lot."

"Clearly. You're like two feet taller." It was nice.

Talking with him, being with him felt natural. Maybe that was because I'd known him all those years ago. Or because I'd talked to him online. Or some combo of the two. Whatever the reason, this was either going to be the biggest mistake or the best thing ever. It was too soon to tell which yet.

The single-story adobe house looked like any other one I'd seen before, only this one had a glowing raven on the door in the same odd color of my tattoo. I'd have to ask about that when I wasn't already feeling totally out of my element.

The interior was decorated in traditional southwestern style. Terra cotta floors and autumn hues dominated the house. Geometric patterns appeared on the walls and accent pieces. The space was open planned, with the living, dining and kitchen in one really large room. All the furniture looked well loved. It didn't smell dusty or old, but no one had been here in at least a few weeks. There wasn't anything out of place. It was like the house had been ripped from a magazine.

I wasn't sure what I'd been expecting, but it definitely wasn't this.

"You okay?" Mona asked. She stood slowly from the worn leather sofa.

"Yeah. Sorry for the freak out. You okay?" I was trying not to be awkward and uncomfortable but failing miserably. Suddenly, all I wanted to do was go back outside, but it was too late for that. I was committed to being here.

"I'm fine," she said, and I nearly winced. Her hands were a little shaky and her skin a little pale. Being my friend was definitely against her best interests. "I didn't know you were a Red," she said.

I blew out a breath. "Yeah, it's not something I really advertise." I looked everywhere but at her. I didn't want to see the rejection that might be on her face.

"I guess that's why you were so closed off when I met you?"

"Yup." I hoped she still wanted to be friends, but if she wanted to bail, I wouldn't blame her. Being friends with me carried a much higher cost than she'd thought.

"Will you zap me if I hug you?"

I cringed and finally looked at her. "I don't think so."

Mona nodded slowly. "Screw it." She crossed the room and wrapped her arms around me. "No more fuckin' secrets, 'kay?"

I hugged her back, and willed myself not to cry. "I'm sorry for dragging you into this. You okay?"

"I'm fine. I swear. That was scary as shit, but we're safe. I trust these guys." She pulled back a little. "It's you I'm worried about."

I took in the other two guys—Dex and Oliver. "Thanks for your help," I said to both of them. "I'm sorry for melting down out there."

"No worries. We're friends with Hunter from way back, so we know the deal," the Dex said. "We haven't been properly introduced. I'm Dex. We've played online before. My handle's TheSurgeon."

I'd asked him about that. The way he talked, it was clear that he probably wasn't an actual surgeon. He said it was because he was a brain surgeon—he got in peoples' heads and messed them up. I'd laughed when

140

he told me since I assumed it was a joke, but now that I knew he was a Blue, maybe he was telling the truth. Something told me there was more to Dex than he let on.

"Right. Nice to meet you in real life." I really knew how to make a stand-out first impression. "Thanks for your help, Oliver." He grunted, but his gaze was trained on Mona. I took a little step away from her, and his shoulders relaxed. He knew how dangerous I could be, and I appreciated that he was looking out for Mona. "So, what's the plan?"

"There are showers," Knight said. "You can take the bed in any of the bedrooms, but I'm sticking close by you." I started to object, but he held up a hand. "I've been searching for you for twelve years. I'm not about to let you out of my sight. I can't give you a chance to run."

I swallowed. The guilt that he'd spent so long trying to find me was a little more than I could handle. I hadn't asked for him to dedicate his life to that. Why would he care so much? It didn't make sense.

As much as I wanted answers, I didn't think I wanted them with an audience, so I settled for a nod.

"Good." He relaxed a little. "Good." His voice was more confident the second time. "Okay. So, I'm going to check in, like I said. If you want to get settled, then we'll get some rest, and before we head out in the morning, we'll check in again. We need the latest intel before we attempt to run."

"Sounds like a decent plan," I said. Getting some rest was a good idea, but I wondered if I'd be able to sleep here. I hadn't slept with people in the same place since I first hit the road.

There was an awkward silence, and I started fidgeting.

"Anyone hungry?" Dex said finally, breaking it.

"Yes," Mona said.

Oliver sat up straight. "I can cook." His cheeks turned a little pink as he glanced at Mona.

Never one to miss a chance to flirt, Mona stepped close to him. "I'll help."

Cute. It was an odd match—his bald head and towering height against her small frame and long, flowing locks—but cute. If something good came out of all of this, I hoped it was the two of them getting together.

I retreated into the bathroom, which was the biggest one I'd ever seen. The shower had ten heads coming out of the walls. I flipped it on nearly as hot as it would go, and a knock sounded at the door.

"Yeah?" I said.

"Clothes. For after your shower."

Everything I wore was damp with sweat from running and being in the trunk. And from nerves. I could use a fresh set. I cracked open the door.

"First thing I could find. They might be a little big. I'll try and find you something else in here before the morning," Knight said.

"That's okay. I'll make this work. Thanks." He looked like he wanted to say something else but he turned and walked away. I closed the door and rested my head against it. Things were going faster than I was comfortable with and yet not fast enough.

I wanted Knight to fill me in on everything that had happened since I knew him as Hunter. What was going through the Trials like? How were those special schools? What kinds of mods did he have? But I was afraid to ask those questions. Any information I learned would make me care about him that much more. Make it that much harder for me to leave him behind when the time came.

And the time would come. It always did.

My parents used to tell me to live in the moment. To cherish every second of happy that I had while I had it, but I sucked at that. I was too busy worrying about the future. Trying to plan life five steps ahead was dumb. No one could predict it. If someone had told me an hour ago that I'd be showering in a monstrosity of a bathroom done in hand-painted tiles, I'd ask them what they'd been smoking.

Yet here I was.

I shed my clothes and tested the water.

Holy crap. It was hot. Like burn-your-skin hot. The Griz's water heater didn't work nearly as well. I quickly turned the knobs and stepped in.

Best shower ever.

The mirror was totally fogged when I got out. I wiped my hand across it and stared at myself. The shampoo in there must've been harsher than my usual stuff. My hair was fading to some horrible combination of strawberry-blond and blue. And it didn't look remotely like purple.

I hadn't seen my normal hair color in forever. For a second I thought about leaving it, but that was probably a bad idea. They were looking for a girl with red hair. Or blue hair. Maybe we could stop somewhere for some dye…

I pulled on the black sweatpants and gray T-shirt

and opened the door. Knight stood across the hall, leaning against the wall.

"Everything okay?" I asked.

"Yeah?"

Weird. "Did I take too long? You can use it now. I'm done."

He blushed a little. "Yes. No. And I don't need it."

I thought for a second. "Then what are you doing in the hallway…oh, right. Making sure I don't run?"

He winced. "Guilty."

I barely held back the sigh. Trust was a two-way street, and I didn't think either of us were totally there yet. "I'm not going to run, but when you watch over me like that, it makes me feel like a prisoner."

He crossed his arms. "You're not a prisoner." He sounded a little insulted.

"I know. And if I ever really feel like I'm one, I will take off." I couldn't hold back the threat. He needed to know what he was up against.

"Well, then I'll do my best to make sure you feel safe and protected, but not smothered."

He didn't seem insulted, which I took as a good sign. "Fine." The sound of Mona's laugh drew my attention. "What's going on?"

"Let's talk. We've got some food."

My stomach rumbled. Food would be good. I followed him into the living room. Mona, Oliver, and Dex were having a hushed conversation on the couches surrounding a coffee table made from a slice of tree trunk. At least they were until I showed up. As soon as I walked in the room, all conversation stopped.

I looked behind me. Was it me or Knight they

were reacting to?

A few pizzas sat on the table. The smell of the too-sweet sauce told me that they were from the freezer, but they'd do.

I sat on one of the armchairs circling the table and cut myself a slice. As soon as I started chewing, I realized no one was talking. "What?"

"Your uncle is tearing up the city looking for you," Dex said. Oliver hit the back of his head, but Dex shrugged. He didn't seem bothered by it.

I dropped my slice on the table. "And? Is it worse than when we left?"

"Much. They've instated martial law."

Suddenly, I wasn't so hungry. The pizza tasted like greasy cardboard anyhow. I grabbed a napkin and wiped my fingers off, but it was like the grease was stuck. Disgusted with everything, I threw the napkin on the table.

Conflicted didn't begin to cover how I felt about the news. That anyone was being hurt or even inconvenienced because of me was horrible. But chaos in the city might keep the Seligo from finding me, so there was no easy solution. "So what do we do now?"

"The same thing we were planning," Knight said. "We knew he was probably going to do this."

I didn't want to let Jack tear apart the Void because of me, but short of turning myself in, I didn't know how I could stop him. "Okay. Now what?"

"We're just outside the limits of the Void. This house is totally off the grid."

"Really?" That was pretty impressive. There were only a few places in this part of the world where you could actually be off the Seligo-monitored utility grids—spots so isolated they weren't worth the resources to regulate them. The only places more remote were dead zones. There was no access to electricity there. No running water. You could get away from the Seligo, but you had to commune with nature to do it.

"It's owned by the Lady," Oliver said. "She's lived a long time—long enough to gather up hiding spots both inside and outside the Voids. We're in the dead zone. Not enough population in this part of the desert to bother with monitoring when they barely have control on the Void cities."

"We shouldn't stay for long, though," Knight said. "Satellites can be repositioned too easily."

"Agreed. Tomorrow, we go pick up the Griz and hit the road," I said.

"No," Knight said. "No way are you going back to that park. He'll be looking for you there. I think we stick with the original plan and split into two groups."

He was right about one thing. Splitting up. And probably right about going back for the Griz. I guessed that could wait, but I felt like a little girl without a safety net if I left my RV behind.

"Splitting up's a horrible idea," Mona said "Whenever that happens in a movie, everything goes to shit. We stick together."

"This isn't a movie," Knight said. It was a little harsher than I would've liked, but Mona needed to be kept safe. Even if she disagreed. "We split up. It's easier to hide two or three than five."

"I'm not leaving Cipher with a bunch of Helixes. No matter how hot you think you are," Mona said.

"You think we're hot?" Dex asked. He tucked his hair behind his ear as he leaned toward Mona.

From the look on Mona's face, she was going to shoot him down hard, and I couldn't wait. Mona really did make things more fun.

"I was talking about the other two. You think a lot of yourself, huh?" Mona said.

Knight maintained his cool, but Oliver had to cover his laugh with a cough.

Dex ran a hand down his chest, stopping to pat his perfectly flat stomach. "Haven't had any complaints," he said.

I was sure he hadn't. Even if he was a goofball, he was a damned hot one.

"Back to the topic," Knight said. "We split up. I have a spot where we can go to ground for a little while. Let the heat wear off before we head to Lady Eva."

This conversation just got ahead of itself. When had I agreed to this plan? "Hold on for one second. You're assuming that I want to go to whatever location you've schemed up."

"We have to go somewhere off the radar so you can learn to control your powers. There aren't a ton of options, and you're dangerous until you know how to find balance. Once you do, we can run without having to worry about the fluctuations around you. Now that they know what they're looking for, they'll find you that much faster. The second you stop running, they'll be on your ass. I have the perfect dead zone island in mind. We can practice your control without having to look over our shoulders too much."

The guy had a point. Although being alone with

him on an island sounded terrifying in a totally different way that I was used to... "Okay."

There was only one more thing bugging me. "If they're focusing on the city right now, then we should just go. Why are we waiting at all?"

"All transpo stations will be under heavy surveillance for the next twelve hours. At this point, everything we do is a risk, but hopefully this will minimize it a bit. It's the best way to get you away safely so you can have a chance at something more. Don't you want that?"

I snorted. "Of course I want a chance at something. It doesn't even have to be something more. I'd settle for a plain-Jane, normal life. One where I don't have to hide all the time. I'd find a nice, quiet house to live in. After that, I don't know. Maybe one day some guy won't mind me and my little defect—maybe have a couple rug rats. As lame as that sounds. For now, I'd just like to be able to sleep a night through without worrying whether someone's coming to kill me." As soon as I finished my little rant, I was instantly embarrassed. I probably should've kept all that to myself.

Knight reached over to me, linking his fingers with mine. "None of that sounds lame. Especially the last part. You'll sleep tonight."

I wasn't touching that. Sleep was hard for me. I kept one ear open, and I liked plenty of light. No one could sneak in when the lights were on. Made it harder to hide, but I'd rather be able to see my enemy than not.

Trusting Knight felt like I was jumping off one of the Voids' tallest scrapers. It might be another stupid decision, but stupid seemed to be the word of the week. I had to start somewhere. "I'll go with you wherever you want. But I need to know that I'm not going to be some lab experiment. I won't be studied or hurt or anything else. I've heard things about a Red who was caught once…I want normal. I want to be left alone. I was serious about that."

"Em. Come on. No one's going to hurt you." His voice was soft and soothing.

I swallowed again. I believed that Knight thought that, but this Eva was a total unknown. Odds were, she'd want whatever knowledge the Ravens could cut out of me.

"Emma, you know as much as I do that there are no guarantees in life. You don't grow up like we did without knowing that. But if I could give you one, I would. I'll call Lady Eva and tell her what you said. I think if you talk to her, you'll feel better. For now, let's all eat and then get some sleep." He shifted his gaze away from me. "Oliver, you're on first watch. I'll take middle. Dex, you're last."

I retreated to the bathroom and found a new toothbrush in the cabinet. When I opened the door again, Knight was in the hall. He didn't say anything, just turned and walked into the next room. I followed him.

"I'll take the floor," he said.

I nodded. Maybe it was dumb to not argue with him, but this was the first time in a long time that I'd had anyone share a room with me. Anyone sleep in the same space as me. It was odd how comfortable I was, but I chalked most of it up to exhaustion—both from anxiety and all the electricity I'd channeled.

Knight still hadn't explained how he'd sucked it from me. I had a feeling that when he told me, my mind would be totally blown. Until then, I was going to live in ignorance.

Hopefully, that wouldn't bite me in the ass, but hoping for things had never made my wishes come true in the past. Not sure why I thought that would change anytime soon.

When my head hit the pillow, I actually started drifting off. He was right. Having him here made a difference. For the first time in my life, I felt like someone actually had my back. Despite everything, it was a good feeling.

Chapter Ten

KNIGHT

I waited on the hard, carpeted floor until Emma's breathing evened out.

I'd found her. I'd really found her.

Those words kept running through my mind. The light was off, but I could see well enough in the dark to make her out. After her shower, more of her strawberry hair peeked through the blue. Her hair was awful, and I hoped she never changed it.

And those tattoos. The piercings. When did Emma Jean Boyd get so freaking hot?

When she'd said what she wanted, I could picture it. The settling down part. Kids. Whole nine yards. Only it was me with her. Even entertaining the idea of her with some other guy made me crazy. Which was a first for me. I never was a guy who wanted more than one night, but Emma made me want everything.

The door cracked open and Oliver stuck his head in. I motioned for him to stay quiet, and snuck out of the room.

"What's up?"

"Got the Lady on the line. She wants to talk to

you."

I nodded. Good.

I made my way to the back room. The security system took up a full wall. A small com screen sat on the desktop in front of them. "Hunter Marquez here," I said when I sat down.

The screen showed the Lady sitting in her lab. Her white coat was a giveaway that she'd been working late. She never really looked tired, and maybe it was the harsh light of the lab, but she had definite circles under her eyes.

"Knight. I'm getting word from Ravens in Parson's circle that he's identified both you and Emma as fugitives. Oliver and Dex have been listed as well as Emma's friend, Mona. They're not as high on the list as you two are. Questioning only for them. Capture for the two of you. Although I think the questioning will get bumped up to capture if you elude them for too long."

Exactly what we'd thought would happen. At least she wasn't reaming me for letting Dex and Oliver destroy their covers. "Understood. I'll let them know."

"Good. They obviously have intel on everyone, but information on Emma remains scarce. They didn't get a clear picture of her, and no one at the gamer bar is giving her up. Apparently that place didn't like to keep surveillance of their clientele?"

You could never guarantee anonymity at a gamer club, but more often than not, they looked the other way to protect their customers. Probably why Wilton had set up shop at Marx's. "That makes sense. Looked like a lot of the regular customers were on the less than honest part of life."

"Well, that worked out for the best. It seems she has a bit of a following there. Even the patrons questioned by Jack himself pled ignorance."

That wasn't expected. Gamers were pretty selfish, but Emma was so little and so good at gaming, I could understand the protective vibe. "Yes, ma'am. She's well known in that community. No one would give her up, not unless they were seriously threatened."

"He's not threatening anyone yet, but he's making life pretty miserable." She paused for a moment, and I wondered what she was considering. I'd follow her orders, but I also wanted to make sure Emma was on board before I made any decisions. "At this point, the news of your escape is classified. All lines of interrogation have remained vague. Jack's still hoping to find the two of you and save face with the Seligo leadership, but that situation will change. What's your status?"

"Holding now at the desert safe house. Plan was to start running in the AM, before daybreak. I wanted to make sure we weren't running into any traps before heading out."

"Smart. The Black Helixes in the area had the highways locked down twenty minutes after they got to the club. They started doing full vehicle searches, no exceptions. Transpo stations were secured five minutes after that. You would've been caught had you kept running tonight. The good news is that the Seligo don't have enough forces in the Void to keep that level of security once day breaks. Not quite a free pass, but your prospects of getting out unharmed will be much stronger tomorrow."

Parson had moved faster than I'd expected.

"Take one of the nearby public transpos when you move. They're searching passengers now, but any agents at the station should move on by zero four hundred hours. Are you planning to stick together or split up?"

I hoped she liked my plan. It was the best I could come up with. "Split up. Easier to hide two smaller groups than one large one."

"Okay. Both you and Emma, and Dex, Oliver, and Emma's friend should make at least three stops using various travel methods before you return to the compound—"

"I was planning to go to my hideaway spot before heading back. She needs to learn to control her powers and I'd like to work on building her trust."

The Lady's lips tilted in a cat-like grin. She didn't do that often. I must've done something right. "Just keep Emma safe. You two need to become a team, but keep me updated on your status. We'll keep our eyes on the area and if someone heads your way, we'll let you know."

"Will do, ma'am."

"Good." She took a breath. "When you arrive, I'm going to put you both through training and then some starter missions. The sooner you're a team, the sooner she'll be stable. Get her prepared for that."

Screw missions. I'd rather tuck Emma away somewhere safe, but that was a discussion for later. "Emma wants a guarantee that you won't study her or stick her in a lab somewhere. She wants to talk to you."

The line was quiet for a moment. I wanted to tell her that if she didn't agree, I'd disappear with Emma and she'd never find us, but I kept my mouth shut.

"I have a few issues to address tonight, but I'll contact you before you head out tomorrow," she said finally. "I'll do my best to put her at ease."

Something about her tone made me feel like I'd be using Emma. Manipulating her. Emma wasn't some tool. She was a person. I cleared my throat. "Yes, ma'am."

"And Knight?"

"Yes, ma'am?" I waited, wondering what else the Lady had up her sleeve. She had a way of surprising me with some new bit of horrible information when I least expected it.

"Get some rest."

That was it? "Yes, ma'am. Thank you."

Before I could disconnect the call, she'd done it for me. That was the Lady's way. Come in like a whirlwind, give a bunch of orders, and then leave the same way. The rest of us were left cleaning up the mess.

One thing was for sure—my doubts about the validity of the pairing program were obliterated. Lady Eva knew her stuff. Although Emma and I had the deck stacked in our favor. My feelings for her were deeper than anything any pheromones could create.

I snuck back into the bedroom. Emma's blanket had slipped down a little, revealing her delicate fingers curled into the sheet. Her shirt was pulled to the side, flashing a hint of collarbone. All I wanted to do was lean down and brush a kiss against it, but instead I pulled the covers up, tucking them under her chin before settling down on my side on the floor.

I wasn't sure I could fall asleep. Not with her in

the same room as me. Instead, I watched her.

Having Emma here safe meant that I'd finally achieved one of my biggest goals, but at the same time, it made my life that much more complicated. As I stared at her straight, pixie-like nose and the long lashes that rested against her cheek, I realized for the millionth time that night that I was toast.

I'd do my absolute best to get her whatever she wanted.

***

Middle watch was the worst. Whoever drew it had their sleep time ripped in half, but I'd offered because I didn't think I'd be able to sleep.

Not true. The sound of Emma's breathing lulled me into the best sleep of my life. When Oliver came into the room I jerked awake so fast that my whole body ached. Stretching as I stood didn't even begin to ease the bone-deep exhaustion.

I met him in the hallway. "Thanks. Get some rest."

"Will do."

I made my way into the security room hidden behind a bookcase. The vid screens showed live feeds from the cameras in and around the house, and the surrounding area. Knowing when someone was coming was half the battle. Then you could make the choice—stay and fight or run.

I was used to keeping an eye out. Being in my element let me relax and focus on work instead of the confusing clusterfuck of emotions spinning through my head.

Dealing with Emma was going to take some

control. A whole lot of it. I didn't want to spook her with what I was feeling.

By the time my alarm went off telling me that it was time to wake Dex, there was no going back to sleep. I moved into the kitchen as he took over, and made a pot of coffee. All we had in the pantry was powdered milk, and I wasn't going to ruin my first cup with that. I drank the bitter brew down, and felt the jolt through my system. I decided to let Dex sleep, but as I was finishing my coffee, he wandered past and went into the security room.

I fixed another cup for myself and one for Dex before following him.

"You not going back to sleep?" He asked.

I shook my head. "You're more than welcome to." There was no way I could, especially when all I wanted to do was climb in bed with Emma and feel her next to me. I had to control myself.

"Nah. I'm already awake." He took the cup from me and sipped. "You want to talk about it?" He asked after a long moment.

"Hell no." Dex was always too perceptive.

"She's cute."

I narrowed my gaze at him. "You're going to want to stop right there."

Dex's grin made me want to break his face. He was going to say something that disgusted me. I just knew it.

"I mean, she's short, but I like that. Perfect height for a SUB-J."

SUB-J. Dex speak for stand-up blow job.

I kicked his chair in just the right way to send it toppling over. Dex landed in a heap on the floor, laughing like a hyena.

"That's what I thought," he said as he picked himself up. "So much for you not having a romantic relationship with your match."

"Fuck." I set down the mug so hard, coffee splashed over the edges.

"What's the deal? I've never seen you lose your shit before."

"I know. I don't like it. Not at all." My dad had always been out of control. I prided myself on keeping everything tucked in its proper spot. And keeping a girl around, that'd been out of the question. Dad loved Mom so much it had destroyed him when she died. I never made myself vulnerable like that. Now I couldn't seem to help myself.

No one had ever messed with my focus as much as Emma did—and she always had. Why I'd thought that could've changed was beyond me. I was losing it.

I relaxed back in my chair. "I'll get used to her being around, and then it'll be okay. I'm just reacting to finally having her after looking for so long. It's bound to mess with a guy's head."

Dex snorted. "If you say so. But I'm pretty sure you're hot for her. She might be your endgame."

I shook my head. My endgame? "What makes you say that?"

"They way you look at her. Who she is. It's all wrapped together with all these feelings. You try to hide them, but I know you too well. She's it for you." He laughed. "You loooove her."

I was going to punch him in the throat if he didn't stop soon. "Shut up."

"Nice come back. Point proven."

It was too soon for all of that. I couldn't go into this expecting everything from her, but I wanted it.

Dex, for all his moronic ways, was right. I wanted her. In every way.

***

At six I went in to wake Emma. She was still sleeping soundly. That shouldn't have shocked me, but it did. If I was lucky, maybe it was because she trusted me. That seemed like a stretch though.

The sunrise peeking through the window gave enough light to see all her features. My favorite was the tiny, heart-shaped freckle just outside the corner of her left eye. I wondered if she'd chosen her nose ring to match it or if that was coincidental. Watching her motionless and vulnerable made her look even younger than she was. She lost that hard edge, and became more the girl I remembered.

I touched her shoulder and she shot up from the bed. Her hand grasped mine and electricity flooded my body. With the jolt she was pumping into me, I wouldn't need another cup of coffee for a long time. I opened myself up and let it crackle along my skin. Wide-eyed with her hair sticking up, I couldn't resist the urge to touch her; I brushed a few strands away from her face. "Morning."

The last sleepiness cleared from her eyes. She gasped and scooted away from me.

"I'm sorry. I'm sorry. I just don't normally wake up with someone else in the room. It was instinct."

I sat down on the edge of the bed. "You didn't hurt me."

She stopped her apologizing to really take me in. "I…That's…You keep doing that, and I don't understand how. Or why."

"Lady Eva gave me an ability that's uniquely suited to being around you." She wasn't ready for the whole truth. Not yet. Instead, I stuck to immediately relevant things. "I found clothes that will fit you a little better in one of the closets. Get dressed. Lady Eva wants to talk to you."

She took the clothes from me, and met my gaze for the first time since she woke up. "She does?"

I nodded. "Yep." The light flickered. "You don't need to be scared. It's going to be fine."

"You don't know that," she snapped.

"Okay." Someone was cranky in the morning. "You should at least know that I won't let anything bad happen to you."

Not giving her a chance to argue, I left and shut the door behind me. Dex and Oliver were getting themselves ready for the road. I assumed one of them had gotten Mona up—she was sleeping in the room next to Oliver's—so it was just me in the kitchen. I tried to busy myself, but there wasn't much to cook. The cabinets were stocked with rations and nonperishables that only needed heating.

This wasn't going how I'd hoped. I'd said I'd be patient, but it stung a little that she wasn't warming up to me a little more.

A few minutes later Emma came into the living room. She stared at the ground for a second before meeting my gaze. Her hands were fisted at her sides. "Sorry. I didn't mean to be so harsh. I'm just not used to anyone waking me up, unless it's someone bad…I reacted poorly. So." She blew out a breath. "I'm sorry." She released her fists as she said the last, like she was setting the apology free.

I leaned back against the counter, trying to look nonthreatening and trustworthy. "You don't need to apologize. Coffee?"

She wiggled her nose from side to side as she thought. "Sure."

I tried not to laugh at that cute move. "How about some breakfast?"

She repeated the gesture. Wiggle, wiggle, scrunch. And a nod. "Okay."

I could watch her decision process play across her face. And yes it was adorable, but survival-wise, it hurt. She'd been alone too long, and didn't have a clue how to school her features. We'd have to work on that.

She sat at the bar in the kitchen and I turned to the toaster, dropping in a few protein pastries. I poured the coffee and handed it to her along with the powdered milk and sugar. She skipped the milk but added enough sugar to make my teeth wince in sympathy.

When the pastry was done, I popped it on a plate and handed it over.

"Thanks," she said. She took a little nibble and then shifted in her seat.

I leaned against the counter again, watching her. She took a few more bites and then scowled at me.

"What did I do now?" I asked.

"Are you going to stand there and watch me eat?"

From the way she was sitting, a little hunched, I knew it was making her uncomfortable, but I couldn't seem to look away. I shrugged. "What would you like me to do?"

"I don't know. Something else. Anything else."

"Okay. I've got a question for you."

She waved her hand in front of her, like an offering. "Go for it. But you might not like my answer."

I grunted. I had a feeling that was probably true. "Why're you so short?"

She choked on her coffee. "Is my being short offensive to you or something?"

I'd only asked to make conversation, but after that reaction I wanted to know the answer. "No, but I want to know why you're so short," I said again. "You should be around five feet eight inches, but I don't think you even hit five feet."

She sat taller in her chair. "I *am* five feet and one *fifth* of an inch."

"One fifth? You're counting *fifths*?"

"When you're my size, every little bit counts." I laughed, but she just talked louder. "Plus, it's not so bad being short. People generally ignore someone they don't think of as intimidating. And those that get a kick out of picking on smaller people, well, they don't expect what I have in store for them."

That sobered me a little. "I'm sure they don't, but you didn't answer my question."

She shrugged. "I didn't know I was supposed to be tall." She flicked her teeth against her lip ring—a nervous habit of hers. "I dunno. I guess I didn't eat much for a while or whatever. That probably affected my growth, right? Malnutrition and all that good stuff."

I didn't like where this was going. How malnourished did someone have to be to stop growing? "What do you mean 'didn't eat much for a while?'"

She shrugged again. "Wasn't much food to be had. Not where I was placed after traveling around with Sally. I didn't want to raise a stink, because then someone might take notice of me. So I stayed. I was only there a few years before protective services arrested the couple. One of the other foster kids got sick and the hospital didn't like what they saw. Nothing like ribs sticking out of a four-year-old to get the doctors in a tizzy. They now have a lovely suite in the Nevada Void's labor camp." She laughed at her own joke, but for the life of me, I couldn't see what the hell was funny about any of this. "I got moved to a much better place. Stayed there for about a year. But that little bit in the godawful trailer must've been when I was supposed to be hitting a major growth spurt." She sipped her coffee. "Mystery solved."

There was so much more to this story that she wasn't telling me. I wanted to know what she was glossing. "How long were you there in that house?"

"The trailer? Uh...three years, eighty-three days, and a handful of hours. Give or take an hour. Not like I was counting." She laughed. She actually laughed at that lame-ass joke. But she still knew exactly how long she'd been in that place. It must've been way worse than she was letting on.

"Don't get your back up for me."

I realized I was gripping the counter so hard my joints were cracking. I forced my fingers to relax.

She set her coffee down and sat up straight. "So,

I'm a little shorter than I was supposed to be. Maybe I went a little hungry for a while, but no one laid a hand on me. You had it way worse than I did."

Who cared what happened to me? I wanted to beat the everlovingshit out of the people who were supposed to be taking care of Emma, but hadn't. "You shouldn't have gone hungry."

She smiled, but it was a sad one. "You shouldn't have gotten hit."

"Touché."

She ate the rest of the toaster pastry in silence.

"You want another?"

She chuckled. I liked the sound of it. "Feeding me now won't make me any taller. I've been on my own for a while, and I eat as much as I want. Who needs to be tall anyhow? Being short rocks."

She was missing the point entirely. "I don't care how tall you are. I'm just glad I found you."

Her cheeks turned an adorable shade of bright red. "Shut up."

Oliver came into the room. "Lady's on the computer. She's asking to speak with Emma."

I glanced at my watch. We needed to get moving. I pushed away from the counter and strode to the security room.

When we walked in, the monitor showed Lady Eva standing in her control room, talking to someone off screen. The white lab coat was gone, and she wore black pants and shirt. Her hair was pulled back in one loose braid.

I cleared my throat. "Good morning, ma'am."

Emma tensed beside me, and I put a hand around her shoulders to reassure her.

Lady Eva gave her full attention to the screen, with a bright smile. "Knight. Emma. It's so nice to see you again."

"Again?" Emma asked.

Her smile dimmed a bit. "I knew your parents a long time ago. I'm sorry for what happened."

"Sure." Her voice was flat. This wasn't going well. The Lady better have something good up her sleeve.

"I've been looking for you since your parents died. I knew them long before you were born and their lives were...a little dramatic...or traumatic. They wanted you to live a normal life, but they didn't understand that from the moment you were born, you were never going to be normal. Getting that Red Helix only set you farther apart from everyone else." Her smile went away fully and she crossed her arms. "Although it may turn you against working with me, I'll be honest—your parents never wanted you to be a Raven. And I don't blame them for that choice, but I really do wish they'd properly prepared you to get to safety in the event of their deaths. You were never supposed to be out there fending for yourself."

No, she wasn't. And now Emma had me. Even if she decided not to join up with the Ravens.

"I got to safety just fine. I'm alive and well."

That was a little debatable, but I kept my mouth shut. Something told me Emma wouldn't appreciate me pointing out anything.

"Are you? You're much shorter than you were supposed to be."

Sometimes the Lady and I were of one mind.

"That leads me to believe that you were not fine for some period of time," the Lady continued. "How bad it was, I have no idea. What I do know is that the Voids hide many horrors. One day, you might tell me your story. Or you might not. That's entirely up to you. I won't push you. You're an adult and it's your choice what to do now."

Emma fisted her hands, and I wanted to step in for her. Being put on the defense wasn't going to endear her to the Lady. "What I want is a normal life. Beyond anything, that's what I want most."

Lady Eva sighed. "You're just like your mother." She held up a hand when Emma bristled at that.

I wanted to shake the Lady. If she continued down this track, she'd lose Emma. And me, if it came down to it.

"It's not a bad thing, but I wish you could compromise a little on your goals," Lady Eva said. "You're not normal. Normal, unmodded people don't harness electricity like you do. You have to find what's normal for *you*." She paused. "But your normal could mean any number of things. I'd love it to encompass coming to my compound, and at the very least learning how to harness and control your ability. Maybe even joining our fight against the Seligo. Knight will help you and guide you. All that I ask is that you give the Ravens a chance. I think you can do good in this world. You could change things if you could learn to view being Red as a blessing instead of a curse."

Emma nodded, but didn't say anything. I wished I knew what she was thinking. All these nods made me want to stay there and question her until she told me what was going through her head. I had to know.

"Good luck, Emma. I hope to see you soon."

Emma stood there, silent, as Lady Eva signed off.

I looked down at Emma, waiting to hear what she said. When she didn't say anything, I decided it was time to break the silence. "What are you thinking about?"

Her brows were pulled tight together as she looked up at me. "She's something, huh?"

"The Lady? Yeah."

The overhead light flickered for a second, but she got it under control before I could reach for her. "Do you think I should give the Ravens a chance?"

I sighed as I sat down in the chair. At her full height standing up, she was as tall as me sitting down. "I know what I should say if I was being a good Raven, but you're not just anyone. You're Emma, the girl who saved me. So, I have to say that I don't give a shit what you do. I just want to make sure you're okay, whatever you decide. And I'd really like it if I could stick by you no matter what that is."

She tilted her head as she stared at me. "Why?"

I shrugged. "Because. I want to." It was as simple as that.

She scrunched her eyebrows. "Okay. But why?"

I laughed. "Just because."

"Just because?"

She wasn't understanding me, but I didn't have more of an explanation. Or at least not one that she was ready for. "Yup. Just because."

She blew out a breath. "I guess we'll have to see what happens."

"I guess we will."

Chapter Eleven

CIPHER

The conversation with Lady Eva left me a little uneasy. My parents hadn't wanted me to be a Raven, but it seemed like joining was my only safe bet.

The fact that I was here, in a safe house with a trio of helixed Ravens and my uncle not far behind, showed how totally messed up this situation was. I was a girl without a ton of options. Especially if I was tired of running.

"Still the same plan?" Oliver said as we sat down.

"Yep. We're splitting up here. We'll meet up with you at the compound. Assume you're being followed and try not to leave the car for a while. Make them think we're still—"

"Hold up. I'm not going anywhere," Mona said.

I knew exactly how she felt. Mona's life had been totally disrupted and it was all my fault.

"You can't stick around here. They'll make the connection between you and Emma soon, and you won't be safe," Oliver said. "You have to come with us."

Mona shook her head. "No way. If I go anywhere

it's with Cipher."

What? She wasn't upset about leaving her place behind? I knew she didn't have any family or friends besides me—we were alike in that way—but I figured she'd at least be a little pissed about abandoning her clothes.

She was upset about not being with me?

"Too dangerous," Knight said. "It's going to be hard enough for the two of us to lose any tail we might have. Adding another person is…"

I didn't want to disappoint Mona, but he was right. She needed to get as far away from me as possible. It wasn't safe for her. I wouldn't ruin her life any more than I already had.

"No—"

"It won't be forever," I said, cutting off her protest.

Mona's eyes were glassy when she turned to me. "You don't know that. People leave all the time and they never come back."

"I won't be like everyone else." My voice was firm and clear, even if I wasn't sure how much of a promise I could make. I'd do my best, but if Jack got to me first… "I'll find my way back to you."

"That's what everyone says. It's a lie. Even if you believe it now, something will happen, something you're not prepared for, and you'll decide I'm not worth the trouble."

I gripped her hand. "You're worth it. I don't forget family. Not ever. Being with me right now isn't safe. But you can't get rid of me that easy. We'll find our way back together." I hoped to God I wasn't lying. I swallowed the lump in my throat. "So, how soon can we leave?" I asked Knight.

He checked his watch. "Next transpo out of New Mexico is in an hour and a half. It's tight, but I think we can make it."

"New Mexico? We can't leave from Arizona?"

"Nope," Dex said. "They were supposed to clear out of the Arizona transpo stations at oh-four hundred hours, but we got word that a force is staying on as a precautionary measure."

"Don't worry," Knight said. "They don't think you got through the Tempe blockade, so the roads from here are clear. The extended transpo station watch really is precautionary. We'll be fine."

My stomach knotted. If we were caught...I didn't want to think what would happen. The longer we waited the worse it was going to get. "Sounds awesome."

"Let's move out," Knight said.

The guys started gathering up stuff and putting equipment away, and they clearly knew what they were doing. They had it all choreographed as they moved from room to room, turning off lights and making it look like no one had been here.

Mona and I moved outside to wait by the car. She hugged me, and it took me a second too long to hug her back. She squeezed so tight, I could barely breathe.

"Stay safe," I said when she finally pulled away.

"We're in this car," Knight said as he motioned to the garage. Inside was a beat-up SUV that looked like a million others on the road. I jumped in the passenger seat.

"You sure they'll be okay?"

"Yeah. Dex and Oliver are used to this kind of thing. They'll take care of Mona. Just focus on staying calm, and if you feel like you're losing control, reach out for me. I'll steady you, okay?"

I stared out the window, unable to meet his gaze as he drove away from the safe house. He thought he wanted to help me, but eventually he'd realize I was more trouble than I was worth. Or he'd die trying to save me.

I wasn't sure I could live through either of those options.

"Okay?" he said again.

I didn't know how to answer that. "Sure."

We didn't talk much on the way to the transpo. I had questions, but opening up right now...I already felt exposed. I tugged on my lip ring as I thought.

"You're going to break your teeth if you keep doing that."

I let go of it, and turned to him. "It's fine. Promise."

"I just don't want you to get hurt."

How had I somehow gained an overprotective guy in my life? "I get that you and I knew each other, and that you feel like there's some kind of debt that you need to repay, but consider us even. Seriously. I don't need protecting. So, let's push that instinct where the sun don't shine. Okay?" I gave him my most angelic smile.

He frowned at me. "What are you doing with your face?"

I was horrible at fake smiling. Why did I keep trying? "I believe it's called a reassuring smile."

"No. That's not a smile. When you smile, your

dimples show, your freckles stand out, and the green shines in your eyes. It's a thing of beauty. When all of those things are absent, it's unsettling. You have dead eyes when you fake smile."

"Dead eyes?"

"Yeah, your mouth is smiling, but your eyes are saying 'I'm going to murder you.' It's creepy." He shuddered.

"What a drama queen." I needed to learn to pretend to be happy better. I could pretend to be pissed off and cry on cue. I had to know how to lie pretty well to survive, but faking a smile had never come easy to me. "So, tell me, oh Wise One, how do I do it correctly?"

"If I have to tell you how, you can't do it. Start with a lot of practice in the mirror."

"Is that how you learned to lie so well?" I winced. That had sounded more bitchy than I meant it to be.

"No. I learned to lie when I was a kid because if I didn't, I'd be dead. Death is usually a pretty great motivator."

He didn't seem upset, so I pressed for more. "Your dad?"

He shrugged. "Took me a while to figure out that it didn't matter what I said or did. If he wanted to kick my ass, he was going to. It didn't really have anything to do with me, but I tried my damnedest to lie and fast talk my way out of fights with him."

Slightly impressive. "You're really well adjusted."

"Yeah, well the school I went to had really fantastic head shrinkers."

I snorted, and then covered my nose.

"Did you just snort?"

This was so embarrassing. "No."

"You totally did, didn't you?"

"Shut up." I laughed again, and snorted in the process.

"There it is again!"

We both started laughing. It was easy to be around him. It always had been, regardless of the version of him I thought back to.

After that, we made small talk about programming and hacking. I asked him about how he built his processors, but he wouldn't share the secret recipe. Before long, we were pulling up to the transpo station. He swiped his ID to get through the gates, and an alias popped up on the vid screen.

"That was fast."

"We've got some good hackers on our team. You might even like some of them," he said with a wink.

The car went through the usual security scan. A bead of sweat rolled down my face as we went through the gates. I was expecting the Black Helixes to come rushing out at us at any second, but no one did. We parked, and everything was fine.

He messed around with something in the trunk, before pulling a backpack over his shoulders. I watched the parking lot, to make sure no one was looking at us, but everyone was going about the day as usuasl.

Knight walked over with a black ball cap in his hand. "Come here."

I stood still as he approached. He tilted my head up and brushed my hair away from my face, before easing the cap over my head. "The cap will limit front-on facial scans to fifty-percent. Ditto for the sides. Sometimes fifty-percent is enough to raise a flag, but not usually. I altered my specs in the system last night and they don't have any on you yet. This is purely precautionary." Knight leaned over me to adjust the cap size before stepping back. "Looking good," he said with a grin. He pulled another hat out of his back pocket, and straightened the folded brim before shoving it over his head.

"Let's go."

The station used to be all white and chrome, but a layer of grime coated everything, turning it shades of gray. I wondered what it would've been like when it was new. Something about the clean lines of the structure made me think it had been beautiful once. The air conditioning in the station hit me as soon as we stepped through the doors, raising goose bumps along my skin. Outside was hot, but inside was freezing.

"You need a jacket?"

The guy noticed everything. "I'm okay."

"This way." He motioned off to the right, and I followed him.

The station was impressive. Different colored lines on the floors marked directions for bus, train, and pod travel. We walked through the security station. Automated kiosks scanned us as we walked into the ticketing area, and I reached for Knight.

My nerves were going crazy, and I didn't want to set off any alarms. This time when he started draining my electricity, the feeling was comforting instead of freaky.

"You sure you're okay?"

I swallowed. "Let's just get where we're going."

"You're doing fine."

I nodded. I didn't want to need the praise, but it helped me calm down as he led me toward the pod docks.

I'd never been in pod station before. I stayed away from transpo stations in general because they had too many cameras. This mega-station had one hanging from every ceiling tile, and I was sure there were more that I couldn't see. Each camera had a flashing red light, meant to draw the eye. I knew this, and yet I still started to look.

Boards hung along the walls, showing destinations, departures, and arrivals. Other vid screens ran ads, alerts, and PSAs. Servers called out from food stalls, trying to catch commuters as they rushed through the station. It was instant sensory overload.

I started to look back up at the cameras and Knight tapped on my brim before the camera could get a full shot of my face. "How about you not look straight at them."

"Accident. I've never actually been in a station like this."

"No? Never taken a pod before?"

I shook my head. "Nope." To be honest, the hyperspeed pods kind of freaked me out. I mean, I knew they almost never failed, but when they did, it was insta-death. And they were expensive. Like thousands of credits. To ride in a deathtrap? Only a helix would be so dumb.

"Well, today's your lucky day."

Right. My nerves started to take hold as we walked through the crowd. People moved in all directions, some hauling giant bags. My feet nearly got creamed by some jerk's rolling trunk. It was too much. Too many people. Too many cameras recording me.

I started to pull away from Knight but he gripped my hand.

He leaned close to me. "I don't want you losing control here. We can't afford for you to cause even the tiniest fluctuation in the electrical grid. The Blacks aren't actively looking for us here, but I guarantee you that every power station on this planet is monitoring local electrical levels. Best way to avoid that attention is to stick close, skin-to-skin. I'll absorb any surges."

I knew that. I wasn't sure why I tried to pull away, other than instinct.

"Plus, I get to hold your hand." He winked.

"Ugh. Dork," I said.

"You say dork, but I think you like it."

"No, I don't." But damned if I wasn't grinning like a fool.

His gaze scanned my face. "Dimples. Green eyes nearly glowing. Yup. Your words might be saying one thing but your face is singing a different song. That smile is gen-u-ine."

I rolled my eyes. Knight walked straight past the ticket kiosks to the gates. "Hey. Forgetting something." I pointed to the long lines.

"Nope. We're already pre-checked in. All we have to do is board."

"Right."

He stopped walking, shoving a hand in his front pocket. "Wait." He laughed. "I actually *did* almost forget something." He slipped a plain gold band over his left ring finger, and then placed a matching ring on me before I could pull away. "Thanks for doing me the honors, Mrs. Vasquez."

Vasquez? Who? What was he doing?

It took me a second to realize what he was talking about. This was our cover. The sight of him putting a ring on my finger must've short-circuited my brain.

When I tried to pull our hands apart to look at the band, Knight's grip firmed. "I know it's not the proposal that you wanted, princess, but I'll make it up to you later."

My heart skipped a beat. "It's just our cover."

"For now."

That wasn't the most reassuring answer. Was it going to be something more than our cover later? Was he actually implying that he wanted to marry me?

The guy was insane. I didn't want to ask that question, no matter how curious I was. Instead, I asked a different one. "Why'd you call me princess?"

"Best to call you what you really are."

"What are you talking about?"

"You don't remember?" He sighed. "Of course you don't. Don't you wonder why I picked Knight?"

"Cause you have a thing for medieval RPGs?" A totally wild guess.

He chuckled. "Nice try, but no. Because you were always going on about these princess stories as a kid. You were convinced some knight in shining armor was going to come save you."

My jaw dropped open. "So, you think you're my knight in shining armor here to save me?"

"But of course, fair maiden." He dipped in a gallant bow, still clutching my hand.

I rolled my eyes dramatically. "I was a lame kid." I started walking again.

"No, you weren't. You saved me. You were my angel. It's only fair that you let me be your knight. At least every once in a while."

What did I even say to that? I was used to taking care of myself. Of doing everything and being the only one I could count on. Maybe sharing the weight—both the burdens of my Red Helix and abilities—would make my life easier for a while, but it was wrong. I had to save myself, or else I wouldn't be worthy of being saved.

"Come on. This way." Knight started toward gateway fifty-two.

A gate agent stood in the pod doorway. The guy was shorter than Knight by a foot, but not as short as me. He was overweight and sweating. In this air conditioning, that took talent. He breathed so loudly that I was worried for his health.

"Automation down?" Knight said as he pressed his finger to the sensor.

"Just doing some routine checks. Got a few fugitives at large. Gotta be extra-secure this morning or the boss'll have my ass."

This was majorly not cool. I glanced up at Knight, but he only grinned at me, like this was totally fine and normal. Meanwhile, I was a complete mess. We could get caught. Right here. Right now.

My heartbeat pounded in my ears.

The gate agent ran through Knight's file for his alias, Juan Vasquez. "Newlyweds, huh?"

"Yes, sir," Knight said, with a shit-eating grin. He pulled me into his side, throwing his arm over my shoulder. "Isn't she just the cutest thing you ever did see?"

He was laying it on way too thick. I poked Knight in the side but he didn't react.

The agent leered at me, giving me a thorough once-over. I wasn't the only one who didn't like the look. Knight was suddenly standing a little too stiff.

"If I had a girl like her, I wouldn't let her see daylight. She'd never leave my bed."

I threw up a little bit in my mouth.

"You and I are on the same page, sir," Knight said. Only the fear of getting caught stopped me from hitting him.

The agent handed us our passes back. "Have a good honeymoon."

"We plan to," Knight said. "Right, sugar?"

Before I could say anything, his lips landed on mine. When I tried to push him away, he held on tighter.

It took me a bit to remember this was our cover. I shouldn't push him away. I should be hamming it up.

I gripped his T-shirt and opened my mouth to him.

Bad call.

The second his tongue brushed against mine I melted. I heard myself moan right before he started to pull my dazed self into the pod.

What the hell just happened?

I stumbled over my feet as Knight found our spot. The pod had twenty gray vinyl seats. Four seats to a row, with a small aisle between them. Five rows in total. I'd always pictured pods to be round, but they were actually more like really tiny train cars. This one looked clean enough, but still had marks of heavy wear. More than half the pod was already full.

Knight pushed me down into a seat in an empty row, fastening my seatbelt across my waist and tightening it. He pushed the shoulder harness and looped the seatbelt through, snapping it into place.

"That was one hell of a kiss," Knight whispered as he sat next to me and buckled in.

I whimpered. "What was that?" I was beyond turned on. Every nerve ending was sensitive. And the heat…

Knight's fingers twined with mine again. "That's us. Only us."

"Is kissing everyone like that?"

"What?"

Oh crap. I hadn't meant to say that aloud.

"That was your first kiss?"

Now I was a different kind of hot. "I uh…didn't have a lot of time for boyfriends. What with the running and the starving and the trying to stay alive. Didn't have a lot of friends period." This was more than a little embarrassing.

"Great time to tell me, princess. Don't worry, I'll make sure the next kiss is even better."

A chill ran along my skin at his promise. "Better?" That was a high bar he was setting.

"Yes."

I didn't think it could get much better, but I was suddenly game to try. "Guess it would be better if it was a real kiss instead of a show for some sleazeball douche?"

"That was a real kiss."

I shook my head. "You know what I mean. Real.

Like you mean it. Like you want to kiss me, not because you have to because of the cover or whatever."

He rubbed his thumb up and down the back of my hand. "That was a real kiss. I wanted to kiss you the second I saw you."

I turned as much as I could. I needed to see his face. "You don't have to pretend."

"I told you not five minutes ago that I'm going to propose to you one day and you still don't believe me about the kiss?"

I opened and closed my mouth a few times as I tried to figure out what to say. Trying to find something that wasn't totally dumb. "You were joking."

"No. No, I wasn't."

I sat back in my chair. The ring on my finger suddenly weighed ten times as much as it had a second ago.

An automated voice announced the countdown to departure through the pod speakers, but I barely heard as Knight's words echoed in my head. It scared me how much I wanted him to be serious. I wanted it so badly my heart ached for it.

It seemed nuts. I hadn't known Knight for long. But I'd also kind of known him forever. Putting all those pieces together in my head, I knew him. And he knew me better than anyone.

I still had a lot to learn about him, but I knew that I hadn't made a bad choice. Sticking around after blowing those transformers was maybe the best decision I'd ever made.

I held on to Knight's hand as the pod took off and

hoped I never had to let go.

Chapter Twelve

KNIGHT

Pod travel only took minutes. I let myself relax into my seat, enjoying these few moments in transit. We'd start being in danger as soon as we arrived in San Diego, but until then, we were safe in the pod. Just being next to Emma meant everything to me.

"How're you doing, Em?"

"I wish you wouldn't call me that," she mumbled.

That was all I wanted to call her. "Why?"

"Because it makes me uncomfortable. Like someone could recognize me." She blew out a harsh breath. "It's not an unusual name, but it's mine. Private. Anything that's mine I've hidden. So hearing it out loud is disarming. Makes me feel...bare." She paused. "I'd rather you not use it. Especially here."

It was a valid fear. "You're on record as Emera Mason-Vasquez. So Em isn't far off."

"Good to know."

Her fingers felt thin and fragile. I rubbed my thumb along the top of her hand so that I remembered not to squeeze it. Not to hurt her. "Okay. So in public, you're Cipher. What about in private?

Can I call you by your real name then?"

Her cheeks reddened. I bet she hated that her skin was so fair. "You think we're going to be in private together a lot?"

I leaned as close to her ear as the restraints would allow. "I sure hope so."

If possible, her face got even redder and she looked away. "How am I supposed to respond to that?"

I didn't want to make her uncomfortable, but I had to make my intentions clear. She had to know I wanted her. Pressuring her wasn't an option, though. "You don't have to. I'm just laying that out there. Okay?"

She breathed in and out hard. "Okay."

I couldn't help the stupid grin. "Okay."

As soon as the pod stopped, announcing our arrival in San Diego. I unhooked myself, and then helped Emma with her belt.

I kept my hand firmly in hers so that she doesn't lose control. "This way."

"Have you been here before?"

"No."

The San Diego station overlooked the water. While inside the pod, I hadn't gotten any com signals, but I didn't want to spare a glance to check it. If something bad was going to happen, I needed my eyes open. I couldn't do that while looking at the screen.

We stepped out of the pod, and I took a breath. If they'd found something wrong with our fake IDs in New Mexico, now was the time we'd find out about it.

I kept Emma close to me, her hand firmly in mine.

We couldn't afford for even the tiniest fluctuation in the electrical grid or the station's security would come down hard.

Officers lined the walls, but I counted only three Black Helixes on site. If we'd been expected, all the big guns would already be out. All the other security guards were low-rent norms.

Jack hadn't stretched this far yet.

We walked calmly to the exit. With each step, we were on safer ground.

Even if I'd never been to this station before, I knew that we had at least three vehicles to choose from in the south parking lot. The Shadow Ravens had escape vehicles planted at every major transpo station.

Emma glanced around as we stepped outside. I tapped on the brim of her hat. "I know it's tempting to look around a new place, but don't."

"Sorry." She walked staring at the ground and I stopped walking, yanking her to a stop, too.

I leaned down to her. "We're going to be okay." I brushed a kiss along her cheek before standing tall again. She was so tiny.

"Let's get out of here."

"This way." I pulled her toward the parking lot, and through the aisles of cars. Raven cars were always on aisle "E" or "5"—depending on what system the lot used. The plates were totally random. The only way to find the car was by the glowing raven painted on the bumper. Thanks to Lady Eva's eye mods, only Ravens could see the shade.

"Are we stealing another car?"

"Not this time."

"Good." She took a deep breath. "That smell. Isn't it amazing? God, I missed the ocean. It's been a long time."

"Why?" A long time ago, we'd lived not far from the beach. She could go anywhere in her RV. Why would she ignore beaches if she loved them?

She shrugged. "I stayed mostly inland. I went along the east coast a few times, but it was always too cold to really enjoy it."

"Well, it's a good thing we're getting some beach time." I finally spotted a car with the raven mark. I pressed my finger to the trunk lock and it disengaged. "Get in."

Emma slid around to the passenger side while I grabbed a bag from the trunk.

"Security code, please," said a silky automated voice as I slid into the driver's seat.

If someone managed to get in without an access code, the car would explode. Good thing I had one. "Marquez, Hunter. Psi one eight three beta seven thirteen."

"Thank you, Shadow Marquez. Security disengaged. Destination?"

"Buckle up." I threw the bag in the backseat. "We're going to get the hell out of here. Fast," I said as I put my seatbelt in place. "Computer. Manual drive, please."

"Manual drive is engaged. Please obey all traffic laws and ordinances, Raven Marquez."

"Yes, ma'am," I said as I put the car in reverse. I didn't like not having control over a vehicle.

I spared a glance at Emma once I was on the road. She was rubbing her hands along the leather seat.

"You okay?"

Her face turned a little pink as she glanced over at me. "This car is legit."

That made me smile. I dug how much she was enjoying the car. "Yeah. Lady likes to travel in style."

"Did she know we were coming here?"

"No." I explained the setup with the cars.

"So, how do we get to the island from here?"

I cleared my throat. She wouldn't like the next part. "We're driving to Los Angeles to catch another pod."

"But isn't there a big citadel outpost there?"

"Yes."

"So, why in the hell would we go there?" She sounded a little pissed, but that was to be expected. She'd avoided the major outpost areas for good reason.

"They're looking for us everywhere, but it's really cursory. You saw how this was. They didn't even have a full Black team out on the platforms." I squeezed her hand. "Don't worry. If something doesn't look right, we'll find a different way to get there. But it'll be worth it. The island in the Virgins that we're headed to is completely uninhabited. It's a natural preserve. We'll stay there a few days. No transformers for you to blow, so we can have some privacy while we work on your control."

Emma turned to face me, straining against the seatbelt. "A few days? Do you think that's enough time to make a difference?"

I wasn't certain, but the Lady said that once the two of us were together, Emma would be able to find her center easier. It wasn't that she couldn't do it on her own, but my influence was supposed to help the process along. All the previous genetic pairs had figured it out quickly. Not in two days, but they hadn't had a vindictive Seligo on their ass.

Taking my eyes off the road for long wasn't an option. I fought against the traffic as I thought about how to answer her question. I didn't want to give her false hope, but I didn't want to shoot her down before we even started trying. "It's not out of the realm of the possible, but first, we need to get to a place where you can practice without calling attention to yourself. As long as your ability is out of control, you'll be in danger."

I glanced at her long enough to see the scowl. The little line between her eyes was begging for a kiss.

"You make it sound so easy, but I've already tried. I got some meditation vids but the more 'chill' I was, the more frustrated I got when I lost control. I had fewer blowouts, but they were worse. So I went the other way. I tried Taekwondo, kickboxing, and krav maga. But the more violent I got, the worse my control was. Littler bursts, but all the time. It left me feeling exhausted. So, I gave up. I am the way that I am. I can't change it. This is as good as it gets."

It sounded like she'd already given up. "Try to keep an open mind. I'm sorry that—"

"Stop apologizing. You have absolutely nothing to be sorry about. You didn't make me this way."

No, I didn't, but I could help her. I knew it. "I wish I could've found you sooner. Before you felt so frustrated."

"I keep telling you, and maybe one day you'll believe me, but I'm not your responsibility. I've been like this my whole life. I've come to terms with the way things are. At least how they are now. But that just gives me a goal to work toward. How boring would life be if I were totally content?"

"Contentment breeds discontent."

"Exactly." She sat straight back in her chair, turning to stare out the window as we passed a shopping center. "I don't know. Maybe. But it's all I've got. Having goals keeps me hopeful and moving toward something." She sighed. "This is a depressing conversation."

Smooth move, Knight. Way to make the girl feel inadequate. At this rate, she was never going to fall for me.

What if she never fell for me?

"I'm not trying to make you feel worse," I said, finally. "I just think you deserve more. Existing isn't enough. I wish you were actually happy."

"Well, why don't you shit in one hand and wish in the other. Let's see which fills up faster." She snort-laughed at her own joke. It was adorable. "I'm not unhappy. I guess I'm not exactly happy either, but I'm surviving. I get by. I don't hate my life. I'm pretty okay with it, but I would like to stop running. I'd like to settle down. I know I was freaking out when I said it last time, but I don't want a lot. I just want what every other person in the Void has. Friends. Family. Freedom…or the illusion of it. A place to live that doesn't have wheels attached to it. I don't think that's too much to ask for."

"It's not too much." That she wanted so little—the basics that other people took for granted—made me want to give her the world. Even if it weren't in my power to give, I'd do my damnedest.

She finally turned away from the window. I felt her gaze on me, and couldn't help the half-smile from sneaking out.

"So, why did you start making the processors?"

"Some girl told me I needed a marketable skill." I winked at her.

"Thank God I was a smart eight-year-old. Your stuff is the best. I'm proud of what you've done with your life." She relaxed a little more, putting her feet on the dash. "It's crazy thinking I had some small part in that."

Small? "You had a huge part in it."

"Nah. Maybe I gave you a push on the path, but you've worked hard for more than a decade to get where you are. That's all you."

"It's not like I had to try too hard to get to a better place. I was pretty much at rock bottom when we met."

"Why didn't you ever ask for help? Turn your father in?"

I hadn't meant to bring that asshole up, but I forced myself to give an honest answer. "Pride. Fear of the unknown. 'Better the devil you know' is a saying for a reason. You know how rough it can be when placed in a foster home."

She was quiet for so long, I wondered if should've kept my mouth shut, but I'd never been good at that. Especially when it came to Emma.

The com on the car buzzed. I accepted the call on speakerphone. "Marquez."

"Saw you picked up a car in San Diego. Lady's asking for your status."

I recognized Samantha's voice. She was hard to read because she was always multi-tasking. I had no doubt she'd be updating Lady and coordinating with half a dozen other teams as we talked. "En route to Los Angeles. Should be there in a couple hours."

"Next step?"

"I'm not sensing that we're being followed. We'll pod to the big island, then take a boat out."

"Do you need tickets? Gear?"

"No on the tickets. Yes on the gear. Camping stuff and supplies for both of us."

She was quiet for a moment. "Lady agrees. We'll set it up at the International Loop Station, Terminal seven. Locker number will be sent to your com in twenty."

"Thanks."

"And Hunter?

I rolled my eyes. "Yes, Samantha?"

"Good luck and stay safe. You still owe me a chance to win back last week's loot."

I'd kicked her ass, and everyone else's, at poker last Friday. "No worries. If something happens, I'll make sure you get your money back."

"Jesus, Hunter. Don't be so morbid. Oh, wait. Lady says she expects you back within a week. She says not to forget what she told you before. I assume you know what she's referring to?"

Emma and I needed to show up at the Ravens compound as a team. I was working on that. "I've got it. Tell her it's in progress."

Some rapid typing on her end.

"She says good. I notified Oliver and Dex with your update. They've just checked back and Oliver says that they're in Emma's RV. They'll be taking the scenic route to the compound. Would you like me to respond with anything?"

"Tell the guys we'll be out of range for a bit. Do you have the latest on Jack?"

"Checking now." There was a brief pause. "Ysenia's still the Raven in charge there. She says that Parson is pissed. He's pushing the Greens in the area to locate Emma and you via coms and tracking. Blacks are still searching on foot and interrogating any suspects. They haven't figured out that you got past the main search area, but the Seligo are looking for your face because no one has an image of Emma yet. They haven't linked Emma to her Cipher identity either. They made moves into the park, but Ollie, Dex, and Emma's friend—MonaLisa Stalimanti…Jesus, that's a name. Anyway, they were long gone before the serious interrogation started."

Nice. "How did they get past the line?"

"Dex. He must've done some of his voodoo stuff. I don't know how he always gets out of a bind, but the dude is slippery." She paused. "If I were you, I'd take your time hooking back up with them. It's too crazy out there."

I'd hoped to meet up with them sooner rather than later, but I trusted Samantha. She was excellent at synthesizing various lines of communication into fact. Her analyses were always spot-on. "Noted. Thanks, Sam."

"No worries. Later, Hunter."

The car was quiet after Samantha hung up. Emma was back to staring out the window, and sat as close to the door as she could without opening it.

Had I said something to upset her? I couldn't come up with anything I'd said to Samantha that would've been rude or insulting.

I was bad at this. I waited a few minutes, thinking I was being too sensitive, but she stayed totally closed down. "You okay?"

"Fine."

From my experience, fine always meant the opposite of fine. "Anything you want to talk about?"

"Not particularly."

Somehow I'd messed up, but I wasn't sure what I'd done.

Being around Emma was odd. I both knew her and didn't. I wanted it to be seamless. For us to magically get what was going on in each other's heads. "Okay. So, are you going to tell me what's wrong or what?"

"Nothing's wrong. Everything's fine."

Her tone of voice was a little too high. It didn't have that lazy rasp that I was getting addicted to. "I can't fix it if I don't know what's wrong."

"Ugh. Will you just leave it alone? I'm fine."

"Fine. Then I guess I'm fine, too." I couldn't keep the frustration from my voice.

"You're so annoying."

The irritation in her voice made me grin. This—being with her—was going to be so much fun. "No, I'm not. I'm handsome and amazing and you are so attracted to me that you don't know what to do."

She laughed. "Ego much?"

"No. Just hopeful."

"Well, don't quit your day job. Mind reading's definitely not your talent. But you could become a driver. That could be your next job if we don't get caught."

We were speeding along the road. There was nothing much to see out here, but strip mall after apartment complex. Most people opted to have the cars drive themselves, but I liked to handle the control. It cut back on delays, and I got a special kind of joy from weaving through the evenly spaced vehicles. "I'd love it, but I think my driving style would make my passengers uneasy."

"There is that. Guess you really should stick to your day job."

"And what is it you think my day job is?"

"I'm still figuring that out. As far as I knew, you built computer parts, hacked, and gamed. But now I know you were also cracking skulls for the Seligo. And I guess for the Ravens, too. Although I can't quite figure out how you have time to do it all."

"I used to work for the Black Helixes. I'd run tech on missions." I gripped the steering wheel so tight my knuckles turned white. She didn't know how much I'd hated that part of my job. "I gave that up six months ago. Now I mostly stay at the Ravens compound, searching for Reds and trying to get to them before the Seligo do." I glanced at her quickly. She was looking at me like I was a hero. I had too much blood on my hands to ever be considered that. "I try to keep the number of crushed skulls to a minimum these days. It's a bitch on my manicure," I said, trying to lighten the mood.

I knew it'd worked when she laughed. "I guess that's good for me. I kind of like my skull the way it is, if given an option."

I gave her my best fake smile. "Noted."

If nothing else, all the years of dirty ops gave me plenty of ideas on what to do to anyone who dreamed of touching Emma.

***

We pulled into the Los Angeles zone in record time. Cars weren't being searched. It was situation normal. The citadel outpost was on the east side of the city, and we were staying far away from that danger. The old Los Angeles airport had been partially transformed to house the hyperspeed pods way before I was born and the lines went anywhere from Asia to Europe. The only air travel left was mostly private. Pods were faster and safer. It would take us two pods and a boat to get to St. John.

We wove through the cars. The smog was low and thick, weighting the air in my lungs. I hated Los Angeles and the bad memories I had here.

Cold air hit us as we walked into the station. It was dirtier and busier than any other station in the world. With all the chaos, it'd be hard for anyone to really track us. Which was another reason we'd headed to this particular station.

I headed straight for the lockers, keeping Em close to my side. It took two seconds to find the right number. It was one of the largest lockers. I pulled out two backpacks loaded with supplies. One was pink. The other was…purple.

Thanks so much, Samantha.

I took the large pink one and gave the purple to Emma.

"You want the pink one?"

"Nope. But you get what you get and you don't get upset. Samantha has a wicked sense of humor. I bet whoever she put up to this had a fun time loading it, too. I'll get even once I find out who helped her."

She cleared her throat. "You and Samantha seem close."

I froze. *This* was the source of the 'fine' comment?

Emma was jealous. I'd never thought jealousy could make me so happy, but this meant she really was interested. "Close as in friends. Not close in any other way. Strictly platonic."

"Sure."

I stopped walking. A little jealousy was okay, but no way was she going to feel insecure if I could do anything about it. "She's more like the little sister I always knew I never wanted."

"What? Is she not attractive?"

"No. She's cute. She's also fourteen. Plus, I have a thing for strawberry blondes."

Her cheeks pinkened. "My hair's blue," she said, finally looking at me.

"For now, but maybe I'll get to see the old strawberry soon?" I touched a lock of her hair that had already been cleaned of the blue dye.

She rolled her eyes. "What's a fourteen-year-old doing working coms?"

I started walking again toward the gate. "She's a genius and a Red. Gotta keep her busy or she gets herself into the craziest situations. This one time she decided she wanted ice cream…from Italy. It took me five days to find her. When I did…well…it wasn't pretty. Took me two weeks of cover-ups and payoffs to fix that mess. Looking out for her is a full-time job."

I logged into the kiosk and grabbed two nonstop tickets to St. John. There were a few security agents walking through the station, but none in black gear. The whole place was completely automated. Not even an agent at the gates to check our passes.

Thank God the Lady's intel had been right on this one, but I'd feel much better once we were on the island.

I stowed the packs overhead and got us buckled in. "Ready?"

She shook her head. "I think I hate pod travel. It makes my brain hurt."

"Really?"

Her bottom lip was adorably fat as she pouted. "Kind of. Don't you feel weird? Like your brain is going to turn to mush and run out your ears?"

I laughed. I'd never felt that way about pod travel. "Nah. I like to get where I'm going to and fast."

"Sometimes the joy is in the journey, not the destination."

"Yeah. And sometimes the destination is where the good stuff is." I winked at her and hoped she'd agree. Once we got to where we were going, good stuff was going to happen. I was sure of it. We needed to become a team. We needed to get her abilities under control. Most of all, I wanted her to really trust me.

And I'd had one kiss. Now I wanted more.

Chapter Thirteen

CIPHER

I was wrong. Pod travel wasn't the worst. Boat rides. Those were the worst fucking thing ever.

The tiny speedboat bumped along the water. Knight held back my hair as I puked again over the edge. *So humiliating.* If I lived through this, I was pretty sure I'd never hear the end of it.

I wiped my face on my shirt. "I think I'm dying."

"You're not dying."

I rested my cheek against the railing. "You don't know that. Are we there yet?"

He ran his hand along the back of my neck, and I closed my eyes. "Nearly," he said.

It was a miracle that the boat was even a little bit seaworthy. The one motor sputtered and spewed smoke as it moved across the water. Waves knocked into us, spraying salty water everywhere. I didn't mind that part, though. It was refreshing after puking my guts out.

I leaned over the railing as I hurled again. *Total misery.*

"I think I'd rather risk having my brain come out

my ears than ever get on another boat," I said once the heaving stopped. He'd have to knock me out if we had to take one back to civilization or we weren't going back. That was just how it was going to be.

Finally, the boat slowed as we entered calmer waters. It was hot, but not totally unbearable; then again, I didn't mind warm weather. The island had a long stretch of pristine white sand, and then beyond that, dense jungle. The little wooden dock was just ahead.

The guy running the boat didn't even tie off. Instead, he ran the boat into the dock and kept the motor gently running in that direction. "I'll be back in three days to pick you up."

I shot my best not-a-chance-in-hell look to Knight. Hopefully he'd get the picture.

"Great. See you then."

I guessed my look wasn't mean enough. "Uh-uh. Helicopter. Plane. Something. Anything. No more boats."

The captain, if he could be called that for driving a piece of floating scrap metal, handed Knight the packs and our water canisters. "No other way off this island. Second time will be easier."

"Liar," I muttered and Knight laughed. "It's not funny!"

Knight put one pack on his back, and carried the other on his front. "It's a little funny."

I stomped my way down the dock to dry land as he said his thank yous and traded fist bump, handshake, and back pats with the asshole.

Now that I was back on the ground, I could relax. I still felt the rolling of the waves, but that would pass.

It had to pass. Right?

The sand was so white, it was nearly blinding in the sunlight. The untouched beach only had bits of seaweed on it. Nothing big though. It was mostly pristine. The water was so clear, even at a hundred feet deep, I could see the bottom. From the shallows, only schools of tiny little fish were visible.

I toed off my shoes and shoved my socks in them. The water was cool on my feet.

I hadn't been swimming in forever, but I hoped Samantha had stuck bathing suits in the packs. If not, I was going to go in my underwear, which was kind of like a bathing suit.

"Enjoying yourself?" Knight said.

"Yes," I said without turning around. "As a matter of fact, I am."

As I moved my feet, the little schools of fish flowed around them. After all the running and hiding, being here felt a little anticlimactic. Like we were waiting for something to happen, and that made me antsy. "What's next?" I said after a long moment.

"We camp out."

"On the beach?"

"That'd be nice, but no. On the off chance that someone moved the satellite feed to cover the island, I'd rather not be so visible. We'll go past the tree line."

I promised myself I'd come back for a dip later, and trudged out of the water. Sand coated my feet, but I didn't care. I picked up my socks and shoes from where I'd dropped them.

"This way."

"You've been here before?"

"A few times. It's one of my favorite hideouts."

It was beautiful, but a little too hard to get to for me. Which meant it would be hard to leave in a pinch. Not exactly comforting. "That's how you knew how to find that boat guy?"

"Jimmy. Yeah. When I need a break, this is where I come. There's a good, flat spot just over here. We'll pitch our tent and get our campsite set up, and then we'll start figuring out your control."

Right. Just like that. Tents. Then control. I shook my head. "And how am I supposed to figure out my control here? There's no electricity."

He set his pack down. "You think the only electricity in the world is the kind running through wires?"

Kind of. "Yeah."

He shook his head. "You're too used to having so much around you, you haven't developed a taste for subtle natural electricity. Once you get that, we'll work up to the big guns."

"Sure." The guy was out of his goddamned mind.

"You don't have to believe me. You just have to give it a try."

I held up my hands in surrender. "Hey. I'm all about trying."

"And there's only one tent."

If that meant what I thought it did, that didn't sound like a good idea. "So you're sleeping outside."

"It's a big tent."

Oh crap. "No way."

He winked at me. "Don't worry. I won't steal your virtue."

I took in the surroundings. There was no one here. Just me and him. Sharing a tent.

This was a horrible idea. Suddenly, I wasn't so worried about him stealing my virtue as I was about me handing it over totally willingly.

***

Setting up the campsite didn't take long, although I wasn't exactly helpful. After trying to put in stakes and totally failing at getting them in at precisely the right angle to meet his standards, Knight put me on watch duty. Meaning I watched him do it. Which was totally fine by me. I'd never camped before and this was his element. At some point, he took off his shirt, and that was more than I could handle. With each rippling movement, I grew more transfixed. I had to distract myself, so I started looking through the packs and organized the supplies.

I could already tell that the little packets of freeze-dried food were going to be completely disgusting. There was no way the powder they held could ever resemble—I checked the nearest packet—spaghetti and meatballs. The rest of our food stock held dried fruit, beef jerky, and nuts. To my surprise, there were two bathing suits for me. Thank you, Samantha. And enough clothes to last a week.

Taking stock of the rest of the gear, I found a first aid kit, some flares, solar-powered LED lanterns, lip balm, and—I grabbed out a small box—condoms. Extra-large size.

Condoms? Extra-large?

Was this Samantha's idea of a joke? And who knew they came in sizes?

How had she known what size to get him?

As my cheeks grew hot, I shoved the offending box to the bottom of the pack. Samantha was nuts. We weren't going to be needing those. Nope. Not gonna happen.

"What's got you so worked up?"

I totally wasn't being nonchalant about this at all. "Nothing." My voice was way too high pitched.

"What's in the pack?"

"Nothing." Damn it. I cleared my throat. "Nothing," I said in a much lower voice. "Just some food and supplies and whatnot." I held up the lantern. "This will come in handy. I have a feeling it gets way too dark out here." I was used to lights. Even on the outskirts of the Voids, the light pollution was pretty bad.

"It won't be that dark. The stars and moon will be out."

Maybe, but I'd rather have motion-activated flood lights. The moon wasn't keeping anyone from ambushing us.

I grabbed the bathing suit. "I'm going for a dip."

"Okay. I'll meet you out there in a few, and then we'll get started."

"Cool."

I moved through the forest to find a spot where I was certain he couldn't see me. No one got to see me without my clothes off. Not even doctors, which I avoided like the nastiest tech virus on earth. One glimpse of the Red Helix and it would be lights out forever.

I changed into a totally respectable black one-piece bathing suit and folded my clothes into a neat pile that I carried to the beach. The sand burned the bottoms of feet, but I didn't mind. I'd always liked the heat. The few times I'd gone north had been disastrous. Snow was a pain in the ass and a bitch to drive in. Worse, it made fast getaways impossible. I had to give the Griz time to warm up, brush off the snow, and scrape the ice…forget that.

But this—clear water, beautiful fish, white sand, heat that sank through my skin, warming my soul—this I could do. For sure. I tilted my head back, savoring the sensation of the sun on my face. I'd get more freckles, but I couldn't be bothered to put on sunblock. Nothing was worth turning back for at this point.

I ran into the warm water, and once it was deep enough, dove under. I swam out until my lungs burned and then came up for air. I treaded water as I looked below. A reef stood off to the side, packed with swarms of colorful fish. If I had a pair of goggles, I'd swim under and get a closer look.

"Hey, mermaid."

I spun around, a retort on the tip of my tongue, but all thoughts faded as I saw him.

That picture did him no justice. In person, shirtless, shoeless, Knight made my brain melt. He stood at the edge of the water, and I realized then and there that I was so out of my league it wasn't even funny.

"Thought you might want these." He tossed something at me.

I closed my eyes as the object hit the water in front of me, splashing my face. The face mask started sinking to the bottom. "Shit!" I dove and grabbed it. "Awesome! Thanks. Where'd you get it?"

"Jimmy. He keeps some gear for me. He added a second pair of goggles and fins when he saw you," Knight said as he swam toward me. "Rub a little bit of spit in the goggles and they won't fog."

"Gross." Although I did it anyway, assuming he knew this nature stuff way better than I did. As soon as the mask was secure, I dove. Knight was swimming to me, but he'd catch up. I couldn't wait to get deeper. My ears popped with the pressure.

This place was paradise. The water in California was so cold that you couldn't really linger in it. And there wasn't snorkeling. Not like this.

When I came up for air, I couldn't help a little squeal of glee. I moved the mask off my eyes, resting it on the top of my head. "There are so many fish! There was this big blue one with this really beautiful fin tipped with bright yellow—"

He treaded water next to me. "Angel."

"What?" Was he calling me an angel? I started swimming toward shore.

"An angel fish."

I was such a moron sometimes. "That's a fitting name."

"The perfect fish for an angel like you to love."

I couldn't help a smile despite the cheesiness of the line. "That was so dumb, but thanks." I took a breath. "And thanks for bringing me here. It's really amazing. On a lot of levels." Here, I could forget—the running, the danger, everything. He'd given me this, in the middle of everything. He'd given me the freedom I'd needed so desperately.

His hand found mine as we hit shallow water. The fear of what I could have and lose hit me hard. "This is a bad idea," I said. "Starting this—" I waved back and forth between us. "It's a bad idea. It'll only end in heartache. Or death. Or both."

"Not everything ends in heartache and death."

I swallowed. "For me it does."

"Not this."

"You don't know that. You can't promise that."

"No. I guess I can't. But there's no gain in life without a little risk. Don't you think you've played it safe for long enough? You say you trust me." Knight pulled me to him, and wrapped my arms around his neck. "So trust me."

I was frozen. My breath came out in short gasps.

"A real kiss. Without anyone watching."

Oh, God. Did he have to say that? Now I was sure I was going to screw this up. Drool all over him or something equally embarrassing.

His fingers tangled in my hair as he pulled me closer.

I closed my eyes and his lips brushed mine. They were soft and warm and tasted a little salty, thanks to the seawater. One touch of his tongue to mine and I opened my lips.

His kiss consumed me. Burned me up. I gave up trying to keep some space between us. I wrapped my arms tighter. Somehow, my legs wrapped around his hips. I felt the brush of him against me. I rubbed along him with a moan, and I knew I was two seconds away from losing it.

I started to pull back from the kiss, but Knight held me to him. Desire swept through me and I had to stop before we did anything more. I pushed away.

"This is a bad idea." I started toward deeper water,

but Knight swam after me. It felt a little like getting chased, but our gazes stayed locked. For the first time in my life, part of me wanted to be caught.

Knight easily closed the distance between us, pulling me in, and his lips briefly touched mine. "Don't be scared. I'm not pushing this. Just enjoy the afternoon. You haven't had a break in a while."

"I take breaks."

"You do?"

"I game with you all the time."

"That's not the same as what we're doing now."

I swallowed. No. It definitely wasn't the same.

***

I'd hoped Knight would forget about the whole gaining-control-of-my-abilities thing, but no such luck. As soon as my fingers started to get pruny, he pulled me from the water. He'd set out two towels on the beach.

"First things first," he tossed me a bottle of sunblock.

I rolled my eyes. "I'm fine."

"You're not fine. You're already getting pink."

I pressed my fingertip to my shoulder. The mark stayed white for two beats before turning pink.

He was right. I was burning. I slathered myself with the lotion, and then let Knight do my back. I tried to ignore the heat that was flaring wherever he touched me, but I couldn't deny it anymore.

My virtue was totally not safe.

"You said before that you tried meditation and yoga?"

I snorted. If this was his approach, we were going to get nowhere. "Sucked."

"What were you thinking of when you meditated?"

"Nothing. That's the point."

"Eh. You can think of stuff. Yoga nidra is all about picturing things as you meditate."

"Yeah, well the yogi I was practicing with said I had to quiet my mind before we moved on to that. Turns out I don't get a lot of quiet in my head." It'd been a major fail. Every time I thought I was getting somewhere, I'd lost control. Epic disaster.

"I have this theory—"

I nudged him with my shoulder. "Sounds dangerous."

"Shut up."

"Shutting up, sir."

"Smartass." He might've sounded serious, but his sea glass green eyes glittered. He was having way too much fun. "I don't think you're very connected to your ability. You've spent so much time trying to get rid of it or shove it away that you've never really embraced it."

The guy had a point. "Go on."

"After I was modified to fit you, I instinctively did the same thing. Lady Eva spent weeks shocking me with electricity. For a while there, she thought the mod didn't work because every time she tested me with strong voltage, I got knocked out. Little stuff was okay. But jolt me with anything substantial and I spent the next day in medical."

"Sounds painful."

"No kidding. But I was bracing against the

electricity. Trying to block it. Stop it. But I couldn't. I had to open myself. Be a conduit. A channel. Absorb it."

"I get what you're saying, but it doesn't work that way for me. It's like I am the electricity and I'm burning everything I touch."

"But fighting it, instead of blocking it, does the opposite. It draws more and more to you until you explode. Right?"

I clicked my lip ring against my teeth as I considered. He was kind of right. The more I tried to stop it, the more power I gathered, and the bigger the eventual explosion. Of course I wanted to stop accumulating it. "I guess. But how is opening myself up to more electricity going to stop me from gathering more? That's totally counterintuitive."

"I think you have to think of yourself as more of a conduit. You're gathering the energy, and you can either hold on to it until you explode, or let it go as it comes. The problem starts when you're blocking it and gather too much. Let it flow through you."

"Right." Because that was what always happened. It flowed through me, and destroyed everything in its wake.

"Let's try something. Do you feel any electricity right now?"

I closed my eyes and tried to feel the waves of electricity, but of course, there was nothing. This island wasn't wired. He was right about it. Total dead zone. "No."

"Yes, you do. I feel it. It moves through me, just in a different way. I dampen it, whereas you amplify it."

I ran my fingers through my tangled and crunchy-with-salt hair. I was sure I looked ridiculous, and I was going to make an ass out of myself trying to 'control' my 'ability,' but I had to give this an honest try.

I closed my eyes again and stayed really quiet. I couldn't expect to feel anything like I did when I was in the city. The power here would be more subtle. As soon as I opened my mind to the possibilities of smaller things, I felt tiny tingles along my skin—the telltale sign that electricity was present.

"Okay. I feel some. From the sun. From the living things around me. In the air. But it's tiny. Barely a whisper along my skin." *See.* I could use my own metaphors.

"Then try gathering it, and passing it to me once you've built up a charge."

I'd never tried gathering it. Not ever. That was way too dangerous.

But I had to start somewhere, and at least here there was no one to hurt. I closed my eyes, feeling the barely there breeze against my skin. The heat of the sun burned against my back. For the longest time, my powers had felt like a drain. It took so much work to keep them down. So much mental energy. Physical strength. Being so far away from the world—with no access to an electrical grid—was a relief. No wonder I'd lost myself underwater. Playing.

I couldn't remember ever playing before. I never relaxed. I could never breathe easy. That pressure to hide what was struggling to break free was always around.

Just sitting in the sunlight, I was rejuvenated.

I let myself relax, and in doing so, drew power to

me. It was there. All around me. I really didn't need wires.

The power grew inside me. When I opened my eyes, my arms had a blue-white glow around them. Brighter than the sunlight.

"Good. Now, try holding on to it for ten seconds. Don't collect any more. Just hold steady."

The more I concentrated on it, the more it filled me up. It was like it was drawn to me. I wasn't sucking the energy in; it just found me.

I shook my head. "I can't. Once I start pulling, it doesn't stop."

"Hold on to what you've got, and let the rest fly past."

"I can't…" If there were lights around, they would've been flickering like mad already. I was full. Ready to blow.

Sharp zaps stung along my legs as the sand formed clumps of glass.

Knight reached for my hand, and this time, instead of feeling like he numbed me, I could feel the electricity going from me into him. He released it back into the area without any big bangs, lightning, or explosions. It just left him.

When he touched me, I was safe. I didn't have to worry about control.

The first time he'd done it, it was disarming. Uncomfortable. That empty feeling was even unnerving. Now I'd grown to appreciate it. Savor the feeling of not needing to have control of everything all the time.

The temptation to let Knight share my burden forever was huge.

But that wouldn't be fair, no matter how badly he might think he wanted it. No one would pick this life. Hiding. Losing control. A second away from total destruction.

I needed to get myself under control. If for no other reason, just so that Knight could finally live his life for himself.

Chapter Fourteen

KNIGHT

As we sat on the beach, I could read every little thought that ran through Emma's head. The girl was ridiculous. She didn't know how to relax. Didn't have a clue how to let go and have fun. Seeing her in the water, chasing fish was truly a sight.

Even when we were kids, she'd always had this weight hanging over her. She was the oldest eight-year-old I'd ever met. As I hit my teens, it had only grown more apparent how strange she acted. How mature she was. But carrying a secret that big meant she had to grow up fast.

She had giggled—*giggled*—as she surfaced from the water. I'd kill to hear her laugh like that every day.

She stared at me in awe—like I'd just saved her at my expense.

It made me want to shake her. She'd saved me at her own expense. That was what you did for the people you l—

Damn it. Dex was going to give me so much shit next time he saw me.

Did she feel the same? Could she possibly trust me

that much? Probably not yet, but I had hopes. I hadn't gotten where I was by thinking negatively.

"It's going to be fine. This was your first try. What do you think you did wrong?"

"I have no idea. I've never done this before. What do you think I did wrong?"

I laughed. "I don't have a clue. This is your ability, not mine."

"Jerk."

"Seriously, though, I think you're fine with gathering. It's the release you need to work on."

Her stare told me she thought I was being dumb. "Clearly. I didn't wipe out the power in the Arizona Void because I had trouble gathering electricity."

"Smartass. I think once we really get down how this works, you'll be able to zap the smallest com without disturbing anything around it."

Her mouth dropped open. "You're out of your mind. I'm lucky if I manage not take out a city block."

My gaze was drawn to her soft, peach-colored lips. That piece of metal. It was like she was both hard and soft. Inside and out. I liked the contrast. I hadn't expected that. But then again, I hadn't expected her.

"Oh, no. Nope. That's not cool," she said.

My gaze rose to her eyes. The green was being taken over by a thick ring of brown around her iris. I'd never seen her eyes this particular color, and I wondered what it meant. What was she thinking?

She kicked out with her foot. "Stop looking at me like that."

"Like what?"

"Like you're starving and I'm a nice piece of apple pie."

"I happen to like apple pie."

"Who doesn't? That doesn't mean I'm *your* apple pie."

I grinned. This was too much fun. "What if I want you to be my apple pie?"

"It doesn't matter what you want. I'm not," Emma said.

"What if you want to be my apple pie?"

"Enough with the fucking apple pie." She stood and grabbed her facemask, snorkel, and fins. "I'm going for a swim. When I come back, have that"—she waved her hand in my direction—"under control."

Under control? Yeah. That wasn't going to happen.

She was running, which was understandable. Emma was the kind of girl who deserved to be chased. "You have fun. I'll be here, getting some sun."

"Put some sunscreen on, you douchebag."

Behind the name-calling—which I was starting to think of as Cipher-style terms of endearment—her soft voice betrayed actual concern for me. I couldn't suppress a smile. "Don't worry so much. I don't burn. I brown." Thanks to my heritage, I'd just get darker and darker the longer I was out. I hadn't been in the sun in a while and my skin was already mocha-colored.

Emma walked into the water like a beautiful, blue-haired siren. She tested me at every turn, but God if I didn't love it. Everything I'd given up for her was worth it, and I'd do it all again in a heartbeat.

I checked my com for any updates. They were still searching for us, but hadn't hit our trail yet. Some choppers had left the coast of Georgia an hour ago, but that was it. We were still good to keep hiding here for a while.

I relaxed on the beach and let the sound of waves crashing on the shore lull me into a nap.

***

That night I built a small fire. The wood was slightly damp and smoked more than I'd like, but it wasn't horrible. Emma was gagging down her dinner.

"Just don't look at it," I said.

She paused with the spoon halfway to her mouth. "How am I not supposed to look at it? I'm eating it."

"Like this." I demonstrated, dipping my spoon into the package and swallowing the bite without breaking eye contact with her.

"You got food on your shirt." Her grin was a little menacing.

I shrugged. "It'll wash."

"It looks like baby diarrhea."

I groaned. "I'm trying to eat here." The little freeze-dried bits tasted like chicken teriyaki, but had the texture of lumpy paste. Emma had already compared it to cat vomit and stewed shit. She was right on all counts, but it had the nutrition we needed.

"Making fun of it is helping me choke it down."

She'd lost her mind. "Comparing your food to baby diarrhea is helping you eat it?"

Emma primly held up her spoon and took a delicate bite. Then made a face as she choked. "It's the texture. I can't handle it."

I laughed at the way her mouth puckered and her nose scrunched as she forced down another bite. She swallowed and then downed half a water bottle. "Ugh. That was so gross. You know, this is the worst date ever."

"This is a date?"

"I hope not. Because really, you suck at showing a girl a good time."

"What about the snorkeling? That has to make up for the food packets."

"No way. Nothing can ever make up for those." She scrunched up her face and then sighed. "It's important to have a sense of humor about these kinds of things. Plus, I've gone hungry before. So, this is really not that bad. But I'm having a really good time grossing you out. So if this *was* a date—which it's not—then maybe it wouldn't totally suck."

I dropped my spoon in the foil packet, and ignored the date comment. If I reacted to it, she'd shy away again. It was a good sign that she was the one who'd brought up the date comparison. "You're good, but you're not *that* good. I'm pretty hard to gross out. You can't say anything that any of the guys hasn't said a million times before." I shook my head. "Trying to gross me out… I don't know why I'm helping you at all."

"Me neither," she muttered so quietly, that even with my modified hearing, I barely heard her.

Those two words were like a stab in the chest. "I didn't mean that. Not even a little bit."

Even in the dim firelight I could see her cheeks redden. "Well, you should. I'm not exactly a safe bet." She stared into the flames to avoid my gaze.

Her words made my heart ache. "I don't want a safe bet. I know what I want, and that's you."

Her gaze met mine for a moment before darting away. "You'll regret it."

No. I wouldn't. Not in a million years. "Why don't you let me worry about that?"

"I can't help but worry about it," she said quietly. That gave me hope.

She worried about me. Since I'd gotten paired with her, there was always a chance that this could be very one-sided, but I was glad it wasn't. Unbelievably glad.

"Not to sound like a broken record, but it's going to be okay."

"You're still saying it like it's a fact. It's not."

"I'm going to make it a fact. And I'm going to keep repeating it until you believe it." I got up. There was no way I was eating another bite of the baby diarrhea. I was off the chicken teriyaki packets for life.

Lord help me if she does the same thing with the curry packet tomorrow.

After disposing of our trash and smothering the fire, I rinsed my hands in the surf. "Let's go to bed. Once the sun rises, it'll be too hot to stay in the tent. We should get some rest."

She stood and rubbed her hands down her legs, brushing off sand. "Fine. But there'll be no funny business."

"Not even a little bit of funny business?" I couldn't help but tease her.

"No!" She sounded scandalized, and I loved it.

I grinned. "How about only moderately amusing business?"

"Shut up."

"How about silly business? Surely we've got time

for that."

"You're a moron," she said, but she was grinning.

"True. But at least I've got my good looks to fall back on," I said.

She laughed, and I nearly patted myself on the back.

Nicely done, Knight. Nicely done.

I climbed inside the tent and she followed. I'd almost zipped the two sleeping bags together to make one big bag, but that would've been presumptuous. I wasn't about to make her more uncomfortable. I clicked on the lantern for her; it might keep me awake, but I doubted I'd be able to sleep alone in the dark with Emma. It was more important that she felt comfortable and relaxed.

I checked the com one more time, and saw we were clear. This was going just as planned. Now, all I needed to do was get Emma to fall for me.

After we settled in, Emma was quiet for a long time. I hoped she was coping. The whole point of being here was to get her to trust me so I could help with her abilities. We were making progress on the former, but the latter...we needed more time and unfortunately, our hours here were numbered.

I laid thinking for so long in the quiet that I was sure she'd already fallen asleep.

"Knight?" She said, surprising me.

"Yes?"

"Thank you. For helping me."

She still didn't get it. "I don't need your thanks." That wasn't why I'd done anything.

"Okay. Well... Just... Thank you anyway. It's been a long time since I've had someone around who cared this much."

That couldn't be true. "What about Mona? It seems like she cares a lot about you."

"Yeah, but she didn't know what I was. You did—do—and you're still helping. No one's done that except my parents. And even then, it was stressful. They were so scared. All the time. It was hard, you know. Being the cause of all of their stress and fear and knowing that there wasn't a damned thing I could do to change it." She was quiet for a second. "Just thanks."

I grabbed her sleeping bag and slid it closer to mine. With the bags to keep us separated, I couldn't get as close to her as I wanted, but I spooned her and kissed the top of her head. "You're welcome." I kissed her again, and she pulled her hand out from inside the sleeping bag to hold mine. I rubbed my thumb along the back of her hand. "Go to sleep, princess. Tomorrow is a new day, full of possibilities."

"Goodnight, Hunter."

That was the first time she'd called me by my real name, and I loved the sound of it. "Goodnight, Emma."

I listened to her breathe for hours, thinking about the huge responsibility she was. Not that I didn't want it. I'd never want anyone to take my place. The idea of that made me seethe. I was glad she was starting to accept my protection, even though she was more than capable of protecting herself. Hell, she'd saved me when I couldn't save myself. I fully knew what she was capable of.

But as much as I wanted to shield her from all the bad things, Jack was headed our way. Both of us would need to use everything we had to stay safe.

I had to help prepare her for that day, so we'd be that much more likely to kick ass.

"Hunter," Emma mumbled in her sleep as she rolled over, and rubbed her nose into my sternum.

"I'm here, princess," I whispered, and pressed a kiss to her forehead. "For as long as you'll have me."

She sighed, and I relaxed, finally allowing sleep to overcome me.

***

I woke to an empty tent. I unzipped the sleeping back and rushed outside, fighting the urge to call out to her. If something had happened, I would've heard.

Biting back *what ifs*, I dashed toward the beach.

Emma lay a few feet from the water in a new bathing suit—still black, but two pieces instead of one. Her flat stomach was bare, and the tiny gold ring in her navel glinted in the sunlight. The low-cut top finally gave me a clear view of the stars that covered half her chest and collarbone. I took a moment to catch my breath as the last of my fear faded.

Well, that was one way to wake up.

I started toward her, and she called out. "I couldn't take anymore diarrhea or vomit." She held up the dried fruit. "Want some?"

"Well, when you make the packets sound so appealing, it's hard to turn them down."

She laughed, and sat up, finally looking at me directly.

In my rush to get dressed, I hadn't changed. I fought the urge to adjust my white boxer briefs under her watch, but it was worth it to see the blush. Pink covered the top half of her body. It was glorious.

I plopped down beside her as she stared, and grabbed a piece of fruit from the bag she held. I took a bite. "Thanks." She stayed frozen for a moment longer before visibly swallowing.

"It's fine," she said in a high-pitched voice. I'd grown to love that tone. She only used it when she was uncomfortable. Sometimes it was worrisome. But not right now.

I grinned. Definitely not right now.

She broke away from my gaze to stare up at the sky like it held all the answers she was searching for. "I was practicing."

"And how did that go?"

"Shitily." She pulled on her lip ring with her delicate fingers. I wanted to bite them, but focused on her words instead.

"Why? What went wrong?"

"Nothing, I guess. I just have a hard time feeling the electricity around me. I did everything the same as yesterday, but nothing happened. Not even a spark."

"What about now?"

"It's everywhere. I can feel it." She shot me a look. "But if I need you around to control this, that doesn't count as having control. I need to be able to be on my own. You can't be around forever."

I wanted to argue that, but it was pointless. She wasn't ready to really hear me. "Maybe I make things easier, but we'll work on it. I'm going to grab some clothes. I'll be back." I stood up and brushed the sand off myself. "Don't worry. We've got a couple more days to figure this out."

"Right. Because that's all it'll take." She snorted and plopped back down on her back.

I kicked sand on her legs. "Good attitude."

She threw a handful back at me. "Asshole."

"What did you call me?" I fake gasped.

She laughed. "With your genetically enhanced hearing, we both know you heard it."

I shook my head at her, trying to look fierce when all I wanted to do was laugh with her. "I sure fuckin' did." I picked her up and threw her over my shoulder, hanging on to her legs, and headed straight for the water.

"No!" She pounded on my back. "Don't you dare throw me in the fucking water!"

"Whoa. Way to talk like a lady." I couldn't resist the urge to slap her on the ass.

She let out a string of curses that made me blush. "I never said I was a lady."

"That's right. You're a princess."

Emma laughed. "Well princesses can say whatever the hell they want."

The water splashed against my legs as I entered the water. "Take a breath."

I threw her into the deep. She screamed, and the water electrified as she hit the surface.

She came up sputtering, pushing the hair from her face. "I stand by my statement. You're a real asshole." She was mostly teasing until she noticed the limp shapes breaking the surface of the water. Her face fell. "And you made me a fish killer."

I nearly laughed at the whine in her voice. There weren't that many fish—maybe twenty—floating around her, but she was probably pissed at herself for losing control again.

I waded out to her, hoping to lighten the mood. "Want me to collect them and do a proper burial?"

"I didn't mean to kill anything." She swam away from the floating fish. "I'm a horrible person."

Suddenly I felt like a total jerk. "Just because you lost control doesn't make you a horrible person."

Her gaze met mine. "Killing people makes me a horrible person."

"So what does that make me?" I'd lost count how many lives I'd taken, knowing it was wrong. All to build my cover. All to help the Ravens, but that didn't ease my conscience.

Her forehead crinkled as she drew her eyebrows down. "It's different."

I gave her a sad smile. "No, it really isn't."

"It is. I never mean to, but everywhere I go, people get hurt." Pain and regret filled her face, and she quickly looked away, hiding from me.

This had gone south fast. "How many?"

"Six."

I hated that. Six times she'd had to defend herself. Six times I should've been there for her. "My dad and…"

"A Seligo, two Black Helixes—different times—this junkie that tried to jump me, and a douchebag that got too handsy."

The first three hardly counted, although I wished I could've protected her. But the last two…

My fists bunched hard. If I'd been there, I would've done so much worse. "You did what you had to do to survive. No one will hold that against you."

Emma laughed, but it wasn't the kind that I loved to hear. The sound was too bitter. Too filled with regret. "I doubt the junkie had anyone who cared whether he lived, but I'm pretty sure the helixes had families. They were just doing their jobs, and I killed them." She finally met my eyes. "There are two things about me that you should never ever forget. I'm not a good person and I'm dangerous."

Anyone with powers as strong as her was dangerous, but nothing she could say would make me think she was bad. "You're the best kind of person. You stood in front of me and protected me at your own expense. You'd do the same for anyone you called a friend." I let that sink in for a moment. "And you're not dangerous to me, Emma. You don't have to worry about hurting me." At least not physically.

"I wiped out five transformers last time, but I've done worse than that. That's a lot of power."

"And I can take it. Believe me. I've been tested. It doesn't do much to me, except make it hard to sleep." I closed the distance between us. "I'll balance you until you can find it on your own. Then, we'll go from there, okay?"

"Fine."

That word again. She wasn't fine, but I'd brought up some bad memories. I'd get her back to that happy place. I hoped. "So, fishy funeral, or let the ocean take care of it?"

She shoved me away. "I'm not eight anymore. Ocean is fine."

"Fair enough." I started to walk toward the shore.

"But, Knight?"

"Yes, Emma?"

229

"Thanks for offering to have the funeral. That was sweet."

"Anytime." I grinned. "Now turn around unless you want to see the show." My briefs were going to be completely see-through when I got out.

"Oh, yuck!" Emma laughed—exactly the sound I wanted to hear.

When I hit the sand, I looked over my shoulder. She was taking in the view.

She whistled. "Nice ass!"

I rolled my hips and walked a little slower.

Chapter Fifteen

CIPHER

Sand exploded around me, hitting my legs and flying outward in a cloud.

This wasn't working. I knew that we didn't have much longer here. Knight was trying to be discreet when he checked his com, but last night some choppers got pretty damned close to the island. He was nervous, and I knew I had to get this down. Both our lives were counting on it.

"Better."

My mouth dropped open. "Are you nuts? That wasn't any better." We'd been at it all afternoon and my patience was totally shot. We'd figured out that when Knight was close to me I could draw ambient power, but when he was more than ten feet away, no dice. I couldn't generate the tiniest spark.

"You only disturbed the sand in a two-foot radius. That's *much* better."

I shook my hair out as I surveyed the area. He was right. When we'd started, the trees were getting singed. We kept moving down the beach as I tried again and again to take control. But I wasn't getting better fast enough. I needed to have a total handle on this. Like yesterday.

"What did you do differently?"

"I don't know!" I yelled, and instantly felt like shit. It wasn't his fault I sucked at my own ability. "Sorry." I was getting crankier by the second. "I'm just tired."

"Or maybe you're gaining control."

I rolled my eyes. "You're too positive. It's annoying."

He grinned and knocked his shoulder against mine. "Eh. It's growing on you."

"Like mold." I quickly braided my hair as I scanned the area. The beach glittered with tiny bits of glass. If I didn't get it together, I was going to ruin the beach for anyone who came after us. "I don't think we're getting anywhere."

"Have some faith. It takes most Reds months to work their powers out. You're trying to do it in a matter of hours. Give it time."

Right. Time. Because we had so much of that.

I'd lived with a certain amount of pressure my whole life. It was part of being a Red. Part of hiding.

Spending time with Knight, that overwhelming burden had lessened for the first time. The thought of going back to life on the run—basically back where I'd started, with no progress on my power…

Can I go back to that now?

I fought a wave of chills. Now that I'd tasted true freedom, I wanted more. So much more.

Being greedy wouldn't get me anywhere. Rushing meant mistakes. Ones I couldn't afford.

"Let's take a break," Knight said.

There wasn't time for a break. Not if I was going

to learn how to control myself in the next twenty-four hours, and I was determined to leave the island with something to show for it. "Let's not. I have to keep pushing."

I closed my eyes once more. Knight sighed, but I ignored it.

The familiar tingle rushed along my skin, tickling me. It came slowly at first, just a whisper, until it grew—making the little hairs on my arms stand on end.

I opened my eyes. The glow along my skin was barely visible in the bright daylight, but it was there. Energy coursed through me and dots danced in my vision.

"Focus. Send it straight to me."

This was where it always went wrong. The energy usually exploded around me in all directions, but I was trying to send it to Knight. It sounded simple to direct the power toward him. Easy even. But we'd been at it for hours and I hadn't gotten any better at hitting the target.

I let out a slow breath and concentrated on Knight. He stood a few feet away, holding his palms out to me, stance wide, waiting to take the hit.

A hit that I didn't want to give.

Maybe that was the problem. "What if you get burned? Or your heart stops? I don't know CPR."

He crossed his arms. "I promise you're not going to hurt me. I can take it."

"I could kill you with this much energy." I'd built so much up that even my teeth were tingling. I didn't know how much it was exactly, but it was more than it took to kill a person.

"No, you can't. I've grounded you before. Why're you hesitating?"

Because I hadn't cared this much about him before. Now I did.

What a jerk.

I knocked my lip ring with my teeth. "This is a supremely bad idea."

"Stop being such a baby and do it. Hit me with it. Do it. Now. Don't be such a chicken—"

I flung my hands in his direction and released the energy—lightning sizzled down my arms, arcing straight for his chest.

Knight grunted as he took the hit, stumbling back a few steps.

Holy crap. *I didn't mean to do that.* It was too much. I knew it was too much. At least he wasn't on the ground.

He bent over with his hands on his thighs for a second, panting, before looking at me with a grin. "Now that's what I call a hit."

My jaw must've been on the ground. "You're okay?"

"Yes, I'm okay."

I closed the distance between us and patted him down, feeling for any injury. I barely even noticed his bare abs as my hands ran over them. "Really? Are you sure? You're not feeling faint? Funny?"

"Oh, I'm feeling really funny."

Something about his tone had me stopping my motions. "You are?"

"Yeah." He drew out the word. "Super funny."

He leaned down like he was going to kiss me and my breath caught. I wanted it. Wanted to feel his lips against mine.

He picked me up and I ran my fingers through his hair. I started to lower my head to his when he took off for the water.

"Not this again! Knight! Seriously?"

His laugh rumbled through me, and I couldn't help it if I held on tighter and never wanted to let go.

***

Knight and I sat on the quiet beach while the sun set. I'd tried a few more times to replicate what I'd done before, but couldn't get it to work. We decided to stop for the day since I was only getting more and more frustrated.

I twisted the fake wedding band around my finger as I thought. It'd become a comfort to me. Which was a dangerous thing. "Do you ever wonder what our lives would've been like if that day hadn't happened? Like, would we still be friends?" Sensing his gaze, I stared straight ahead, watching the sun disappear behind the horizon.

"Of course we'd still be friends. We're friends now, aren't we?"

I blew out a breath. "I guess."

"You guess?" The tease in his question was thick.

I gave him a half-smile. "Okay. We're friends."

He snorted. "You don't have to keep that wall up, Em. It's just you and me here. We know all of each other's secrets."

Not even close. I hadn't been willing to tell him when I thought he was just Knight, but even now there were things he didn't need to know. As soon as he'd freaked about why I was short, I'd known I had to protect him from the rest of my past. Besides, he hadn't told me much about what he'd gone through at the Trials or helix school.

Hunter or Knight—I knew who he was inside, and he knew me. "Just in case I don't get a chance to tell you, thanks."

"For?"

"For being you."

He laughed. "Okay."

I was hedging and he knew it, but opening up even that much was a struggle. Losing everyone I'd ever cared about had done a number on me. "For not forgetting about me. For getting your DNA altered for me. That was kind of a crazy move."

"Necessary."

"What?"

"Necessary move. Not crazy. I needed help, so you helped me. Now you need help, so I'm helping you. No agenda. That's what friends do." He paused. "I asked Lady Eva to pair me with you. Most Reds need a balancing person for their ability. As soon as I found out, I wanted to be there for you like you were there for me. I probably should've waited and asked you first, but…"

I didn't know what to say to that. He'd changed everything for me. Given up so much. He kept saying that he owed me, but I was finally understanding how much I owed him.

I cleared my throat. "So, how long do we get to stay here exactly?"

"Until we get the call that we can go back."

"How close are Jack's choppers?"

"Last night they were pretty close, but today they're gone. We'll probably head out tomorrow afternoon. Next day at the latest." He bumped his shoulder against mine. "Sick of me already?"

"What? No!"

"I was joking."

"Right." The guy made me stupid. My cheeks burned. "Really I was thinking about the packets. I'm hungry and I don't know how much more of that crap I can eat. I'd kill for a bean and cheese burrito right about now."

"We'll get you some good food as soon as we get back to civilization. Promise." He stood and held a hand down to me. As soon as I put my hand in his, everything quieted. Even if the noise was faint on the island, I always felt it buzzing.

When Knight touched me, it was like being covered in a warm blanket.

Peaceful.

At first, I'd found it disorienting, but now I was afraid I was getting addicted. It was like Knight could erase my helix with one touch. If I weren't careful, he'd end up a crutch instead of a crush.

"How about an omelet?"

"No! Breakfast is my favorite meal. One packet and it'll be ruined forever."

"Okay. I have mac and cheese. Beef stroganoff. Or more chicken teriyaki."

"I'll take the chicken. I'm already ruined for life on that one."

"You got it."

As we ate, I thought about all the times we'd hung out online. "Did you ever think you knew me from somewhere else when we gamed?"

"I really thought you were a guy." He stabbed his spoon in the bag a few times. "It's a little creepy when you think about it. I'm attracted to someone I used to think was a guy."

That was too funny. "So my cover is full-on mindfucking you?"

He jabbed at me with the spoon. "It's not funny. If we weren't childhood friends, I'd be seriously annoyed."

I barely swallowed down another bite of the chicken mush. "All right. I think I'm done. I'm not full but not hungry anymore. I can't stand this stuff."

Knight reached for my packet. "It's not that bad." He took a bite and made a face. "Okay. Maybe it is that bad."

"Yeah. Don't give me any of that nonsense. Anyone with taste buds would know it was disgusting."

"Meet you in the tent? I'll clean up."

As I got ready for bed, nerves twisted in my stomach.

It felt like we were leading up to being more than friends, and I was already getting too attached. If I slept with Knight, like really slept with him, then I'd never let him go.

I wasn't that strong.

When he unzipped the tent flap, I pretended to be asleep. Avoidance seemed the best way to go about things.

I stayed still on my side, facing away from him. I kept my breathing as steady and even as possible, but I wasn't prepared for him to plaster himself to my back. His arm slid across my stomach.

"Good night, Em." He brushed a kiss to the top of my head. "I…"

My heart picked up its pace until it thundered in my ears.

He wasn't going to say what he thought.

"I'll see you in the morning."

I let out a breath, and was surprised to realize that it hurt that he didn't say the words I wanted.

But how could I ask for those words when I couldn't say them in return?

Chapter Sixteen

KNIGHT

Choppers.

The rhythmic sound of blades cutting air jolted me awake.

They'd found us. The only way off this island would be stealing one of their rides.

This one fuck up was going to cost me everything.

"Cipher."

Her eyes fluttered open and she shot up as soon as she heard the noise. "Let's go." She jammed on her shoes and started to grab the pack.

"Leave it." I pulled out weapons, jamming one gun in back of my waistband, and leaving another to carry. The spare ammo went in my pockets. Anything more and it would slow us down. We couldn't afford that, and we were way beyond needing to hide the camp.

They already knew we were here.

I unzipped the tent and stepped toward the beach. Still dark. Five beams of lights meant five choppers overhead. They'd be on the ground in minutes.

We only had two options, and I hated one of

them. Really fucking hated.

Emma stood beside me. "What now? We're stuck here. Sitting ducks."

"I know." I made sure one bullet was in the chamber of my gun before turning back towards the trees. "There's a cave not far from here." I grabbed two water bottles with filters and some jerky from the tent. It wouldn't last us long, but it was the best I could do.

Emma could hide in relative safety while I separated the strike force, taking them out one by one.

Still a crapshoot. We were too outnumbered.

But the second option…

Not yet. I wouldn't even consider it.

"The cave is our best shot. It's deep and the rock should block their tech from sensing us." I pulled Emma behind me, moving deeper into the trees. Emma's footsteps trampled the ground.

The only thing going for us was that it was night. The jungle drowned out most of the light. Emma tripped and I caught her.

"I can't move this fast. I can't see anything," she said.

I squatted down. "Hop on."

"What? No. You can't carry me."

"Yes, I can. You weigh a lot less than my pack. We don't have time to argue. Hop on." She jumped and I caught her legs around my waist. "Just hold on so I can keep my hands free."

"Okay." Her legs squeezed and I pushed away the unavoidable flash of desire. Now wasn't the time, even if my body had a different opinion.

I could already hear the teams moving through the woods behind us. I knew the route, but with each passing second, we lost ground. They were going to catch us.

I was going to fail. I had Emma here, and I was going to fail.

Sweat rolled down my face, and I pushed myself harder.

Gunfire hit the tree next to me.

"Down," I said, and Emma dropped off my back. I took cover and spotted three guys coming our way. All dressed in black.

Three shots and they were down. The sound echoed among the trees, silencing the night for a moment before more shouts rang out.

They knew where we were now. We were out of time. Complete and total fear gripped me. Adrenaline raced through my body and I knew we needed to run. Fast.

"Move," I said and Emma didn't hesitate.

We raced through the trees like the hounds of hell were after us.

Another shot rang out as we jumped over a fallen tree. Shattered bark bit against my cheek.

That was too fucking close.

I kept moving but Emma stopped. She stood next to the fallen tree, eyes wide in fear, cheeks flushed from running.

What the hell is she doing?

I raced back to her, pulling her down into a crouch, hidden in the brush. "Are you hit?" *Please don't say yes. Please don't say yes.*

She panted and shook. I tried to run my hands

over her, but she swatted me away. "You have to hide."

My blood chilled. "We. We have to hide." She'd figured out the other option, and I couldn't let her agree to it.

She shook her head. "We're not getting out of this alive. I'll surrender and go with them. But you have to come get me. You have to find me again."

No. This was a bad idea. A really seriously bad idea. I couldn't let the Seligo have Emma. Not for a day, not for a minute. They'd only let her live long enough to torture her as they probed her genetics. "No. We go together or not at all."

Her gaze met mine, both determined and bright with fear. "It's not your choice. It's mine. They're taking me either way, but if I go and you stay, then there's a chance that we both survive."

I searched for something—anything—that would change her mind. "Mona would disagree. Splitting up is a terrible idea."

Emma gripped my hand. "It's the only option. You'll be safe. If I go, you'll be safe."

"No—"

"Find me."

Terror gripped my gut, and I froze. She couldn't do this. I wouldn't let her. "No. Emma—"

She dropped my hand and lunged, heading for the beach.

My training said to stay. She was right—we needed to make this sacrifice.

Fuck that.

"No. Emma!" I raced after her until I caught her hand.

"Don't make this any harder," she whispered harshly. Then Emma closed the distance between us, pressing her lips to mine.

I sank into the feel of her. It wasn't enough. This wasn't enough time. I wanted more. Life couldn't be this unfair—to give me a couple perfect days and then rip Emma away from me.

"I refuse to watch you die," she said as she pulled away. "I'm trusting you with my life. You find me. Save me."

Shouts rang out nearby. It was either let her go or both of us died here.

My stomach dropped to my feet, and I couldn't breathe. "You stay alive. You do what you have to stay alive."

She nodded, and then spun. Racing toward danger.

I ducked behind a tree. It took everything I had not to charge after her.

Logic said I should run the other way, but I stalked through the trees, following the sounds as quietly as possible.

Black Helixes surrounded her in a clearing lit by chemlights.

Jack Parson broke through the trees in a rubberized protective vest. "Be careful. She's dangerous even without wires around."

The teams slowly closed in. Always in a circle. No one letting her out of sight.

Then a shot rang out.

Emma hit the ground, and I bit my hand so hard I tasted blood.

A man in a lab coat broke through the ring of

security and pressed a med device to her wrist. "She's fine. She'll be out for the next twelve hours or so. Enough for us to get her to the facility."

I breathed out a sigh of relief. At least she was alive. They needed her too much to really hurt her.

"Good. Let's move."

"What about Marquez?" one of the men in black said. I recognized the voice. Colonel Santiago.

"Let him go. We have what we need, and he's dead the next time he steps foot on Seligo-controlled land."

I slid to the ground as I watched Santiago carry her away. Her head lolled down over his arm, blue hair spilling over.

Every instinct screamed to take her from him.

But I couldn't. I clenched my teeth so hard my jaw cracked.

I couldn't fight now and win. I had to wait. I had twelve hours to find out where they were taking her. Twelve hours to get to her before she woke up and they started experimenting.

As the sound of choppers faded in the distance, I placed the call. Emma had been taken. I needed pick-up.

After everything I'd been through, nothing compared.

I'd rather be twelve years old again, letting my father kick the shit out of me a thousand times than see her hurt.

And I'd just let her sell herself for my life.

I stood, brushing grass from my knees.

I'd get her back or die trying.

Chapter Seventeen

CIPHER

I faded in and out. Lights were bright and then there were none. It was dark. Motion rocked me. But no matter how much I struggled, I couldn't wake up.

Every time I grew close, I was sucked back down into the darkness.

***

I woke up strapped to a bed. The room smelled of dust, rust, and concrete. Clear plastic walls that had to be ten inches thick formed my square prison. The hospital bed I was strapped to took up the center and a few rolling carts and IV stands surrounded it. Gas lamps lit the room.

"She's awake," said a voice off to my left, but I couldn't see the man who spoke.

How much time had passed since the island? It could've been hours or weeks.

I swallowed back panic. I hoped it hadn't been weeks.

Uncle Jack stepped through the plastic. He'd

always been tall and lanky, but now he was much too thin. His cheekbones stuck out and his eyes were sunken in. The hair along his temples had grayed. My dear uncle looked like hell warmed up. Someone had been keeping the serums from him. No wonder he was so desperate to catch me. Bringing in a Red would be more than enough to put him back in Nagi's good graces.

"I had this room made especially for you," he said. "Not a lick of electricity within a mile radius."

I tried to push away the fear that chilled my skin, but I couldn't. I was stuck here, at his mercy. I couldn't believe I was related to him.

I reached out, trying to feel even the littlest trickle of electricity, but nothing was there. My hands shook in their bonds, and I closed them in fists. He'd put me in an empty landscape with nothing for me to pull from. How in the hell had he found a lab in a dead zone?

Only one possibility explained it. He hadn't found the dead zone. He'd made it. I really was in a Seligo facility made just for me.

My breathing quickened. I tried not to tug on the restraints, but I couldn't help myself. My stomach turned as I struggled. I couldn't even get an inch of wiggle room.

My uncle's laughter echoed through the warehouse.

I stilled, my breath coming in gasps.

"Notice something about this room, niece of mine?"

"Fuck off!"

"Now that wasn't polite."

I could nearly hear the smile in his voice, but he'd stepped far enough away that I couldn't see him.

"I've done my research. I had this whole base built especially for your capture years ago. Totally off the grid."

He couldn't be serious.

I suddenly felt cold.

This was a nightmare. I was tied down, with no weapons, no abilities, nothing. I was completely at my crazy-ass uncle's mercy.

My breath came in short pants as I struggled not to totally lose it. I wanted to go home. I wanted to go back to Knight. Where in the hell was he?

"Where is Dr. Grozdan?"

"I'll go check, sir," someone answered from beyond the plastic.

"I want guards around her at all times. She won't get away from us this time." He spun around and strode from the room.

I lay back and closed my eyes, trying to think of a happy place, but for the life of me I couldn't. The only thing I felt was fear. Mind-numbing fear.

Who the hell was Dr. Grozdan and what was he going to do to me?

Chapter Eighteen

KNIGHT

I pulled up to the Ravens' compound, and jumped off my bike. It'd taken me three days to get back to Colorado. Three days of dodging Helix security.

Three days that Emma was with them, and I wasn't there to save her.

My muscles ached with tension. I needed to be loose, calm, and decisive, but my emotions didn't give a fuck about cooperating.

I tried to think of this as just another of the countless missions I'd been on, but it wasn't. It couldn't be when Emma was involved, and I knew my judgment was suffering for it.

I made my way through the maze in the main compound building. When I found the right door, I placed my hand on the lock, and gave the computer my access code.

The doors slid open, revealing the central control unit, ringed by rows of desks. An intel agent sat at each desk, typing furiously.

I strode toward Samantha. She sat close to the center of the action, next to the Lady's empty desk, where she was scanning through info on a massive screen. Her fingertips guided intel across the glass, sorting it into subcategories.

Her hair was hot pink today. Emma would love that.

My breath caught. Every time I thought of her, it was a like a stab to the heart.

Sam hopped down from her post. "Knight." She wrapped her arms around me and squeezed for a second before letting go. "You okay?"

I gave her a hard look.

"No. You're not. That's what I thought."

"I didn't expect to see you here, kiddo." She liked to run coms from her own office, but that meant she couldn't coordinate with other Ravens as easily.

She climbed back into her seat. "You need the best. I've got your back."

I let out a breath. I did need the best, and Samantha was that. Even if it put that much more responsibility on her, there was no way I'd turn down her help.

"Sam!" A Raven called from the back of the room. "I've got something."

People moved out of the way as I half-ran to the screen. "Report!"

"There was a sign of power fluctuations two hours ago at the Mission Street facility."

"Sam, can we get a video feed—"

"Already on it." She was typing away on a nearby screen. "Listen, Knight. We only have one operative in this building. It's rarely used, and we didn't see the need to place more than one Raven on site. He's on his way to see what's making the power grid go crazy, but he can't blow his cover."

I wanted to call bullshit, but I knew blowing more Ravens' covers wasn't an option. Not anymore. Plus, I might need someone on the inside to help me get her out of wherever she'd been stashed. "I understand."

"Playback is from a while ago," Sam said as a security cam feed filled up the screen.

A team of Black Helixes loaded Emma into an elevator. She lay limp on a stretcher, freckles stark against her bloodless face. I nearly threw up.

I never threw up. Not on any of my missions. But seeing her there, so vulnerable...

Samantha fast-forwarded the feed. When the team stepped off the elevator, the screen went blank.

"Sam?"

"I'm trying to pull up the feed for that floor." Her fingers were almost blurs as she worked. "The cameras on this floor were turned off twelve hours, twenty-eight minutes, and forty-two seconds before this. I'm guessing our enemies are taking extra precautions now that you, Dex, and Oliver have been confirmed as Ravens."

I crossed my arms to stop myself from punching the screen.

More thumbnail feeds popped up. Video coverage for the Seligo facility. One by one, the screens went blank. "Everything goes out an hour after Emma got there. I'm guessing this place was a diversion while they moved her somewhere more secure, but we have to wait for our agent to confirm."

Spots danced in my vision.

She's gone.

"Find her," I spat the words and regretted it. This

wasn't Sam's fault. I was the one who went to that island. I was the one who let her take the fall.

My father had been right. I was nothing but a loser.

"I'll find her. It's only a matter of time." Sam turned to the room. "Everyone, start scanning for cars leaving the area. Should be a train of them. Start at—" She shouted orders, and people scrambled.

I paced the room as I waited. I wanted to take over. To start searching, too. But there wasn't an open space, and I wasn't sure my brain was working right. I was losing my mind a little.

Or a lot.

"Hunter," Sam said.

I jolted free of my thoughts. "What've you got?"

Sam tapped her screen. "We've narrowed it down to three vehicles. She has to be in one of these. But I think this car's your best bet." She pointed to a car weaving through traffic. "I was able to follow it into a dead zone."

I nodded. "That'd be a good place to stash Emma. She'd be totally helpless. Cut off from her abilities." Except they didn't know we'd been working on the island for that exact scenario.

"Exactly. We pulled in everyone we could spare for you on this op. It's not a lot, but it's the best we can do right now. The team's waiting in the briefing room. Dex is on lead."

Good. I wasn't in any kind of mental place to take on commanding this, even if I wanted to. Dex wouldn't let me down. "Got it." I squeezed Samantha's shoulder. "Get us a location, and we'll take it from there."

Down the hall, a team of seven Ravens was waiting. None of them had helixes except me and Dex, but I'd helped train many of them and they were good operatives. The room had screens in the front and rows of seats. Each chair had a com attached to it. Dex stood in front of the room talking to the group assembled.

"Fox, your team is first in the air. Rico, your team's second. I'll let you pick who has the third and fourth spot. I want you in formation. Once we get Emma, we're going to have to haul ass out. We need you covering our asses all the way back to the Colorado station."

I cleared my throat and Dex turned to me. "You found her?" He asked me.

"Yes," I said. "What do we have for resources?"

"Five ground teams en route. Plus four air. Won't be here for another day, though."

I shook my head. That wasn't fast enough, but we'd have to do. "Where's Oliver?"

Dex rolled his eyes. "With Mona. Says he's out for the next week. Doesn't want to abandon her in an unknown place."

Dex wasn't hiding his disgust at all. "I'd do the same if the situation was reversed."

"No, you wouldn't."

I slapped his back. "Let it go, man. We need to get moving."

"We're going in civie cars," Dex said, and then paused for objections. The room stayed silent. "Not the best, but I don't want us getting spotted on the way. Sam is covering intel. Once she finds our in, we move."

I cleared my throat. "My Red is in there, and I won't have her turned into some fucking science experiment."

The group shouted agreement.

"This is a dangerous mission. We're going into the den and pulling one of our own out. And it's personal to me. As much as I'd like it not to be, that will color my judgment. Shit goes down, look to Dex." I clapped him on the shoulder. "Let's move."

**

Four hours later, I was outside a warehouse on my stomach. "What's the readout say?"

"Five heat sigs inside." Dex's sensor unit beeped. "One could be Cipher. More outside, but nothing big. We can be in and out in fifteen. Gives us enough time to cover our tracks before the Seligo jump on it."

"Good. Let's do this."

I started to move, but Dex grabbed my arm. "You're not seriously going in first."

"Why the fuck wouldn't I?" Although I knew perfectly well why I shouldn't. I wasn't running this show. Dex was.

But I didn't give a shit about procedure right now.

Dex rolled his eyes. "Fuck it. Let's go."

I gave the signal and we moved.

Moving through the security was easy. Too easy. We moved through the compound with little to no resistance, taking down a few token guards. When we reached the room with the heat sigs, I busted through first.

Shots rang out, and I stepped back through the

doorway, using it as a shield.

I popped around again to another chorus of gunfire. This time I paid attention to where the shots were coming from.

When I popped out a third time, I fired first, and didn't slow my stride. Four shots was all it took. The bodies hit the ground and I stepped over one to get to the chair in the center of the room. A girl with strawberry blond hair was strapped down, but from across the room I knew this wasn't Emma. The girl wore a short skirt and a skimpy top, and she was too tall, even sitting down.

She was hunched over, but looked up as I approached. Not Emma. Not even close. Her eyes were dark brown. No freckles. Makeup smeared down her face.

I squatted down next to her and pulled out one of my knives. She flinched, but when I cut her free, she relaxed enough to start crying and throw herself at me.

I didn't want her gratitude. I wanted to get the hell out of here. "Sullivan?"

"Yes, sir."

"You and your team are on cleanup. Make sure she gets taken care of." I passed the girl off and hurried out of the room. I jammed the buttons on my com, fingers shaking. "Sam. What the fuck."

"I'm sorry. I could've sworn that was the right one. The other went to a building in the city. I checked the video feeds just now. It's definitely not her."

"And the last one?"

"You're not going to like this."

"I already hate everything about this. Just tell me."

"The car disappeared in the Nevada desert, and I haven't been able to find it."

"What do you mean disappeared?"

"It's not just in the dead zone, it's off the grid entirely. Short of moving some satellites into Seligo occupied space, I can't track her."

I stopped walking and started sprinting. "Everyone move. Now. I want you in the cars and ready to move five minutes ago!"

As soon as I was in the car, I took off. Dex was still half outside.

"Fucking shit, Hunter. Are you trying to kill me?"

"I can't help it if you're slow."

He muttered something and I didn't give a shit what it was. He was quiet for a second. "That's a lot of desert to search."

"I know."

"There's no power there. No surveillance."

My knuckles turned white on the steering wheel. "I know."

"She'll be cut off from her ability."

I ground my teeth. "I know."

"So how are we going to find her?"

"I don't fucking know, okay. I don't know." I shouted at him and cringed. "Sorry."

"We'll get her back."

That sickening feeling in my stomach was back. I gripped the steering wheel and pressed on the gas. The desert was massive. We'd have to get lucky with the air team to have any clue where Emma was being held.

I gripped the steering wheel hard.

This was royally fucked.

Chapter Nineteen

CIPHER

My heart was beating so fast in my chest that I was pretty sure I was going to have a heart attack if it didn't slow down. I started meditating, or tried to, but a man strode through the plastic, killing my concentration dead. Dr. Grozdan. His white lab coat billowed behind him as he speed-walked toward me. His eyes were deep set and dark, and his hair was slicked back.

I wasn't sure how long I'd been here. Days maybe? The Black Helix goons had knocked me out a few times. I'd been in and out of consciousness for a while, but now I was awake.

I wasn't sure what I was more afraid of—being awake or being knocked out.

Dr. Grozdan moved to the closest rolling cart and opened a drawer of implements. Metal clanked on metal as he searched for his torture device of choice.

He turned back around with a needle.

No way. An injection? We had technology. It was easier to put on a patch that delivered whatever straight to your bloodstream. "What the hell?"

"It's a shot." He wasn't mocking me, simply stating a fact.

"I see that, but it's got a real needle on it. It's older than Nagi."

He petted the syringe like it was something to be revered. "It's perfectly safe, and has no electricity for you to pull from."

"I don't care about it being safe. Get that thing away from me. Go get a normal non-prehistoric torture device. Hell, I'll take last decade's injection gun over that."

"Those run on power, and aren't allowed in this room. This will have to do." He stepped toward me. "I've heard that it will only hurt for a moment."

Bullshit. No one had used an actual needle in forever. He had no data to back up his dumb-as-fuck statement.

He wiped my arm with some sort of chemical and then stabbed the long-ass-needle into my bicep.

I gasped as my eyes crossed. "Holy shit that hurts."

"Oh yes, I was supposed to tell you to breathe out. It's supposed to make it not hurt as much. Well, next time…"

Next time? Next time!

He pulled the needle out much slower than it went in. Was he trying to prolong the discomfort? Pain traveled through my arm as whatever was in the injection made its way through my body. I ground my teeth until it was bearable. "What was in that?"

"A microbe. It's a biological information gathering system. We inject it, and then after three hours, take a sample of your blood. It'll tell us more about your current genetic status and the extent of your…powers. Once I know more about your DNA sequencing, then I can tailor a second batch to really get into the nitty-gritty of how you are the way that you are. If this yields the data I need to prove my thesis, I can finally be elevated to Seligo." His matter-of-fact way of talking made me want to punch him. If I ever got free from the table, I'd make sure to do just that. "You might experience some discomfort as the microbe makes its way through your system, but it shouldn't be more than you can bear."

More than I could bear? My blood was on fire, like he'd injected acid into my veins. "This is more than discomfort."

He grunted. "Well, I can't give you any pain inhibitors. There's always the chance they could interfere with the results. You'll just have to take it." He patted my leg. "Don't forget to breathe."

I clenched my jaw and tried to focus on not swallowing my tongue.

I heard myself whimper. My eyes started to tear up, so I closed them and focused on my time with Knight on the island. On how he made me feel. The sound of the waves on the beach.

He would find me. I knew it. He wouldn't give up. I couldn't either.

Thinking of him made me feel better. It didn't hurt as much. Or at least he was enough of a distraction to get me through it. So I thought about his dimples. His bright blue eyes and how they changed shade depending on his mood. About his neatness. And his sensitivity. And his abs. I could dream about those abs forever.

I missed the jerk.

But he was safe. Far, far away from whatever hellhole I was in. He'd be pissed that I left. Maybe even looking for me by now.

I wondered if he'd ever find me.

If I'd ever get out.

The pain was getting worse. What happened at the end of three hours? Would whatever was left in me die out? Or would this pain be a fun new addition to my life?

No. It had to go away.

Something brushed my hand and I whimpered again, squeezing my eyes tight.

The lab-dick was back. So was my uncle. They were arguing, but I couldn't focus on their words. The pain was too much.

Sweat soaked through my clothes and I started to shake.

I choked as my body tried to rid itself of the chemicals. Suddenly I was rolled to my side, free of my bindings, as the contents of my stomach came back up. Just my luck I wasn't in any state to try to get away.

Another needle stabbed my bicep.

Then there was nothing but darkness.

***

The next time I awoke I was blessedly alone. The bindings were back, but that was to be expected. My mouth tasted like something had died in it. I could've killed for a toothbrush, some super minty toothpaste, and an ice-cold glass of water.

The only positive was that I could feel a faint twinkling of energy. It made zero sense. It was barely there, so much so that at first I thought it was my imagination. But then, a dusting of electricity hit my fingertips when I tried to pull it and I knew it was real.

How could there be electricity here, when Jack had cleared the space to hold me?

I tried to focus on what Knight had taught me on the island. Everything in nature had a base electrical current. Electrons moved. I tried to feel it, to pull the energy toward me, but without him here to ground me, it was so much harder. It was like I could see what I needed just outside of my peripheral vision, but couldn't reach it.

I struggled against the bonds that held me to the bed, and suddenly it didn't matter where the electricity was coming from, only that it was there. That little buzzing along the outskirts of my senses boosted my confidence. Even if I could grab it, it wasn't enough to stop a heart or even bust a lightbulb. But if I could get it to come to me, then maybe I could scare the guards. Keep the sadist and his needles away from me.

I smacked my lips and blinked. My vision was going a little fuzzy around the edges, even lying down. That cold glass of water was becoming more of a necessity by the second.

"Hey," I said. My voice was raspy and much quieter than it should be when it felt like I was yelling. Whatever Grozdan had given me was seriously gnarly.

Rustling noises came from beyond the plastic

curtains.

"Hey! I need some water!"

No one came.

"Hey!" I put a little more force behind it. "Water! Please! I'm dying over here."

"We're not supposed to go beyond the barrier. You're going to have to go without," said a deep voice.

"You scared of little ole me?" Chicken. If he came over here, I could try to give him a little shock. "Come on. There are how many of you—"

"Forty-one."

"Jeez. Forty-one to watch one little girl who's strapped to a bed and helpless. And not one of you is brave enough to get me a glass of water. Someone never learned their manners…"

A hushed argument echoed through the plastic and then someone strode through the sheets. The guy who stepped around the bed was tall and Asian, and held a glass of water.

"Thanks."

"My mother raised me correctly, but you're a prisoner for a reason. Reds are dangerous."

"Not me. Not here."

The beige plastic glass had a straw in it.

He held the straw to my lips and I tried to sit up a little so that I wouldn't choke. As I sucked the lukewarm water down, I focused those tiny little specks of electricity along the straw. I held a little bit of water in my mouth and coughed, using it to conduct a tiny bit of electricity as it splattered him.

"Motherfucker," he said as the cup crashed to the ground. "The bitch shocked me."

"Come on. There's nothing here for me to use.

Even the lamps are gas."

"Get back here, Chu."

Chu looked around the room, then to the glass, and finally back to me. He didn't understand what'd happened. I didn't need him to. It was enough for me to know.

"What are you doing in there?" Dr. Grozdan sounded pissed. "I gave orders no one was to go near her."

"I only gave her a sip of water."

"Out. Get out now." Dr. Grozdan came toward me. "You're up."

Way to state the obvious, Dr. Dumbass. "As up as I can get while being strapped to a bed."

"It's time for another injection. I've changed the formula again. This one should give us more information. If I'd…" He trailed off but I didn't care. All I could do was stare at that needle.

The last one had hurt when I got it, but it was the effect after that I had zero desire to relive. "Please. I'll do whatever you want. Just not another shot."

He grasped my arm. "It's necessary."

The needle shoved in and I screamed. This one was so much worse than the last time.

One second I was screaming, the next I was dead to the world.

***

When I woke again, I felt even shittier, if that were possible, but at least I wasn't hooked up anymore. I lay curled on my side, every muscle in my body aching. Even my fingernails hurt. I wasn't sure if I could move, but I gathered myself and sat up.

The room spun around me. Someone whispered something, but I couldn't hear what they said. The second piece of good news was that the little fuzzies that had been on the fringe were now full force in front of me.

One of Jack's men came through the curtain. He tossed a plastic water bottle at me, and I let it hit me in the chest.

An ache rolled through me, but I ignored it. "It's hard for me to move."

The guard inched forward and picked up the water bottle. His eyes stayed on me the whole time he bent over. He moved to me, wary of what I might do.

I didn't know why they were suddenly so scared of me. I'd barely even shocked the last guy. Static electricity did worse.

Maybe I was giving something away with my face. Maybe he could see through me.

As soon as he reached out, I grasped his wrist and let the electricity flow. Just enough to fibrillate his heart. He gasped and his body thudded to the ground.

For a moment I watched him twitching there, and regretted it, but this wasn't the time to feel guilty. I swung my legs over the edge of the bed.

"Don't move," one of the guards shouted from beyond the plastic curtain. The barrel of a rifle peeked through.

He wasn't going to shoot me. And if he was, I wasn't sure I cared. I wanted out. It was a game of chicken, and I was more than ready to call their bluff.

I stood up from the bed on wobbly knees.

"Don't move."

I kept walking and heard the guys scrambling.

"Keep a safe distance from her. She might want a stroll but she's not going anywhere. There's nowhere for her to go."

I moved past the plastic barrier. My plastic cube stood in the middle of a massive hangar. Over forty Black Helixes surrounded me, weapons drawn.

The guys stepped back each time I stepped forward. I needed a plan. If I could find a car, and knock all these guys out, then maybe I could run. Maybe I could get away. I could—

An explosion rocked the building. The instruments on the carts rattled as my plastic prison shook. Jack's men shouted orders at each other, but I couldn't do anything but grin as another explosion rattled the steel walls.

I wobbled, almost biting it, but a burst of adrenaline rushed through my body, taking away the pain. Smoke rolled through the hangar, licking along the walls. Gunshots nearby rang in my ears.

I looked down at the glowing tattoo on my hand. Somehow I knew.

Hunter had found me.

Chapter Twenty

KNIGHT

Chaos rang in the night as we moved through the old storage facility. "I want a hangar by hangar sweep. Capture anyone who doesn't resist. I don't give a shit what you do with the rest. Any computer, any drive, any bit of information—I want it. All of it. Let's make this clean."

Dex moved in front of me and threw a grenade. I protected my ears and took cover as I waited for the explosion, and then jumped him.

"What the fuck! She could be in there."

"You're losing it." He pulled free from me. "She's not in there. It's already been checked. But there were seventeen hostiles. Now none. Let's move."

He was right. I was losing it. If she wasn't here, I didn't know what I was going to do.

"We have her," I heard through the link in my ear. "You'll want to see this."

I forced myself to take calm, even footsteps that echoed in the suddenly quiet warehouse. Bodies dressed in black lay on the floor—either knocked out or dead. I wasn't sure which. I barely spared them a glance.

Emma stood in front of me.

I closed my eyes and let out a breath. I could finally breathe again.

I stepped closer. The entire facility was only lit by gas lanterns, but even in the dull light, I knew it was her. Smart, but I'd taught my girl well if she was up and around.

As I stepped closer, the hairs on my arms lifted in alarm. Emma wobbled on her feet, and I closed the distance in a few steps. I wiped a thumb across her brow, and it came back pink.

There was blood in her sweat.

She grabbed my hand. "You're bleeding? Where are you bleeding?" She started patting me down, until I grabbed her wrists.

I swallowed. "I'm not bleeding."

"Don't lie to me. You're hurt."

I sighed, not knowing what would upset her more—thinking the blood was mine or hers. But I had to tell her the truth. "The blood is yours."

I watched the emotions cross her face. Shock. Disbelief. Fear. Finally, she ran a finger down her forearm, coating it in a fine layer of blood. She looked up at me. "I'm sweating blood." She swallowed. "Well…that's disgusting."

I laughed and pressed my forehead to hers. "It's so good to see you, princess. I don't think I've ever been so scared." I picked her up before I said anything else, pulling her close to my body as I spoke into my com. "Dex. We're heading to the med-v. We're moving out. Now." Seeing her, I was glad Sam had made me add the med-v to our convoy; the small RV was outfitted with a full suite of medical supplies.

Dex was already in the driver's seat when we got there. "What the fuck happened to her?"

"I don't know. Drive." I carried her into the bathroom and set her on her feet. She wobbled a little bit. "You able to stand?"

"I think so."

As soon as I let go, she started to crumple. I grabbed her before she could bang her head, keeping a firm grip on her shoulders.

"Maybe not so ready to stand on my own?"

I nodded, unable to say anything. The rage was there, boiling under the surface, but not at her. Never at her.

I flipped the toilet lid shut, and sat her down. I needed to relax. I closed my eyes for a second. "Are you really okay?" I asked.

She was quiet for a while, but I waited. I needed to know the truth.

"Not really, but I will be now that I'm with you."

I squatted down in front of her. "Don't do that again."

"You're mad."

"Fuck yes, I'm mad. Not at you, but you scared the shit out of me. Next time, no splitting up. I can't handle it."

A tear rolled down her cheek, clearing away a line of red from her face. "It wasn't easy for me either."

I was being a dick again. "I know. I know." I paused until she looked me in the eyes. "Don't do that again. I don't think I'd survive it."

Her smile was a little watery. "Okay."

"You're stuck with me forever now. No running

away without me. No turning yourself in to spare me. If you have a problem, we deal with it together." I tugged at her feet, and pulled off her shoes.

When I started to lift up her shirt, she grabbed my hands, voice panicky. "What are you doing?"

"You're covered in blood. I want to put you in bed, but you have to rinse off first."

"But…"

"I've seen you in a bathing suit, and I won't be taking advantage of you. Not right now. Trust me, okay?"

She looked at me with her big hazel-green eyes. "I trust you."

"Thank you." I knew how hard those words were for her. She let me finish stripping the blood-soaked clothes away. When I started pulling off my own clothes, Emma grabbed me again. "There isn't room for two in there."

"We'll squeeze." No way was I leaving her alone when she could barely stand.

"The water tank won't be that big. We won't have much time."

"It'll be enough."

"But—"

"Emma. Stop." I placed my finger across her lips. "We're going to rinse you off. I'm going to tuck you into bed. And then I'm going to get us to someplace safe so I can make sure you're okay. Please don't argue." I needed to take care of her. I had to know that she was okay.

"Okay." She reached her arms up, and I pulled her to her feet.

The water wasn't as warm as I would've liked, but

we made do. She rested against the stall as I soaped us both up. In other circumstances, I would've enjoyed a co-shower, but with the water running down pink, all I felt was regret.

I grabbed two towels from the cabinet, and wrapped her up before sitting her back down on the toilet seat.

"There's my girl." I smiled down at her as I quickly toweled myself off. Most of the blue was gone from her hair, and I could see all of her freckles. She looked so little, all wet and huddled in the towel. I could finally see some of the Emma I used to know in her. "How are you feeling?"

She blushed. "Weak and woozy."

My smile faded. How could I fix this?

"Sorry," she said.

"You're taking my line, princess." I brushed her hair away from her face. "You did what you thought you had to do. Next time we'll talk before you make a crazy decision." I picked her up, easing her into my arms. "We'll get you feeling better. I don't know what they did to you—"

"It was some sort of injection—a bio agent that was supposed to figure out the limits of my conductivity."

"I don't like the sound of that." The long-term effects of whatever they'd injected her could be pretty bad. I'd seen stuff like that before. We needed to get her to the Lady and fast.

"Me neither. It hurt like a bitch. At least it did until they knocked me out."

Dex was talking to someone on the com, but quieted as we exited the bathroom. I carried Emma back to her bedroom and tucked her into the bed. "I'll contact the Lady, and see if she knows anything." I kissed her forehead and turned to go.

She grabbed my hand. "Can you…"

"What?"

Her cheeks heated beautifully and she shook her head. "Never mind. It's stupid."

Suddenly all the panic, the fear, the weight in my chest was gone. If she wanted me, I was there.

I climbed into bed next to her, and pulled her close. "Come here." She rested her head on my chest. "Sleep, princess," I said as I ran my hands through her wet hair. The scent of her shampoo and the feel of her in my arms was like a balm. I could lay with her forever.

"Thanks." Her breathing evened out after a few minutes, and I stayed there, motionless. I didn't want to wake her, even if I had people to coordinate. Dex could handle it for a bit. All I could do was thank the gods that I had her. That she was safe and still alive.

I watched her sleep for a while. Her skin was clammy. When I brushed my fingertip down her face, it came back wet and pink.

She was still losing blood.

I swallowed. I didn't think it was enough for her to need a transfusion. Not yet, but I went ahead and put her on a fluid drip. She was so exhausted she didn't wake when I strapped the membrane patch around her arm. I got up, kissed her cheek, and tucked the covers around her.

The door closed with a soft click behind me. "She's sleeping," I said to the Dex. "I'm going to do some digging around. See if I can figure out what they put in her."

"She looks like shit."

"I know."

"We need to get her checked out. By a real doctor."

"I know." What did he think? That I was purposefully keeping her from getting medical care?

"Those experiments go bad sometimes. Remember when we picked up Allison—"

"I fucking know." The words were a whisper, but barely. Allison was a twelve-year-old Red we'd found a year ago. She'd been held in one of the labs for a week, but seemed okay. She'd been tired, but she'd been through an ordeal.

Then she took a nap and never woke up.

Fear clawed my insides. "That's not going to happen with Emma. She's strong."

"Allison—"

"Shut up about Allison. She's not fucking Allison, okay?"

Dex held up his hands. "Okay, man. Okay. She's not Allison."

I let out a shaky breath. "How are we doing?"

"Good. No one's on our ass yet. That won't last, but for now we're fine. Air teams are keeping watch. Sam says nothing's come up on the wire yet, so we're solid."

"You okay to keep driving?"

"Sure thing."

"Great. Thanks." I sat down at the nook in the kitchen and dug into my pack. I grabbed out my comp and hooked up one of the drives I'd taken from the facility.

Its security was total bullshit. Took me two seconds to break in, and then I found the research. I wasn't fully getting all of it, but it looked like the doctor who'd examined Emma was trying to isolate Red Helix mutations. Nagi had been trying to make super soldiers for years but he didn't have anything like the Reds. Only Lady Eva had been successful working with that kind of DNA, and even then, she could only stabilize it—not replicate it.

That was why she was the lead scientist, and Nagi had been in her shadow. Not many people knew he'd stolen her research and used it to his own profit. He'd tried to kill her off, but she was smart. Resourceful.

If one of Nagi's doctors had somehow poisoned Emma, Lady Eva was the only one I trusted to fix it. The more I read the research, the more I didn't like it.

I clicked on my com.

"Knight," Sam's voice came through. "Been waiting to hear from you."

"Had to get her settled. We're taking the scenic route back your way." I paused. "And I'm sending you some files. Emma was pumped full of some drug that was supposed to isolate the Red mutation. She's sweating blood."

"Send me the data."

I clicked a few buttons, logging into the Ravens' network. "It's up now."

She was quiet for a few minutes. "You're right. This looks bad. Hang on."

I tapped my finger on the table as I waited.

"Knight," Lady Eva said.

I sat up straight. Lady Eva had been busy the past week. If she was coming on screen, something wasn't right. "Yes, ma'am."

"You need to watch Emma closely. That drug is highly unstable and can undo what I did for her. Is she lucid?"

My heart sped up. "She's sleeping now, but she was fine earlier. Should I wake her up?"

"No. It's good that she's sleeping. Get here fast."

"But we're probably going to catch a tail soon, it's not—"

"I'm sounding a warning and we'll be ready to move the compound if necessary. Don't worry about the tail. Just stay close to Emma and monitor her. If her system is compromised, she may pull more electricity than you can handle."

What was I supposed to do? Let her explode with power?

No. If it came to that, I'd take what I could. She'd stepped in for me, and I had no qualms about reciprocating.

"I'll take care of her."

"If she starts to lose control…" Lady Eva's voice dropped, deadly serious. "We can't have another New York."

"Don't worry. I won't let it come to that."

"I'm serious, Knight. If the situation gets out of hand, I need to know that you'll take care of it."

Emma wasn't a fucking situation. She was a person.

"I understand what you mean. I won't let her get that far."

"Fine. See you soon." It was an order.

"Yes, ma'am."

I clicked off the com. "Fuck." Running my fingers

through my hair, I stood to pace back and forth in the narrow galley.

"Everything okay?" Dex asked.

"No. It's not fucking okay."

The only question was what I could tell Emma. It didn't take long to decide. She was already worried about containing her abilities. If I told her she was at risk, chances were she'd lose control faster.

"Well, I'm afraid I've got some bad news," Dex said.

Perfect. Like the day could get any worse. "Go ahead."

"We're being followed."

That I could handle. I was trained for this. "How many? How far?"

"Three trucks and two choppers. We have our own choppers in the air flying low to stay under the radar, but they won't be able to stay hidden long. We need to decide what to do, and soon."

That's the question. *Do we make a stand? Or keep running?*

We were going to have to confront Jack and his goons at some point. The real question was, could we lose them fast enough to make it to Lady Eva's before Emma lost control?

"Call in some reinforcements. Let's see if we can switch vehicles and shake our tail. We need to get Emma to the Lady as soon as possible."

"What did the Lady say?"

I ignored the question I couldn't answer. Instead, I walked back to the bedroom. "I'll be with her. Update me when we're ready to switch."

"You got it."

Emma was still sound asleep. Plus, she was glowing, and not in a figurative way. Like she was being lit from inside. I slid into bed next to her. As soon as my hand touched her face, my teeth started tingling. I breathed through the jolt as she sighed and rolled into me. "Rest, princess," I said as I kissed her forehead. My only hope was that the drug would wear off, and she'd find balance again.

Until then, I'd stick by her. There was no way I'd hurt Emma if she got into a 'situation.' That wasn't happening. Ever.

The stream of electricity running into me was low, but steady. I could take this all week. Sure, I wouldn't be able to sleep, but that wasn't any different than normal.

Emma was mine, and I wasn't ever letting her go again.

***

A few hours later, I felt the med-v slow. A soft knock sounded before Dex stuck his head in the room. He must've switched the drive controls over to auto.

"We're ready."

"Good."

I slid out from under Emma, and the second I wasn't touching her, her skin lit up.

"Holy shit. What's going on?"

"Later." I lifted the IV bag off its stand, and Emma finally stirred when I scooped her into my arms.

"What's happening?" She mumbled.

"We're changing vehicles."

"I can walk," Emma said, but I tightened my arms as I cradled her.

"It's fine. I got you. We're going to a different med-v. There are a few more. Each one is going to break off in a different direction. We're hoping to lose your uncle in the mix up."

"Sounds like a plan." Her words garbled and she blinked so slowly, it was like her lids were too heavy to hold open.

"Relax, princess. I've got you. You can sleep. I'll tuck you back in soon."

"Will you stay with me?"

My heart swelled. "Forever."

"Do you mean it?"

"Yes."

"Okay."

I smiled. "Okay."

She sighed and let her eyes close. Emma's breaths had evened out by the time we stepped outside into the parking lot. Except for us and four idling med-v's, the area was empty.

A crew of four stepped from the nearest med-v and hopped into ours.

I stepped into our new med-v. It wasn't as nice as the last one. The inside was an obnoxious shade of orange, and smelled moldy, but we didn't have the luxury of being picky.

A blanket was folded over the foot of the bed in the back. I didn't want to disturb Emma too much, so I quickly hung up the IV bag, then eased us down and pulled the blanket over us both. It wasn't a minute before the RV started moving.

Dex came into the room and knelt by the bed.

"Sam says all the switched med-v's are being followed, but I think we can lose the tail. The other med-v's are moving a little faster than us. One's pushing it to make it clear they're running. It's got the most attention so far."

I nodded. "Thanks for handling this."

"You okay?"

"More or less." I stroked Emma's shoulder. "She's constantly pulling energy. It's okay right now, but if we don't get back soon, I'm afraid she'll go nuclear."

Dex whistled. "Should we just knock her out?"

I shook my head. "She's already dead to the world and that's not helping." I paused. "I'm good for now, but you'd better retreat. Just being around her is dangerous."

"I got that. You sure you can handle it, man?"

There weren't a hell of a lot of options. "Yeah. I got this."

Dex nodded slowly. He'd known me long enough to know when I was bullshitting, but he wasn't going to say a damned thing about it. "Holler if you need anything. I'm going to go back to driving on manual controls now, but I can go auto anytime."

"Thanks."

He left and I forced myself to close my eyes. My teeth were tingling again and my whole body was jittery. The truth was, I wasn't sure how much I could take. If it took much longer to get to the compound…

I might be in trouble.

Chapter Twenty-One

CIPHER

I woke up feeling much less zombie-like. Every time I'd come to for a few seconds, Knight had been there holding me, and it was nice. Beyond nice not to have to worry about losing control. But I had to get out of bed at some point. Knight shook, itching to get up.

When I rolled out of bed, he looked at me for a long moment. "You okay?"

"Yeah." I stretched. "A little weak, but better." I noticed the IV strapped to my arm. "What the hell?"

"Hang on. I'll take it out." He gently cradled my arm and unstrapped the device. "How's the energy?"

"Sizzling along my edges." I paused to assess, and opened my eyes. "I have it under control. I'll be okay."

He nodded once, but made no move to get up.

"I'm going to go to the bathroom."

When I peeked back in, he was positioned on the floor doing push-ups so fast my arms ached in sympathy. I left him to it and made my way to the front of the med-v.

The whole thing was a piece of shit. The road

noise was constant and loud, and the windows rattled as we flew down the freeway, passing cars on both sides. Not easy to do in any med-v, especially such a hunk of junk. Dex was doing some badass maneuvering.

The bathroom was tinier than the one in the Griz, but it had bunks on either side of the walls. More room for injured soldiers. Cabinets took up the space between the bottom bunk and the floor. Even if the vehicle was old, I'd bet every shelf was fully stocked with supplies.

I sat in the passenger seat and propped my feet up on the dashboard. I'd been online friends with Dex for as long as Knight, but Knight and I had always clicked a little more.

Still, it was fun to talk face to face. That I hadn't realized how much human contact mattered showed how deeply I'd fallen into my persona. It was like the cloud had finally cleared and I could maybe be happy.

I might've been on the run and feeling off, but I had friends. I had Knight.

Which was awesome. And terrifying.

Having something to lose also meant I had something to fight for. For him. And us.

"How's it going?"

"Good," Dex said. "How are you doing?"

"Better. I think." The roads were pretty quiet as we moved through the nighttime desert.

"That's good."

"We're still being followed?"

"Not anymore. They fell back. They've apparently ruled us out."

Twenty minutes later, Dex had me cracking up as

he told me stories from just after he and Knight had gotten their helixes.

"—and then Knight said, 'Ma'am, please put the uzi down.' In that calm voice of his. She's totally off her ass on drugs, and pointing some serious shit at him, but man, that guy has iron intestines. I was nearly shitting myself and I wasn't the one in front of her."

I snorted. "So, what did he do?"

"You're not seriously telling her this story," Knight strode out of the bedroom.

"Hells yes I am. So then—"

An explosion overhead rocked the med-v.

"Fuck!" Dex slammed the gas, swerving around falling debris.

"Turn right!" Knight shouted from the back.

He turned hard, nearly flipping the med-v. I hadn't even realized there was a chopper above us until it crashed down.

"Check in. I want to know if that was one of ours?" Dex asked.

Knight was quiet for a second. "Yes, it was ours."

"Who was in her?" Dex asked.

"Mendleson. DeLuna. O'Brien." Knight's voice was cold, unemotional. "Get this med-v moving, Dex. There's more coming our way."

Adrenaline flooded my system and I knew Knight was right. We had to get the hell out of here.

Dex gunned the engine. As we took off down the highway, gunshots peppered the med-v.

"Michaels says we've got six trucks coming up on us and two choppers in the air. Their team is fighting in the air, but we have to lose the trucks or find a defensible spot. Fast," Knight said.

My hands shook. The power of the explosion and chaos had my control slipping, and my skin tingled as electricity ran along my body.

Something slammed into the side of the med-v, knocking us to the side.

"Wrong move, asshole," Dex muttered. He switched gears, and slammed back.

I grabbed the 'oh, shit' bar beside my head, and tried to stay calm.

"We can't outrun them in this rig," Dex said.

"So what's the plan?" Knight squatted between the driver and passenger seats, keeping a hand on me. "I'm open to suggestions."

Right. We couldn't outrun them. We couldn't outgun them. We were surrounded in the middle of nowhere with no cover and we couldn't stop to find any.

The only advantage we had was me, but Knight wouldn't hand me over.

That only left one thing for me to do. Fight.

I unlocked my seatbelt. Dex was busy hauling ass and avoiding getting slammed again. The med-v was swerving so much it was like being wasted, but I managed to stay on my feet.

"Where are you going?"

"The power's building too much. I'm going to blow. It'd be better if I was outside when it does. Maybe I can direct it."

Knight shook his head. "What exactly do you think you're going to do up there?"

"I'm gonna, you know, zap 'em."

"Your control isn't that good. You could blow all

of us up."

"I know. Always tried to keep myself under control, but this seems like a good time to let loose. Especially since I'm barely hanging on. Maybe I can direct it this time?" I hoped I wasn't out of my mind or this would be a majorly stupid move.

Knight spun to Dex. "Rope?"

"In my pack."

Knight grabbed a thick coil from Dex's backpack. He wrapped the rope around my waist, and tested the knot three times.

His gaze met mine. "This is a terrible idea." He handed the slack to Dex. "You lose this line, I will slit your throat. If you hear me yell, you pull her back in."

Dex wrapped the end around his forearm, and then went back to gripping the steering wheel. "Great. Defensive driving and keeping lifelines. Anything else you need me to do?"

"That's it for now," Knight said, and then he turned to me. "I'll go out first and cover you. Then you go out. You need help harnessing, you put your hand on my skin. I'll help you focus." His words were firm and clear, but I could see the fear in his eyes.

I blew out a breath. I didn't want to put him in danger for my dumb plan. "It'd be better if I went up by myself."

"No." He went back to Dex's pack and pulled out a com, putting it in his ear. "When we get up there, you do what I say, okay?"

"Okay."

He climbed up to the top bunk and removed the ceiling hatch. He popped up, and then back down quickly as a shot rang out. He pressed on the com.

"I'm going on top of the rig. Give me cover and then get the fuck out of there."

My heart raced. I wiped a bead of pink-tinged sweat from my brow.

Shots echoed in the night. Knight winked at me and then disappeared through the hatch, big-ass gun in hand.

My breath caught. I climbed up the bunks and poked my head out.

All I could see were headlights and Knight as he lay on his stomach, aiming. He fired, a tire blew, and the first truck rolled. The headlights spun and an explosion blasted through the night.

I lifted myself onto the roof. Wind blew across my face, and I was glad I'd thought to pull my hair back.

Then the gunfire stopped.

"Emma Jean." Uncle Jack's voice boomed over a loudspeaker.

Was he in one of the trucks?

No. There was no way he'd take that kind of risk. He had to be watching from some safe distance.

"Stop running. Don't let any more people get killed trying to avoid the inevitable. I will always find you."

I copied Knight's move and lay down on my stomach. The metal roof was cool against my chin.

For once, Jack was right. He would always find me, and three Ravens were already dead because of me. Was my life really worth this?

"Don't listen to him," Knight yelled over the noise. I could barely hear him, but barely hearing was enough. "We're all Ravens. He won't let any of us go without killing us."

Knight was right. Maybe if they hadn't broken me out of that warehouse, but it was too late to go back. The second the Ravens showed up, they'd signed up for this fight. I'd already tried the whole running away thing, and it hadn't worked out well for anyone.

Now my plan wasn't about running. It was about fighting.

My uncle continued to talk, but I wasn't paying attention. It didn't matter what he said. I wouldn't go to him again. If I did, Knight would keep coming after me.

Sticking to my plan was the only option. I closed my eyes.

I breathed out two steady breaths and I could feel the little balls of energy that fueled the trucks. They were like burning candles in the night. All it would take was a burst of thought from me, and they'd explode.

I went for the one farthest away first, just in case I went out of control. The truck was fourth back in the convoy—the last one. I thought of the truck like a light bulb. I'd blown more bulbs than I could count in my life, and the truck was no different.

I magnified the energy with my power, speeding up the pulsing signal and overloading the truck's systems with electricity. I felt the explosion in my bones. Smoke and debris flew overhead.

I was reaching for the next truck before I could stop myself. It was moving too fast. Much too fast. The second truck exploded, and another blast of heat licked along my skin, closer this time.

Before I knew what was happening, another explosion rocked the night. I opened my eyes as a chopper fell from the sky. The metal crunched into the ground and a wave of heat blazed overhead.

Oh shit. I couldn't contain it.

The smell of fuel and burning cars filled the night.

"Emma." Knight's voice broke through the chaos. "Emma Jean Boyd. Snap out of it!" He started firing on the three remaining trucks as they fired at us. "Grab me. I'll ground it."

I scooched closer to him on my belly.

Another truck blew. This one was closer. I blocked my face from the heat. The med-v tipped over on two wheels from the force of the explosion.

"Shit." Knight started sliding off the roof. He pulled a knife from his belt and stabbed the metal, holding himself in place until the tires met the ground again. "Get our cover away." He yelled into his com. "She's lost control of her powers. Assume twice the safe distance." Another copter fell from the sky. I covered my ears from the crash.

"Fuck." I screamed, but I couldn't hear it over all the noise.

"Not one of ours," he said, but my ears were still ringing. "But get it under control, Em."

"I can't." I was too afraid to move. What felt like a never-ending stream of electricity was zinging through my body. I was too upset. Too angry with my uncle. Every bullet that plunked against the med-v set me off.

"If you can't, then get over to me. I can't stop firing at them. You're a foot away. Just reach out for me. You can do this." He kept his sight on the approaching trucks.

This was dumb. I was dumb. I knew I needed to

get control, but the more panicked I was, the more angry I became, and the worse my control got. "No. I can't move. I'm losing it."

"I can't get over to you." He shot off three more bullets and then reloaded. "Come to me."

Another truck exploded.

"Cy, if you're doing this, you gotta make sure you don't blow us up," Dex yelled from inside the med-v.

"Trying."

Energy built in my core. It ran through my veins, overpowering me. Searing its way through me.

There was only one more truck left. It was right next to us.

My teeth tingled with a surge of power. I couldn't get control.

The explosion rocked the med-v. Dex tried to correct us to keep her from rolling, but I was about to fly off the roof.

Knight was already airborne.

I leaped for him. Our hands met in the air. The energy running through me was instantly quieted. Tires squealed as Dex righted the med-v.

The rope caught around my waist, slamming me back into the roof. All of the air was knocked from me, but I held onto Knight with all I had.

He was over the side of the med-v. And he was slipping.

"Slow down, Dex. Knight. Don't." I reached for him with my other hand, but it was no use. He was going to fall. He was going to die and I hadn't told him how I felt about him. "I love you! Please don't leave me!"

"I love you, too. But don't worry so much."

What? Don't worry? He loved me, but don't worry? We were going as fast as this stupid vehicle could go and he was about to become roadkill.

He kicked away from the side of the med-v. My hands slipped the last little bit. I screamed.

Glass shattered as Knight's foot hit the window. He slid-fell into the med-v.

My heartbeat pounded in my ears. I laid my cheek back down against the metal as my breath wheezed in and out of my lungs.

I'd never been so scared before. And the asshole had done it on purpose.

"Get back inside, Emma," Knight said.

Nope. I wasn't moving. The dickola would just have to wait.

The rope tugged at my waist, pulling me back toward the hatch. I grumbled to myself, and then made my way down to the top bunk. Hands came around my waist and set me on my feet.

I stared hard into Knight's beautiful green eyes, and then slapped him across the face. It only took that split second of skin-on-skin for the electricity to dissipate.

He scrunched up his face. "What was that for?"

"For scaring the crap out of me. You let go! What the hell was that?"

He grinned. "That was my patented let's-not-become-roadkill move."

I shoved him. "Give me some warning next time, you asshole. I nearly had a heart attack up there. And you're here all fine and dandy laughing." He laughed harder. "Not cool. You can't promise me a future and then throw yourself from a moving vehicle at high speed."

His grin softened. "Emma." He wrapped his arms around me, and I listened to his heartbeat. "See. I'm fine."

I squeezed him harder. The overreaction said everything that needed saying.

"I love you, too, princess. And I'm not letting you go. I won't die on you. We'll get through this."

Knight was in too deep, and I couldn't let him go anymore.

Chapter Twenty-Two

KNIGHT

I soaked in the feel of Emma for a second.

She'd nearly lost control out there. Lady Eva wasn't stupid. She would have told the whole team the danger. If Emma had really lost it, someone would've shot her. Even though she was a Red. Even though she was insanely powerful. Even though I loved her, they would've shot her dead.

There was no hope for the Ravens if another Red publicly lost control. No one would care what Nagi did as long as he eliminated the danger. It'd happened after New York, and it had taken Lady Eva decades to rebuild her cause.

Emma had been out in the open. Glowing.

Thank God she was okay. We were okay.

But we weren't out of danger.

I held onto her hand as I looked to Dex. "Who's left?"

"We've got two teams behind us. One in the air."

That meant three air teams were down. Three ground. Jack knew our location. It wasn't about outrunning him anymore. We were going to have to make a stand. "Where's the closest defensible spot?"

"How much time do we have before they're on us again?" Emma asked.

"Fifteen minutes. Max."

She looked at the GPS. "We're kind of in the middle of bumfuck nowhere, but there's an abandoned military base about five miles west of here, if you take the third exit."

I turned to her. "How do you know?"

She shrugged. "Sally. Plus, spent a lot of time roaming on my own. It's good to have a few hiding spots here and there. Spent the night on the base a couple years ago. It's creepy, but it could work."

Creepy was probably a different thing for her than it was for me. Still, I didn't like to hear that she was sleeping in abandoned military bases.

If she knew about it, then so did other people.

I connected a call to Sam. "We're heading to the abandoned base."

"What? No. You should keep moving. We've got reinforcements on the way, and if you can hold off, I think we can get you in the clear."

There was a little bit of desperation in Sam's voice. She was still way too young to have this job. "No." However smart she was, she didn't have the level of experience that came with living life and loving.

"But, Hunter," she said. "She was glowing. You could see it in all the feeds. You can't engage. She'll lose control. You'll lose her."

"We both know that help won't come in time. It's better to stop and make a stand from a defensible position. How many of them are en route?"

She blew out a breath. "That's the only good news.

Y'all aren't close to any outposts. That part of the Void is really hard to get to, which is why they stashed Emma there. Parson and his goon squad have to get to you by air, but none of them will be fast enough. If you can end this in…under ten minutes, you'll be okay. Otherwise, you're fucked. If that happens, surrender. Stay alive. We'll get you out as fast as we can."

Surrendering wasn't an option. I'd rather die than get picked up as a dual-helix traitor. They'd already hurt Emma once, and probably had about as much information as they were going to get out of her. If Jack got his hands on her again, she wouldn't last long.

Yeah. No. That wasn't happening. "We've got this."

"You're being dumb, Hunter. If you'd just—"

"Sam." I was done listening to her.

"Fine. But if you die, I'm going to be seriously pissed off."

"See you soon." I clicked before she could start arguing again. I didn't run by committee. It was my choice what to do next, for better or worse. Luckily, all the options sucked. It was about choosing the least sucky one.

I hated being on the defensive. We needed to turn the tables.

One more exit to go before the base. I started to coordinate the men we had left, shoving away any grief for loss of life.

That would be dealt with later.

I rolled my shoulders, and prayed I wasn't making a bad decision.

***

The base was a series of buildings, some more than twenty stories high. The base plans that Sam had sent showed a landing strip that took up a good swath in the back of the base. An air control tower sat off to the side.

If we stayed by the tower, then we could be in a good position to wait for the Ravens' jet.

I called Sam. "There's room for Eva's—"

"Plane. Yeah. Already on it. ETA is nineteen minutes, forty-three seconds. Parson's squad will be there in less than five."

"Thanks, Sam." I knew she thought I was making a foolish mistake, so it mattered that she still had my back.

"Where to?" Dex said as he swerved between buildings. "I need to know where I'm going."

"The runway. We'll take cover in the control tower." I directed him where to go.

"We've got four trucks behind us," Dex said. He opened one of the windows and stuck his head and shoulders out. "They're not quite in firing range, but we slow down, and they will be. We have to move fast." He was coming up on the tower quick. He spun the wheel as he braked hard. The med-v stopped with a jerk next to the control tower's door.

Time to move.

I jumped out of the door, weapon in hand. "Everyone out." The two teams behind us tore in and followed suit.

The door was coded, but it opened after a bullet

and a firm kick. I checked the stairwell before motioning everyone in. "Let's move." The guys moved as a team, surrounding Emma. Her skin was barely glowing. If you didn't know she wasn't normally that brightly pale, you'd never notice the difference. But I could see it.

I stood against the wall as the men moved past, cutting in the center to grab Emma's hand. The zing of power was painful for the first second, but I relaxed, letting it flow through me. "You've gotta get control, Emma. I need both hands."

Her face turned a nice shade of pink. "You say that like it's easy. I'm doing my best."

If I didn't have skin contact, she really would've been glowing. I had to stay calm. Collected. Like always. "Don't get upset. Breathe deep. You can do this."

She nodded sharply once. Her breathing became slow and steady as we walked up the stairs, and my bones finally stopped aching.

"That's good," I said.

"Are you okay?"

"Yes." I wouldn't tell her that I had so much energy that I was suddenly exhausted. I could handle this.

Cold sweat rolled down my spine. This was either going to be a really good idea or a fucking bad one.

The top of the tower was surrounded with large glass windows. Busted com consoles ran along the edges, where air traffic controllers used to work. Two long tables with equipment took up the center of the room. I pushed Emma into one of the chairs. "I'll be right back." Leaving her without skin contact was bad, but she was holding it together so far.

"Okay."

I stared at her for a second, waiting to see if she could hold it together. Her skin seemed her normal white with a dusting of freckles. "Okay," I said as I strode to Dex. "How's it looking?"

"Four Black Helix teams are on the ground and closing in fast. There's an enemy chopper heading our way and Seligo plane en route, but if the Lady's gets here in the next eighteen, we'll miss it. We need to take off again as soon as the jet lands."

"Got it." I looked out the window. Trucks were already rolling in from the east side of the tower. "We're up high. We've got the advantage."

Men in all black hopped out of the vehicles, weapons ready.

Predictable.

But I wasn't expecting the rocket launcher.

"They won't use it. Emma's here."

I said that a second too late. As the rocket flew from the barrel, I raced to Emma, throwing my body over hers.

Shards of glass rained down on us.

Something slammed into my head.

Chapter Twenty-Three

CIPHER

My ears were ringing and Knight slumped on top of me. "Knight?"

He didn't respond.

"Knight?"

I rocked my body, trying to get out from under him. "Knight!"

Oh God. He wasn't answering. I slid out from under him. Blood dripped down his face. I pushed until he was on his back. "Hunter." I whispered. "Wake up." I slapped his face lightly. I didn't want to hurt him more, but panic gripped my heart in a fist. "Hunter. Please wake up." I shook him.

A fire spread over one of the com consoles. Water rained down from the few of the old sprinkler heads that still worked. The windows were completely shattered and half the roof was gone. Blown to bits. They'd aimed a little high, which had probably saved our lives.

I felt Hunter's pulse. Weak, but there. He was breathing, but he wasn't waking up.

A few of the guys stirred. Dex sat up, shaking his

body.

"Dex," I said. "He's not waking up. He's not waking up!"

He knelt beside Knight, feeling for a pulse. "Give him a minute. Looks like he took a hit to the head. I'm sure he'll be okay."

"Why would he do that?"

"Do what?"

"Cover me like that. Why would he do that?"

Dex gave me a look that was perilously close to pity. "Because he loves you."

Bullets pinged against the wall, and Dex pushed me under one of the console desks. "Stay here with him. Let us take care of this."

As I watched, one of the guys I didn't even know took a hit in the neck.

The others scrambled. Dex yelled orders to the group, but I couldn't hear them. The wind was too loud.

A chopper shined a light down into the half-missing roof. "Emma," Jack called. "Time for you to do what you promised. We'll leave all these boys alone if you walk out of that tower now."

My vision was blurring. I heard someone yell at me to calm down, but I couldn't. There was too much going on. I looked down at Knight, as he lay there prone on the floor.

A muffled scream burst as another Raven was hit.

I couldn't do this. I couldn't sit here and do nothing. I stood and the room spun.

Shaking off the dizziness, I focused. I had to get outside. Risking any more of these guys wasn't an option. I took off, running down the stairs two at a time. The guys shouted behind me, but I ignored them.

The metal stairs sizzled as I jumped down the last three steps.

The first Black Helix came at me, gun raised. I lifted my hand.

"Slowly step this way," he said.

He thought I was surrendering. Not going to happen. I'd burn myself out before I'd surrender.

But I wasn't going to hurt the guys in the tower either.

I stepped further away from the metal structure, letting the Black Helixes surround me. They stood shoulder to shoulder, each one pointing a gun at me.

"No one touch her. She can't hurt you unless you touch her," Jack said.

That was entirely inaccurate. I focused on gathering all the electricity I could reach. It built in me until my skin tingled as it raced through my body and my hands glowed.

"Get down on the ground," one of the Blacks yelled as he stepped forward.

I knelt down, and pictured a ball of energy forming around me. I let it grow. Fed it with my fear. With my anger.

When the guy stepped toward me again, I let the ball explode outward in a deafening crackle. I was dizzy for a second as the energy flew out of me and I squeezed my eyes tight. I didn't need to see to know that every single one of the Blacks was now on the ground.

"Emma. Don't make me shoot you. I'm here to help," Jack said from above. He was in the chopper, waiting to see if I'd surrender.

"You're not here to help me. You never were. As soon as you found out I was a Red, you murdered my parents. Your own sister. How could you? Are you that fucking selfish? You want to be a Seligo that badly?"

"You're dangerous. Look what you've done here!"

He was right. Thirty men lay on the ground because of me, but I was done blaming myself. If not for Jack's obsession, none of this would've happened.

That was the worst part. All of this could have been avoided.

I didn't realize that I was gathering so much power until I blinked. The energy flooding me was so bright, making my skin glow a swirling blue and white. It was almost as if night were turning to day and I was the sun.

"You've got to the count of three to turn it off, and then I'm firing."

"Three," I said as I released everything I'd been holding inside. I focused it toward the helicopter overhead.

The energy burst from me so fast that I slammed down on my knees. I wanted to cover my ears to block the roar of the explosion, but my body wouldn't move. I was dead weight, my limbs suddenly too heavy for my body. Pieces of metal crashed into the ground, and I closed my eyes. I didn't have any energy left for me. Not even enough to roll myself out of the way.

Heat licked along my skin as the chopper burned out, and I knew that Jack was dead.

For the first time in a long time, I smiled. Really

smiled.

He was gone. I didn't have to worry anymore.

A pair of hands ran down my face, but I couldn't open my eyes. I didn't need to. I knew it was Knight.

"Emma!" His voice rang out. "Princess. Open your eyes for me."

I managed a moan. "Tired."

Something wet plopped on my face. "Okay. Sleep. I've got you."

I felt weightless. Like I was floating. It soothed me, and my mind shut off.

***

When I woke next, the sheets were soft against my skin, without the stink of mold and mildew. The shake of turbulence had me sitting up and the world went cattywompus. I was in a tiny room with a tiny bed. A curtain made up one wall. I peeked out the window and saw clouds.

I was on the Ravens' jet.

"Whoa." I steadied myself before trying to move again. I walked slowly out of the room.

Knight jumped up from his chair. "How're you feeling?"

"Honestly, really weak. I hate it."

He laughed. "You need food. You've been sleeping for the last three hours."

"Holy shit," I said, using Mona's favorite phrase. It was the only thing that fit. "What happened?"

Knight backed me into a plush leather chair and then reached into the mini-fridge along the wall. "You took out the whole Black Helix team by yourself, and then blew up your uncle's helicopter with him in it."

"I remember that bit." I took the sandwich he gave me and took a bite. "What about the rest?"

"We took off. You burned out the power for all of the Western Voids. They're still working on power getting restored. We're about an hour away from the Lady's compound." He pushed an electrolyte drink at me. "Have some."

I rolled my eyes, but took a long drink. "What happens when we get to the compound? Is Mona there?"

"Yes, Mona is there. I'm sure she's dying to see you, but first we'll get you checked out. I'm still worried about whatever they pumped you full of. You're not glowing anymore, so I think it got all burned out of your system, but we're not fucking around with that. The Lady will do a full scan of you and your DNA."

"Hmm." I wasn't sure I liked the sound of that, but I didn't have much choice. I wasn't feeling well, and the only person who could help was the Lady. And I'd get to see Mona. So, there was that.

I ran my finger over a bandage on Knight's head. "You okay?"

He smiled. "Thank God I have a hard head."

I started to laugh, but stopped. "Don't do that again."

"What?"

"Put your life in front of mine. What were you thinking throwing yourself over me like that?"

"Not a chance. I will always put you first. It's my job. My privilege to protect you."

"Privilege. Bullshit. That's dumb."

He reclined in his seat. "Not dumb. Smart."

I didn't have the energy or brainpower to do anything else, so I finished off my sandwich.

"Better?"

"I feel off." I blew out a breath. "Might just be tired, but don't know how that's possible because I slept."

"Give yourself a break. You harnessed an amazing amount of electricity with that awful cocktail running through your body." Knight stood up and pulled me with him. "Want to go back to bed? Or we could watch a vid?"

"A vid would be good." I looked around as we moved back to the room I'd been sleeping in. "Where's Dex?" I lay down on the bed and Knight slid in behind me.

"Taking a nap up front. He's been out since we got on board." Knight pulled out a screen from the wall beside the bed, and started scrolling through the list of movies. "What do you what to watch?"

"Anything." My eyes were getting heavy again.

Knight ran his fingers through my hair and kissed my forehead. "Relax. I've got you."

The funny thing was, I knew he did.

Jack was gone. Knight was safe. I was maybe a little sick, but I didn't care.

The movie started and I let the steady noise lull me into the first deep, dreamless sleep I'd had in years.

***

It wasn't until the next day that we got to the

Lady's compound. The jet had to land in a special hidden airstrip and we switched to a med-v for the last leg of the trip.

I was sitting in the passenger seat again. This time with Knight driving. I'd gone full-on pathetic. I didn't like being apart from him at all. I sat across the seat, with my feet resting against his legs. When he wasn't using both hands to drive, he lazily rubbed up and down my calf.

The dizziness and weakness were slowly fading away. I didn't feel like I needed to sleep twenty-four seven anymore. I wasn't back to my normal self, but I was getting there. Knight was definitely helping.

I'd never realized what happy was. I'd probably been as happy as a kid on the run could be when my parents were alive. They'd tried their best to shelter me, but life was stressful. We'd always been looking behind, wondering if we'd tipped ourselves off in any way.

After their deaths, I'd lived a half-life. I got by. But barely.

As I watched Knight's profile, the weight lifted. The burden of being who I was—what I was—seemed infinitely lighter. Although it wasn't all good. The Ravens we'd lost still hung over my head. I didn't think I'd ever feel like my life was worth theirs. The sacrifice…it didn't sit well with me. But I couldn't change the past. I had to focus on the future. Even though I still had questions about the Shadow Ravens, I wanted to try helping. For myself but also for the other Reds out there and for the guys who'd given their lives trying to help me.

I was going to figure out how to really control my

powers, and Lady Eva was going to help with that.

Knight glanced my way and winked.

I nudged him twice with my foot. "Watch the road."

"Then stop distracting me." He pinched my calf. "We're here."

I spun in my chair. All I saw were trees. And mountains. There was nothing on this random dirt road. "Am I missing something? Because I thought you said we were here…"

He pulled off to the side, and parked the med-v. Dex exited behind us. We walked toward the tree line, and then it was like a door opened in the forest. I gasped. "Holy shit. It's an illusion."

"Yup," Knight said. "One of the best."

Beyond the square, I could see people walking around. Cars driving. Buildings. But around the square, it still looked like a forest.

I was so blown away by the Lady's compound that I didn't even notice who opened the gate.

"Bitch. You coming in or what?"

I spun to see Mona standing against the gate, one hip cocked to the side.

"Holy shit. You're here!" I said. I closed the distance between us and hugged her before I could think twice of it.

"Holy shit. She hugged me?"

I stepped back and Knight pulled me to his side.

"I take it this is your doing?" Mona said to Knight.

He looked down at me with a grin. "I think so?"

Mona held out her fist and he bumped it with a laugh. "I'm so glad you're here. It's been boring without you guys."

"What? Oliver hasn't been keeping you busy?" Mona laughed, and that made me smile. It was good seeing her so happy. I'd been worried that I'd ruined her life, but maybe not so much. "I'm glad to be here. Told you it wouldn't be forever."

Oliver stepped through the doorway, and Mona grinned as he pulled her to his side.

Inside the compound was amazing. It was like a whole city hidden in the forest. Three- and four-story buildings were sprinkled among small one-story ones. A playground stood off to the left of the entrance. Kids filled the space, yelling and playing without paying attention to anything else.

"Come on, Emma," Knight said. "Let's go see the Lady. Get you checked out. We'll both feel better once we know that junk is working its way out of your system. And then we can relax."

"Relax?"

He nodded.

That sounded amazing. Knight tugged my hand until I fell in step beside him. As he led me through the buildings, it occurred to me that I didn't know where I was going. For the first time, I didn't have an escape plan. I wasn't thinking about how I'd run. How to get away. As long as I was with Knight, I had a feeling it would be okay.

It was nice not being alone.

Knight looked down at me as we walked. "Everything okay?"

I squeezed our linked hands. "Yeah. Everything's great."

For the first time in as long as I could remember, I actually meant it.

For the Readers:

Thank you to everyone who read this book. The Shadow Ravens has been in Ink Monster collaboration from the start. Christina Bauer, Lola Dodge, and myself came up with the world and each of our superheroines. I hope you liked the first installment!

Each of us is telling our superheroines' stories:

Out October 13, 2015: *Quanta* by Lola Dodge.
Out October 11, 2016: *Maker* by Christina Bauer.
Out October 10, 2017: *The Shadow Ravens* by Aileen Erin, Christina Bauer, and Lola Dodge, featuring all three Reds!

But don't worry! If you want more of Cipher, there just might be some short stories and a novella between now and her return in The Shadow Ravens! So keep a watch on Twitter, Facebook, and our blog!

xoxo,
Aileen

The Shadow Ravens Saga continues with Quanta by Lola Dodge.
Out October 13, 2015.

For more information on the series, go to:
http://inkmonster.net/books/shadow-ravens

Also by Aileen Erin, The Alpha Girl Series.
Book one: Becoming Alpha.

Also available, *Avoiding Alpha*, *Alpha Divided*, and for
preorder, *Bruja and Alpha Unleashed*.
For more information and updates about the series, go to:
www.inkmonster.net/alphagirl

Acknowledgments

I'm big on writing with lots of feedback from my editors and beta-readers, but this one was really a team effort. It's the first Ink Monster collaboration and took a lot of coordinating between writers to get the world-building figured out. It was a feat, but with Christina Bauer and Lola Dodge on my side, we got it done! Huzzah, ladies!

So, thank you to the lovely Christina Bauer and Lola Dodge. We did it! Now, for two more novels and then the group one... Not thinking about that one yet... ;)

Christina: Another release date done! We're killing it, sistah!

Lola: You're an editing genius. I've said it before and I'll say it another million times, I can't write anything without your fabulous feedback and comments. Bet you didn't realize when you got me at SHU that you were going to be stuck with me forever.

To all of the lovely ladies at INscribe: Thank you for everything that you do. Working with you is like magic! Christina and I and Ink Monster wouldn't be where we are today without you.

To my Halcyon Bastards: Thanks for helping me maintain my sanity. You're all amazing writers and I'm lucky to call you friends. Counting down till our next chat. Big hugs.

To the lovely Kristi Latcham: Thank you for all of your support and proofing! And being sweet about doing it on an extreeeeeemly tight deadline. You're the best.

To Kime Heller-Neal: Thank you for reading and listening to my bitching. You're amazing! Hope you're busy writing! :)

To my family and friends: Thank you for all of your support. I know I turn into a bit of a hermit when I'm writing and on a deadline, and more so the past few months! Sorry I checked out, but I'm baaaa-aaaack. I love you all. Now, it's time to go out and have that glass of wine (or three) that I've been talking about!

To everyone at Seton Hill University's Writing Popular Fiction program, big hugs! I'm lucky to be part of such an amazing writing community.

Last, but most importantly, to my husband: Thank you for everything you do. From making sure I get out of the house to making sure I see the sun, I love you. I can't do it with out you. You're my everything. And you do take such good care of your pet writer. ;)

Aileen Erin is half-Irish, half-Mexican, and 100% nerd—
from Star Wars (prequels don't count) to Star Trek (TNG
FTW), she reads Quenya and some Sindarin, and has a
severe fascination with the supernatural. Aileen has a BS in
Radio-TV-Film from the University of Texas at Austin,
and an MFA in Writing Popular Fiction from Seton Hill
University. She lives with her husband in Los Angeles, and
spends her days doing her favorite things: reading books,
creating worlds, and kicking ass.

65378715R00183

Made in the USA
Lexington, KY
10 July 2017